I0629384

# Chaos at the Christmas Tree
## An Emerson Fox Mystery

## Jennifer Shaw Wolf

JS Wolf Publishing LLC

Cover design by Angelica Hagerman

Cover Art by Arianna Smith

JS Wolf Publishing

jennifershawwolf.com

# Contents

## Chapter 1

# Stranger in Town

"These were your mother's favorites." Ramona pulled out a box of hand-blown glass ornaments. There were blue and silver balls, diamonds and star-shaped ornaments in red and green. They were delicate and old-fashioned, and beautiful. "Your father didn't want them, but I thought I would keep them for you."

Emmy, Ramona, and Pierce stood in front of the boxes in the back room of the bookshop. It was another neatly hidden nook built into the bookshop's design. There were boxes and boxes of ornaments, decorations, and lights that had once decorated the Sharp Island Town Hall and lit up the giant pine tree in the center of the town square.

"The larger ornaments are farther back. These are for your own tree."

"Thank you. They're perfect." Emmy ran her hand over the smooth surface of the ornament. She wasn't sure she was going to put a tree up in her apartment. She wasn't sure what to think of the upcoming holiday season. Last year, she had been up to her neck in wedding planning and had been so swept up in that—and in the innumerable holiday celebrations that her fiancé Collin and his family attended that she hadn't been able to do much but go along for the ride.

Last year had been chaotic, but at that point she had welcomed the chaos. Her dad had already been in jail for a couple of years for embezzling money from his company, and her stepmom had broken off all contact. She'd looked forward to a Christmas with what she'd thought would be her new family, but it turned out to be just as lonely as the years she'd spent alone.

Ramona directed Pierce toward a wooden box at the back of the top shelf. He pushed the boxes aside to retrieve it. Emmy didn't regret breaking off her engagement for a heartbeat. The events and choices she'd made in the last few months had led her on a far different path than she'd ever imagined, but she felt like she was finally going in the right direction. She had Pierce, Ramona, Ginny, Madelyn, and really all of Sharp Island to celebrate with this year.

As well as being less lonely, she hoped this year would be less crazy. Emmy had talked the island event planner Kirsten down to one week for "An Island Christmas." There would be a tree lighting, a holiday bazaar, and a lighted boat parade in the harbor. The island was doing better than it had for a long time, but it wouldn't hurt to have a little more tourist revenue coming in over the holidays.

Ramona took the wooden box from Pierce, wiped off the dust, and opened it with a little gold key. "And this, this has been at the top of every Christmas tree in the town square for generations."

Emmy leaned close as Ramona unwrapped the dark velvet surrounding a beautiful star. "Oh," was all she could say. The star appeared to be covered in crystals, but as she looked closer, she wasn't so sure. "Are those..."

"The real deal? Yes, they are, in fact, diamonds. George Sharp had it designed for his wife for their first Christmas on the island."

"Wow." Emmy lifted the star from its wrappings. As she did, a diamond came loose, fell onto the floor, and bounced behind the boxes.

"I've got it." Pierce got down on his hands and knees and retrieved the diamond. He turned and presented it to her while he was on one knee.

Emmy blushed, and Ramona chuckled at the image. "You might want to get that taken care of sooner rather than later."

"Taken care of?" Emmy asked.

"The loose diamond. You should have it fixed. In fact, I'd take the whole thing to a jeweler before it's put up at the tree lighting. It's worth tens of thousands of dollars."

Emmy looked at the tiny diamond in her hand and then at the star again. "Where was this when I was trying to find a way to pay for the repairs on the water system?"

"Safely tucked away in this box." Ramona took the star from her, wrapped the velvet back around it, tucked the diamond among the wrappings, and locked the box again. "Some things are priceless not because they're expensive, but because they have more value than what they can be sold for."

Emmy wondered if that was really true. The star had sentimental value as a family heirloom, but was it really priceless? If she had known about it before, would she have sold it to save the island? She was grateful she didn't have to make that choice.

Pierce stood and brushed the dust from his knees. "I didn't realize it was real. If it's that valuable, why was it just hung out in the open for anyone to steal?"

"Have you seen the size of the tree in the town square?" Ramona smoothed her yellow and red poinsettia-print skirt as she stood. "You'd have to be Spider-Man to steal the star once it's in place, and most people don't know it's real."

Pierce turned to Emmy. "It's still a bad idea. You aren't seriously thinking of putting it up this year, are you?"

Emmy didn't know how to answer. Following a heartfelt PowerPoint presentation from Kirsten, the Founder's Council had decided to honor the old town traditions that had died when her Uncle Edward took over the island. The tree lighting was a big part of that, but did the star at the top really matter?

Before she could decide what to say, Anjuli, owner of the Patisserie, came in.

"There you are." She looked at Emmy impatiently. "There's a woman in my shop who would like to talk to you. Something about the bazaar. She wants to know if the mess is going to be cleaned up in time to make it worth her while."

By mess, Anjuli could only mean the wreck that was left of the Town Hall that had all but burned down a couple of months ago. There was no way to do the reconstruction on it before next spring. It was a huge eyesore and, as far as Emmy was concerned, a good reason not to have tourists in town for the holidays.

Kirsten had promised she had something spectacular in mind to do with the space. She'd put the town maintenance guy, Landon, to work building her vision. Emmy still didn't exactly trust him, but he was a skilled carpenter. His budding relationship with Kirsten had been good for him, if a bit distracting for her.

They were creating a kind of open-air bazaar in the space the burned building had left behind. Emmy had pointed out that winter open-air markets weren't practical in the Pacific Northwest, where it was sure to rain more days than not, but Kirsten had only taken that as a further challenge.

"Kirsten sent out all the information to the vendors already," Emmy said. "It's really her thing."

"The woman said she stopped by Kirsten's office, but Kirsten wasn't there." Anjuli rolled her eyes. "And she said she preferred to talk to you. She wanted to go straight to the top."

"I'll go talk to her." Emmy started out the door and toward the shop.

Anjuli gave a sharp nod. "There is also a man who has been asking about you. I didn't give him any information. He appears to be..." she paused, "what is the appropriate term now? Unhomed?"

"You mean unhoused?" Emmy asked.

"Yes, a street person. Here, on Sharp Island. Can you imagine?" She shook her head. "I called Officer Peters, but he didn't answer."

Pierce joined them. "He's on vacation for the next week. I'm doing his patrols until he gets back. Did the man eat and not pay or..."

"No, he just looks," Anjuli paused as if searching for the right term, "like he doesn't belong."

Pierce turned to Emmy with a question in his blue eyes. "I'm sure it's fine." Emmy said. The man was probably harmless. Everyone looked rough by Anjuli's standards.

Pierce nodded. "If something comes up, call me; otherwise, I need to head to the far side of the island for a stray dog call."

Anjuli looked offended that a stray dog took precedence over a stray human, but since the man had done nothing wrong, Emmy agreed with Pierce's decision.

The smell of gingerbread and sugar cookies greeted Emmy as she pushed the door to the patisserie open. Christmas was just getting started, but the Sharp Islanders were already showing their holiday spirit. Anjuli had a whole new menu of Christmas treats, and Ms.

Lee of Ms. Lee's Teas had replaced the myriad of pumpkin beverages with her newest winter brews.

Sitting at one of the back tables was a large man with a white beard. Maybe it was because Christmas was on her mind, but Emmy thought he bore a striking resemblance to Santa Claus. This must be the man Anjuli believed to be "unhoused."

Before she could get a closer look, a middle-aged woman in dark slacks and an unapologetically crafty Christmas vest moved in front of her view.

"Are you Emerson Fox?" she asked. A pair of crocheted holly leaf earrings dangled from her ears.

"Yes," Emmy answered. She could feel the eyes of the man from the back table watching her, but she didn't dare break eye contact with the woman in front of her.

The woman extended her hand. A knitted and beaded bracelet slid down her wrist. She was slim, with a long, pointed nose. Her light brown hair was short and sensible. There wasn't a hair out of place.

"I'm Penelope Carmichael." She shook Emmy's hand firmly. "I'm about all things Christmas and crafty and craft and Christmassy. I specialize in hand-knitted and crocheted apparel. When I saw you were holding a bazaar, I signed up immediately. I was promised a premium booth. I'd like to see where the booth will be located, so I can be sure it will suit my needs."

Emmy stepped back, blinking. "The booths aren't finished yet. The bazaar is still a couple of weeks away. Perhaps Ms. Loche told you—"

"Oh, she did, she did, when we talked over the phone, but I wanted to make sure I had a prime location, so I got right on the ferry and came on out in person. I like to be proactive, so I don't have any unpleasant surprises. She said you would discuss the bazaar at tomorrow's meeting, and I wanted to ensure they would have time to address any concerns I had."

"What issues do you have?" Emmy asked.

The woman lit up like a Christmas tree. Clearly, coming up with issues was her favorite thing to do. "What will keep me and my wares dry in an open-air market?"

"My event planner assures me—"

"And what about heat? It can get chilly this time of year. And traffic flow? What guarantees can you give me that there will be enough business to make the whole thing worth my while?"

"We haven't done this for many years, so we can't be sure—"

"I would like to see the finished booths as soon as possible. I'm willing to take a room at the Inn for the night."

"I'm afraid we won't have anything ready by tom–"

"Well, as soon as you have it ready, I expect to be notified."

"Of course," Emmy said. "I'll make sure Ms. Lo–"

"In the meantime, I'd like to preview your list of vendors. I've been in this business for years, and I can tell you who the most desirable vendors are and those you should watch out for. You should be very picky about what is being sold and who is selling it. Vendors can make or break a Christmas bazaar."

The woman's sense of superiority and the need to eliminate the undesirables, or more likely, any competition the other vendors might pose, put Emmy off. "Thank you for your offer, Mrs. Carmichael. But all of this is still—"

"It's Ms., actually. I'm afraid I'm married to my work."

The man in the corner coughed, but to Emmy it sounded as if he was trying to cover a laugh. Her gaze moved back to him. His back was to her, but there was something familiar about him. She couldn't decide what it was.

"Perhaps Ms. Loche told you we're signing up vendors on a first-come, first-served basis, since this is our first–"

"Oh, that's a mistake. You never know what you'll get when you do it that way. My advice would be to have vendors put in an application and then have a stringent vetting process. I can tell you how I would do it if it were me."

"Right, of course. But that's really a discussion you should have with Ms. Loche." The man in the back cough-snickered again. Emmy lost her train of thought. What was it about that man?

"Oh, I always go straight to the top. No use wasting time and energy talking to some underling. I've been in this business for nearly twenty-five seasons, and I can tell you—"

The man stood, then turned to face her. The rush of blood in Emmy's ears drowned out everything Penelope had been saying.

Her breath caught in her throat as one word came out.

"Daddy?"

## Chapter 2

# Home for the Holidays

E mmy stared in disbelief. The last time she had seen her dad, he had been trim and handsome. His hair had been light brown. He had been clean shaven. But it was definitely him. He looked as if he had aged about twenty years during his last three years in prison.

Penelope stopped talking and stared at the two of them. "This man is your father?" She peered closer, studying him. "Don't I kno–"

Anjuli moved to the woman. "I think maybe she has something else on her mind. Could I interest you in a petit four? It's one of my specialties."

Emmy missed whatever Ms. Carmichael said in response. She was vaguely aware of the woman complaining as Anjuli directed her toward the front counter.

Her dad stepped closer and held out his arms. "Baby."

She embraced him. Even with the added girth and other changes in his appearance, the hug still felt like him. "What are you doing here?"

Suddenly she was wary and guilty at the same time. She hadn't spoken to her father in months. There'd been a strain between them ever since she found out he'd lied about her mother's death. With all she had to do to keep the island going, she hadn't kept in touch like she had when he first went to jail.

He stood back and looked at her. "You look beautiful, so mature, so...I don't know. More grown-up than the last time I saw you."

"I have grown up."

"I can see that. And you have your own private island." There was a gleam in his eyes when he mentioned the island. Money had always been important to her father. Too important. They sent him to jail for defrauding clients and embezzling money from his company.

"It's a lot of work, but I like it here." She took a breath. "What are you doing here...how did you...?"

"Get out of jail?" He finished for her. "I was working in the laundry area and I saw the chance to get under one of those covered carts and climb into a bag of dirty laundry. They did the laundry off-site, so someone loaded the bag into a truck that left the prison. When the truck stopped, I jumped out and made a run for it."

Emmy stared at him, dumbfounded.

He laughed. "Still as sweet and gullible as ever. I saw that in a movie once. They paroled me. I would have told you before, but I wanted it to be a-"

Pierce came in, out of breath. "Emmy, I just heard that your dad was—"

"Paroled, yeah, I figured it out." She turned and stood between them. "Dad, this is my boyfriend, Detective Pierce Hamilton. Pierce, this is my dad, Wayne Fox."

They stared at each other for a long moment. Finally, her father extended his hand. "I'm happy to finally meet you. Emmy has told me so much about you."

It was a lie, one that rolled off his tongue easily, the way all his past lies had. She hadn't been dating Pierce the last time they spoke, but there was no point in calling him on the lie.

"And thanks to the parole board's generosity in letting me out, we get to spend Christmas together." He reached to pull Emmy into another hug.

Emmy hugged him back, but her mind was racing. She loved her dad and had always been daddy's little girl, but had she really known him? She didn't know the man who had committed fraud and embezzled money for years. She didn't know the man who had lied to her for years about what happened to her mother or where all their money had come from. After all that had happened to her since he went to prison, she wasn't sure that he knew her anymore, either.

"This is where you live now?" Her dad said as Emmy opened the door to her apartment. Pierce had stayed behind after giving her dad a few wary glances.

It felt as if he were appraising everything in the room as he circled it. She'd changed little about the apartment since she'd moved in. There wasn't a lot of time in her life for interior decorating, and she felt like the retro, comfortable vibe suited her.

"It's nice...but I expected it to be bigger and the furniture to be newer. I can only imagine what Donna would say."

Emmy stiffened at the mention of her stepmother. The only mother she had ever known had left them both pretty quickly once the money ran out.

"You have a beautiful view," he said as he peered out the window.

"You can put your things in the guest room." Emmy led the way into the back bedroom.

"I don't have much to put anywhere." Her dad lifted the black duffel bag he had brought with him. Everything about him appeared to droop with age and the weight of his time behind bars. "It's ironic that I used to give you everything, and now I'm the one on the receiving end. I guess I should be thankful I have a multi-millionaire daughter who is willing to help me get back on my feet."

Emmy didn't answer that. No one had asked her if she wanted to help him. As for her being a multi-millionaire, she had most of her money tied up in the island. She wasn't sure her dad understood that. "You have your own bathroom. If you need more clothes, we'll have to go to the mainland. There's only one clothing store on the island, and I'm not sure it really fits your style."

"Not much style left. I'm good with anything so long as it's not an orange jumpsuit." Her dad chuckled bitterly. Before going to jail, her dad had dressed impeccably. His hair was always in place. He was always clean-shaven. Now he wore a stretched-out t-shirt, a pair of worn jeans, and a full beard.

"We'll take a trip to the mainland in a day or so. We can get whatever you need then."

"It will need to be tomorrow," her dad said, sitting on the bed. "I have my first meeting with my parole officer at nine o'clock in the morning."

"Tomorrow?" Emmy looked at him with dismay. "I have meetings all day. We're working on plans for the island's holiday celebration."

"Unfortunately, I can't go alone. They need to make sure I have a place to live and a sponsor. Otherwise, they'll ship me off to a halfway house."

"Can we change the meeting with the parole officer, or can I attend virtually? Running the island is my job now. These meetings are important."

"More important than me?" he asked.

"I didn't say that," Emmy said. She suddenly felt like a teenager again. Back then, she didn't understand how good her father was at emotional manipulation. She took a breath. "If I had known you were coming and that I needed to be at the meeting with your parole officer, I could have rearranged my schedule. If you had called—"

"Called." He stroked his beard in a mock-thoughtful gesture. "Now that would have been nice. But I guess once you received your inheritance, you didn't need me anymore." He stood. "It's okay. I can go to the halfway house. It was good to see you, Em. What time is the next ferry?"

"Sit down." She was impressed with the authority in her own voice. "You're not going to a halfway house. I'll tell the committee members I have a family emergency and send Ramona to my place."

"Ramona." He shook his head. "That old bat."

"Ramona is one of my best friends here, and she's been my legal representative, even though she's supposed to be retired."

"Well, she never liked me. Are you sure about the family emergency thing? I don't want to disrupt your important business."

She didn't like the way he said, "important business," as if she were playing at being a businessperson, like she had been when she went to visit his office when she was a little girl. She let it go. "I'll make it work. Get settled while I make a few phone calls. Then I can make you something to eat."

"You're going to cook?" he chuckled. "Do you remember the time you forgot to put water in the ramen noodles and almost caught the house on fire? Wouldn't you rather go to the White Sails? The food there used to be pretty good."

"The White Sails is temporarily closed pending a change in management," Emmy said.

"Oh yeah? What's going on with Artie? Did he finally drive away all his customers with his terrible service?"

"No, he..." But Emmy didn't want to get into all the reasons Artie wasn't managing the White Sails anymore. "I can cook. I took a few culinary arts classes in college."

"But you didn't stick with it," he said.

"I got past the point where they taught us to put water in the ramen, so I think I can handle it." She walked out before she said anything she'd regret.

She went to the far corner of her room and dialed Ramona's number. "So, he's back?" Ramona said without even saying hello. "Did you have any idea he was getting out?"

"None whatsoever." Emmy sank onto the settee in her room. "I should have stayed in touch with him better, but..."

"But you've been busy and your father is a manipulative ogre, and it was probably better that you stayed away from him."

A protective indignation rose in Emmy. "He's my dad. I love him. He spent his whole life trying to make me happy. Even if his methods weren't good, his motives were—"

"Bull. You may know a different side of Wayne than I did, but don't fool yourself into believing he did anything for your sake."

Emmy didn't want to listen to a catalog of her dad's faults from Ramona, so she moved on to the reason she was calling. "I need a favor. I need you to take over things at the Founder's Meeting and at the planning committee meeting tomorrow."

"You want me to sit in while the council bickers about how to best spend the settlement money from Khonico and try to rein in Kirsten so she doesn't spend it all on one event?"

"That about sums it up. I'd really appreciate it if you would do that for me. I'll owe you big time."

"You already do." Ramona sighed. "Where are you going to be?"

"Meeting with my dad's parole officer. He needs me there to show he has a place to live and a sponsor."

"Does this mean he's going to be staying with you?" Ramona asked.

"We didn't talk about it, but I guess so, at least until he gets on his feet and finds a job and his own place to live."

Ramona tutted from the other end of the line. "Are you sure this is what you want?"

Emmy sighed. "Right now, I don't have a choice."

"There's always a choice," Ramona said. "But I get you can't just throw him out into the cold. I mean, I could, but you're not me."

"So you'll cover for me?" Emmy asked.

"Why not? I've been dealing with this lot for thirty years. What's one more meeting?"

"You're the best," Emmy said.

"I know." Ramona took a breath. "Don't let him get to you, Emmy. Don't let him make you feel small. You're a strong, independent woman with a lot going for you. Make him see that if you're going to have any kind of relationship with him. He's your dad, but that doesn't mean he can manipulate you into doing whatever he wants."

"Right," Emmy said. She heard her dad rummaging around in the fridge. "I need to go, and thank you. I'll call you for the report as soon as I get back to the island."

"Don't forget what I said," Ramona said, and then hung up.

"That wasn't half bad." Her dad leaned back on the couch and patted his full stomach. "Maybe a tad dry, and if it were me, I wouldn't have put so much tarragon on the salmon."

"I like the bit of licorice flavor it gives it," Emmy said. She was grateful she had the right food in the house to at least semi-impress her dad. Usually, she just had what it took to make her own simple meals. She'd bought the salmon to make something special for Pierce. She'd have to do that later.

"Give me a good alder plank-smoked salmon and I'm happy. I don't need all of that extra stuff. But this was a definite improvement over the fire-roasted ramen."

Emmy felt as though he was implying that her salmon wasn't quite adequate. She shook off the feeling and went to clear the dishes. "I'm glad you liked it."

"So tell me everything about what's been going on in your life. For example, when did you start dating a cop?"

"A few months ago." Emmy focused on putting the dishes in the dishwasher. She didn't want to talk about Pierce, or the island, or her inheritance right now. "What's the meeting tomorrow going to be about?"

"I imagine it's all about what it's going to take to keep me on parole and out of jail—a place to stay, a job, all the things I took for granted before it all came crashing down." He seemed resigned to whatever fate was waiting for him. Too resigned maybe. Her dad always had a plan. Emmy didn't know what to think of the dad who had come home versus the one who had left.

"You're all I have left in the world, baby girl. I know I screwed up, but I thought I was doing what I needed to do to provide you with the life you deserved. After your mom died, I had to fill the void. I guess I just–"

"Stop." Emmy stood up. She'd heard this argument from him and from her stepmother before. She'd even let herself feel guilty for what he had done, but she'd learned a lot since then. "I'm not taking responsibility for your bad choices. You chose to steal the money, and for whatever reason you thought you had, you were wrong. I didn't care about the money. You made your own choices. Don't drag me into it." She took a breath, waiting for him to defend himself, to go over all the things he had done to make sure she had the best of everything. For once, he remained silent.

"But you're still my dad, and I love you. I'll help you. But as long as you live under my roof..." she let a smile spread across her face.

"I'll live by your rules. Got it." He gave her a long hug before he let her go. Emmy had the distinct impression that there was a lot her dad was not going to let go of.

Chapter 3

# Chapter 3: Bazaar Plans

"How did the meeting go?" Emmy asked Ramona as soon as she walked into her office. Belle, Ramona's red hound dog, raised her head, and Emmy scratched her behind her soft, floppy ears.

"Kirsten is out of control again. But other than that, not bad." Ramona held up a pile of sketches. "This is her plan to make the Town Hall site into 'a Christmas bazaar dreams are made of.'"

Emmy studied the drawings. There was a canopy stretched across the lower level of what used to be the town hall. Landon had left the wooden floor intact, but with a more rustic feel. There were lights strewn along the ornate walls and a path of lights that led to the pine tree in the center of the square, which had been traditionally lit to start the Christmas season.

"She already has vendors lined up to set up booths."

"I know," Emmy said. "I already met one crazy craft lady." Emmy flipped through the drawings again. "What did the council say?"

"She has them eating out of her hands, even Brighton, though he'd never admit it. He agreed to head up the boat parade. Speaking of eating out of your hands, did you see the drawings of the petting zoo? She's promising a real reindeer, maybe even a camel."

"I'm sure getting the animals here will be a delightful ferry ride for someone who is not me," Emmy said.

"She's got the high school band playing and some strolling Victorian carolers." Ramond turned the page. "Oh, and a comedy troupe–The Three Wise Guys–she's trying to get them to agree to do a nightly holiday-themed show here."

"Hopefully that goes over better than the whole ghost hunter thing went."

"Agreed. They're supposed to be pretty good," Ramona said. "One of them was once quite famous." She looked through her notes. "Franklin or Clark, something like that…"

"Clark Franklin, the British guy from *Comedy Train*?"

"Yeah, that's him."

"My stepmother used to watch his show. She was obsessed with him. She said his accent was 'sexy.'" Emmy rolled her eyes at the memory.

"Those Brits know how to do comedy–if you get it. But I agree with the accent thing."

"Sounds like Kirsten has everything under control," Emmy said. "Thanks to a quick settlement with Khonico, we actually have the money to do it. I'm sure Kirsten will make it amazing."

"You don't seem to be too into it," Ramona said.

"Just tired." She stifled a yawn. It had been a mostly sleepless night listening to her dad snore. She hadn't known how thin the walls were in her apartment until she had a guest. "And I have a lot on my mind."

Ramona nodded sympathetically. "How did your meeting go with your dad's parole officer?"

"Okay, I guess. He has to find a job soon and…he's required to wear an ankle bracelet."

"Oh," Ramona said, "I guess that means he'll need a permanent place to stay."

"Yeah," Emmy swallowed. "He'll be staying with me."

"With you?" Ramona sounded surprised. "How do you feel about that?"

Emmy shrugged. "He's my dad. He needs me. What else is there to feel?"

"How about betrayed, angry, frustrated, hurt? It's okay to feel all of those things."

"Maybe. But maybe I just need to let go of all of that. I'm happy to see him and I'm happy to get to spend the holidays with him."

"I'm glad to hear it, and I hope it all works out for your sake. But don't let go of too much. Family relationships can get complicated. If anyone understands that, I do."

"I get that," Emmy said. "I'm just hoping everything else stays simple."

Ramona snorted. "With Kirsten at the helm?"

"Well, as long as it's just the normal craziness and no one dies this time, it will be okay."

---

"Landon said he could have it together by next weekend—the canopy, the booths, the whole thing. He's quite talented." Kirsten's eyes shone, and Ginny and Emmy exchanged a glance over at their teacups. Somehow, Kirsten and Landon had gone from two people vying for the same piece of the island through tenuous family ties to a romantic relationship that was at best odd, and at worst, nauseating.

Kirsten scrolled through the list on her tablet. "The petting zoo is ready to go—some sheep, three reindeer, a camel, and some adoptable animals from the shelter. I've already filled almost all the booths. The Victorian carolers are on board for two nights. Brighton has agreed to head up the lighted ship parade at the end of the week. I booked the comedy troupe. The lights for the tree will go up and the tree topper will be the crowning touch."

Emmy held up her hand. "I haven't agreed to that one yet. I'm not sure it's a great idea to put my priceless family heirloom out in the open at the top of a thirty-foot tree."

Kirsten smiled her best public relations smile. "I understand your concern, but we talked about it at the council meeting. It will be just the thing to bring the whole celebration together. Mrs. Hamilton said it topped the tree in the town for years before they discontinued the lighting. We'll make sure it's safe. As long as it's secured to the tree, there shouldn't be any problem."

"And how exactly do you plan on keeping it safe?" Emmy asked.

"Madelyn is on it. She's going to install one of her high-tech security systems. Besides, who would climb to the top of a tree to steal a star? Especially since no one outside of the family and a few council members knows it's real."

"I'm sure there are lots of people who would scale the tree for what that star is worth." Emmy sighed. "I'll think about it."

Kirsten's phone rang. She looked down at the caller ID and smiled. "I need to take this. Landon," she cooed as she stood up. "Right, exactly the way the plans say. No, I hadn't considered adding booths on the north side. They'd be a bit more open, but I think it's a brilliant idea." Kirsten walked away, still talking to Landon.

Emmy's dad walked into the shop. He looked much more put-together in the polo shirt and new jeans they'd bought. He hadn't shaved his beard, though. "I woke up, and you were gone. Why didn't you tell me where you were going?"

Emmy suddenly felt like a teenager being reprimanded for sneaking out. "I had a breakfast meeting scheduled." She gestured at the tea and scones on the table. "I didn't want to wake you up."

"Right," He pulled over an empty chair. "What are we discussing?"

"*We*," Emmy emphasized the word so that he would get that 'we' didn't include him, "were talking about our holiday bazaar and tree lighting."

"Sounds interesting. What's the plan?" He directed his remarks to Ginny, as if she were in charge.

"I'm just here for the pastries," Ginny said. "Kirsten and Emmy have control of this one."

Emmy's dad turned to her with a wide smile. "That's great! I love that you're taking a hands-on approach to managing your island." He probably meant the comment to be encouraging, but it felt more like he was being condescending. "What kind of bizarre celebration do you have planned?"

"A bazaar," Emmy corrected, "like a place for vendors and craft people to—"

"I know what a bazaar is, Pumpkin," her dad said. "I was just playing with you."

"I love the idea of having Santa's village at the end of the lane, just under the tree." Kirsten walked by, still talking to Landon. "I can't wait to see it. I know it will be perfect. If only we can find the right Sant—" she stopped, facing their table. "Hold on. I'll call you back."

"Hello." Kirsten approached the table with a wide smile. "Emmy, you haven't introduced me to your gentleman friend."

For a minute, Emmy couldn't figure out who Kirsten was talking about. Then she realized. "Kirsten, this is my dad. Dad, this is our island events coordinator, Kirsten Loche."

"Your dad?" Kirsten said. "Here for Christmas? That's wonderful."

Emmy's dad stood and extended his hand. "It's a pleasure to meet you, Kirsten."

Kirsten held onto his hand as she sat at the table. "The pleasure is all mine, Mr. Fox."

"Call me Wayne," he insisted.

"Of course, Wayne. I was just talking to my carpenter about our plans for the Christmas village and Santa's workshop."

"I saw that on the plans." Wayne said, sliding his chair closer to Kirsten and moving the drawings from their place in front of Emmy. "This should create a nice traffic flow from the stage to the vendors. It's always a good idea to have something for the kiddos. It gets more families out."

"I agree," Kirsten said. "That's why I've set up the petting zoo here." She put her finger on the map.

"Interesting. Have you considered moving it to the east side?" Wayne said. "Then you'd have more traffic flow into the businesses in town."

"No, I hadn't thought of that. That's a fantastic idea. It won't take much to move it."

"Of course it is. I have a lot of good ideas. I was a successful businessman for many years and, you know, business is business." He turned to Emmy. "Could you grab me a croissant? One with that cream stuff in the middle." Without waiting for her reply, he went back to the drawing. "Now tell me about your plans for the Christmas Village."

Emmy felt like she was a child being edged out of an adult conversation, or at the very least, a secretary being sent on an errand.

"Oh, it will be amazing—colorful lights, giant candy canes, the town in miniature—the works." She looked at Emmy's dad intently. "We're just missing one thing, something that I think you can help us with, Wayne."

"And what is that, Ms. Loche?" Mr. Fox had turned on the charm. It was an attitude Emmy knew well.

"Kirsten, please." She smiled at him again. "I was hoping you might be willing to play Santa Claus."

"Absolutely not," Emmy said after her dad had said the idea intrigued him and he'd think about it.

He had left to go for a walk. He said he'd spent a lot of time hiking around the island and wanted to see what had changed. Emmy and Ginny went with Kirsten to meet up with Landon so they could check on the work he'd done so far.

"Why not?" Kirsten said. "He'd be perfect for the part. He wouldn't even need a fake beard."

"You did say he needed a steady job," Ginny pointed out.

Emmy shook her head. "Because it's not in his nature to be a jolly old elf. His idea of playing Santa for me as a child was buying me off with a bunch of expensive gifts he made sure I knew were from him and then heading off for a cruise with my stepmother while I stayed home with the nanny."

"He's a good actor, though, right?" Ginny said. "How else did he convince all of those people that investing in his phony fund was a good idea?"

"Phony fund?" Kirsten asked.

"Yeah, the con he ran for years while embezzling money from his company. My dad is a felon, so unless you want to explain to everyone why we have a Santa with an ankle monitor..."

Kirsten sighed. "Okay, I can see where that might be an issue. One vendor recommended someone she's worked with before. I guess I can follow up with her. What's the deal with you and Pierce and your ex-con parents?"

Emmy ignored the question, but she was sure it was something that would come up again and again. She'd been so caught up in building her own life that she hadn't considered what would happen when her dad became part of it again.

## Chapter 4

# Power Strips

"You've done it again," Emmy said to Kirsten. Although she expected nothing less from Kirsten, she was impressed. The square was a flurry of activity as the Christmas bazaar came together. At one end, Landon had built a smaller 'Christmas Village' replica of the town, including Santa's workshop. The animals for the petting zoo had arrived on the last ferry and were getting settled into their pens–all but a very stubborn camel. It had sat down in the center of everything, beneath the big pine tree that was getting ready to be decorated and lit.

"Balthazar!" The trainer was prodding the camel with the toe of his boot while his assistant pulled on the creature's halter. The camel chewed thoughtfully, as if he didn't understand what the fuss was all about.

Emmy shook her head and moved to check out the vendor's area. She couldn't believe it was the remains of a burned-out building. There were booths on both sides, full of crafts and food and all sorts of Christmassy things. Penelope Carmichael, the crazy craft lady, had her premium center booth. She was hanging up sweaters like the one she had worn when Emmy first met her.

The one she was wearing this time was a deep red. On the front was a large crocheted Christmas tree covered in ornaments of every kind and color. Underneath the tree was an impressive array of presents. There was so much going on with the sweater that it made Emmy dizzy to look at it.

"Ms. Fox, Ms. Fox." Ms. Carmichael hurried to Emmy as soon as she spotted her. "I was told this booth would have access to electricity, yet I have only partial access. I'm forced to share an outlet with the adjacent booth."

Emmy turned to her with the accommodating smile she'd seen Kirsten use. "I'm sure we could locate a power strip for you if you need to plug in more."

"Oh, I have one. I just wanted to point out that I have only partial access. Maybe you should have said 'shared access' on the contract under 'electrical.' That seems like it might be more accurate, don't you think?"

"I'm sorry. I'm not sure what the problem is, then?" Emmy asked.

The woman moved closer to Emmy. Her stance looked intimidating, despite her slight frame. "The problem is, I received unclear documents. What if I needed an additional outlet?"

"Two power strips worth?" Emmy asked.

"It wasn't clear." The woman put her hands on her hips. "I've been doing craft shows for many, many years and I can spot a hole in the contract from a mile away."

Emmy looked around desperately for Kirsten, but she'd disappeared. Emmy sighed. "What can we do to make it right?"

The woman pursed her lips. "How about a ten percent discount on my booth rental?"

"Ten percent is way too much for such a slight error." Emmy's dad had come up behind her. She didn't know he was here or how long he'd been listening. "Especially since it's not a difficult problem to fix. Ms. Fox offered you a power strip. I suggest you take it and continue with your setup."

"Well, I need to be compensated in some way for—" The woman stopped, staring at Emmy's father for a long moment. "Don't I know you?"

Mr. Fox seemed taken aback. "I don't believe so."

"Hmmm," the woman stared at him over her horn-rimmed glasses. "I know we've met before. I never forget a face. Especially one from an unpleasant encounter. It will come to me."

Emmy's dad stepped back and appeared to duck his head. Emmy got the impression that he was trying to keep Ms. Carmichael from seeing his face clearly.

"While you're racking your brains on that one, I suggest you leave Ms. Fox to her many duties. You will not be getting any kind of discount on your booth fee. If you would like to surrender your contract, we can give you a full refund. We have a waiting list for the space, so I'd ask that you decide quickly."

The woman was still looking at Emmy's dad with suspicion. "No. I'll compromise on this one point, and this one point only. But if something else comes up..."

"You can speak directly to me," Emmy's father said.

The woman huffed and then went back to her booth.

Once she was gone, Emmy turned to her dad. "You didn't need to do that. I can handle—"

"Of course I did. You were about to give her the discount. I could see it in your eyes. You don't know how these kinds of people work. You're too nice. I've dealt with a thousand people like her. They get their feathers ruffled and think they can weasel their way into a discount. It doesn't matter if they're talking about pennies off at a restaurant or a cool million in the stock market. They always want something more than what you're willing to give them. It's important to be firm with people like her."

"What if she had walked away? She paid for one of the premium booths. And I know for a fact we don't have a waitlist. Her booth would have been glaringly vacant."

"A little white lie now and then doesn't hurt when it comes to business."

Emmy bit her tongue to keep from reminding him that what he called "little white lies" had hurt a lot more than just his business. Instead, she said, "Thanks for the help, Dad, but I think we have things under control here."

"No problem, and I'm happy to stick around and help where I can. I may not have much experience running a little side show like this, but like I said, business is business."

## Chapter 5
# Three Wise Guys

"I found him!" Kirsten sang out. She reappeared as soon as Ms. Carmichael had gone back to her booth. Emmy's dad wandered off to see who else he could give advice to.

"Who? The love of your life?" Emmy guessed.

"No," Kirsten said. But she blushed, and Emmy wondered how close to the mark she'd hit.

"Who did you find?" Emmy finally asked.

"Our Santa Claus. He's jolly and round-faced, and he has his own beard. He's pretty much everything I want in a Santa."

"Great, that checks one off the list. When do we get to meet this Santa Claus?" Emmy asked.

"He said he'd be here tomorrow. We conducted the interview online, so I haven't actually met him yet. I hope he's good. A good Santa can make or break a Christmas event."

Emmy decided she would have to take her word for it.

"Right on time." Kirsten waved to three men getting out of a rented van. "Our live performers have just arrived. Let's go meet them."

They walked across the square toward the men. Emmy's dad was already there, shaking their hands when she and Kirsten reached them.

"Emmy, Kirsten, I'd like you to meet The Three Wise Guys," her dad made the introduction as if he were the reason the men were there.

"Hello ladies." The oldest man in the group extended his hand. "I'm Clark 'Franklin Sense' and these are my fellow wise guys, Jay Gold and Dennis Mirr."□

"Nice to meet you," Kirsten shook his hand.

"And you must be the lovely heiress, Emerson Fox." Clark bowed to Emmy and took her hand. She wasn't sure if he was going to kiss it or shake it.

She blushed and said, "I recognize you from your old show, *Comedy Train*. I used to watch it with my stepmother."

"Old?" Clark said, pressing her hand. His eyes crinkled as he smiled. Clark was still handsome. Emmy's stepmother had swooned over more than his accent back in the day, and he still had the same chiseled jaw and rugged good looks, even if it was now paired with a full head of silver hair.

The second man, Jay, was close to Emmy's age. He had dark hair and a ready smile. He reached out his hand to Emmy. "Thanks for the opportunity to perform. You have a beautiful little island."

"Thanks," Emmy said. She turned to the third man, but he was staring at her dad with a strange look on his face.

"Wayne Fox," he said, grasping her dad's hand. "It has been years, but it's so good to see you."

"Dennis? Is that you?" Her dad looked at the man in disbelief. "What the hell are you doing on our island, and as part of a comedy troupe of all things?" He turned to Emmy. "Dennis was the most promising up-and-coming investor in our firm. The last time I saw him, he was securely on his way up the corporate ladder." He looked at the man again. "What happened?"

"I made it all the way up that ladder. I was the top dog in a big investment firm, but then I had a change of heart, almost literally. A heart attack a couple of years ago prompted reflection on my life's direction and purpose. People always found me funny. I always wanted to try my hand at comedy, and since I had a substantial nest egg, I decided, 'What the heck?' I've been following this crazy dream for the last fifteen months."

"Wow, that's...interesting." Wayne Fox didn't seem to know what to make of someone who would leave riches behind to follow a dream.

"And what about you?" Dennis asked. "I heard a rumor that you got into a little trouble with the law. Whatever happened with that?"

Mr. Fox waved his hand dismissively. "That was all cleared up a long time ago. I live here now. This is my daughter, Emerson. My late wife's family founded the island. Emmy and I are running things around here now. I guess you could say going into the family business represents my retirement."

"Glad to hear it," Dennis replied. "I knew whatever it was, you'd land on your feet."

Emmy turned to look at her father, flabbergasted at what he had just said about the two of them running the island together. Kirsten was looking at Emmy for guidance, but Emmy didn't want to call him out and embarrass him.

Clark approached Emmy's dad. "We have some questions about our contract."

"For those, you'll need to talk with our events manager, Kirsten. I try not to get too sucked into the minutiae of events like these. There are so many other facets of the business that require my attention."

"I get that," Clark said. He turned to Kirsten. "We weren't sure about the social media pieces in the contract. Will our performances be broadcast or shared online?" He laughed. "I know little about that kind of marketing, but Jay thinks we should go over that."

"Of course," Kirsten said. "We can talk about it over a cup of hot tea. Wait until you try Ms. Lee's. She's almost got me off my four-a-day coffee habit."

"It sounds lovely. As a Brit, you know I always appreciate a good cup of tea," Clark took Kirsten's arm. He nodded toward the still unmoving camel. "Stubborn beasts. Remind me to tell you about the time I was on tour in the Middle East and I rode a camel from one show to the next."

The four of them drifted toward the tea shop. Emmy turned to her father, intending to confront him on the embellishments he'd just told Dennis.

Before she could say anything, something that sounded like cats screeching turned her attention back to the booths. She was horrified when she realized it wasn't cats fighting, but two of the vendors.

## Chapter 6
# Bazaar Conflict

Two older women—Penelope Carmichael and a silver-haired woman in dark slacks, red high heels, and a red sweater sparkling with fake jewels—were standing in the middle of the booths screaming at each other. The women were so close as they shouted at each other that Ms. Carmichael's long, narrow nose was almost touching the other woman's short, turned-up one.

"Looks like you have another problem on your hands," her dad said. "Would you like me to?—"

"No," Emmy said firmly as she strode toward the disturbance. "I can handle this."

"What is she doing here?" Penelope asked as soon as she saw Emmy approaching. "I was told I would have exclusive rights to the Christmas sweater sales at the bazaar."

The other woman drew herself up proudly. "I do not sell Christmas sweaters. I sell bedazzled apparel. My wares are of a much higher caliber than this woman's poor offerings."

"You mean you buy cheap sweaters and throw a little bling on them and try to pass them off as fine clothing?"

"At least I don't incorporate every kind of yarn and every color of the rainbow in my crafts."

"At least you can call mine crafts. You apply a bunch of cheap sparkles with a glue gun. A five-year-old could do what you do."

"At least mine have class," the other woman retorted.

"Ladies, ladies." Emmy stood between them. She was aware of everyone watching her. The other vendors, her dad, even Kirsten and the comedy troupe, had stopped on their way to the tea shop. They all wanted to see what she was going to do.

She took a breath and forced a smile. "There is more than enough room at this bazaar for two ugly Christmas sweater booths. It's such a trend right now that—"

"Ugly?" Ms. Carmichael and Estelle were, for one brief second, united in the word and in the horrified expressions on their faces.

Emmy realized her mistake immediately. "I don't mean to say that they are actually ugly. It's just, well, that's just how they've been branded."

Estelle drew herself up in a way that reminded Emmy of an overbearing hen in a yard of chicken underlings. "Don't confuse my craft with the cheap manufactured garbage that everyone seems to have picked up on."

"I'm sorry, I didn't mean to–"

"My sweaters are not ugly. Each one is handmade by me, a skilled artisan, the height of craftiness," Ms. Carmichael added.

"Right, of course, you put a lot of skill into your...um...creations, and it shows." Emmy stumbled over her words in an attempt to smooth things over. She wished she had Kirsten's gift of soothing frayed nerves and hurt feelings. Both women still appeared offended.

"What I meant to say was, although there are similarities, clearly you have different crafts, so the two of you working at the same bazaar shouldn't be a problem. You both have your own unique styles."

"Style," Estelle sniffed. "Clearly, only one of us possesses that particular gift."

Ms. Carmichael pushed her pointed nose closer to Emmy's face. "I paid extra money for a *premium booth,* so I shouldn't have to share airspace with people like her."

"You and your premium booth." Estelle rolled her eyes. "You always edge in on your premium booth. A premium booth will not help you sell your trash."

"You're calling my work trash? Do you know how much care I knit into every stitch?" Ms. Carmichael said.

"I know every stitch has 'hideous' knitted into it," Estelle replied.

"Hideous? Why I should—" Ms. Carmichael brandished one of her knitting needles.

The other woman backed up in horror. "Did you see? Did you see? Now she's threatening me."

Emmy stepped between them. "Ladies, ladies. I'm sure we can work this out."

Ms. Carmichael moved closer to Emmy. "I will not be in a booth next to that woman! Estelle Pearson is one of those vendors we spoke about. One of those undesirables I told you about. The kind of vendor who can turn a holiday bazaar into a holiday nightmare."

"Holiday nightmare? Estelle said. "At least I'm not wearing a sweater that looks like Christmas threw up on it."

Emmy raised her voice. "Ladies, maybe if we moved one of you to another spot, somewhere farther away–"

Emmy's dad stepped forward. An odd look spread across Penelope's face. She sank back as if she were afraid of him.

"The problem here isn't that you sell wares that are too similar, or even that you ladies can't seem to be in the room together without fighting. The problem is you have no Christmas spirit, no sense of responsibility for your actions, and no thought for other people. My daughter here has worked hard to make this bazaar possible. She put her whole heart into it. This is her first time out of the gate with an extensive project like this. Now, can't we just get along and make the whole thing easier on her?"

Emmy's face flamed. She was mortified. Her dad made her sound like she was a fifth grader at her first science fair and her dad was saying to the judges, "We know her project completely failed, but she's done her best, can't you at least give her a participation ribbon?"

Emmy wanted to crawl under the table, any table. Even one that wasn't in a premium spot. But she needed to show all of them, especially her father, that she had it in her to be a leader.

She raised her voice over the din, working to keep it steady. "You can choose to stay, or you can choose to go. If you're unhappy with your placement or someone else's, or if you simply can't get along, then you're welcome to leave. Your contract states that if you withdraw on your own accord, you won't get back any of the money you put on the booth."

The women turned their arguments to Emmy, but she held up her hand. "That was what was in the contract you both signed. There is no exclusivity agreement, so there is no way for you to get out of it. You have two choices. You can leave your money on the table and leave the bazaar, or you can stay and try to make money and make the most of it with the rest of the people here."

"There is an open spot around the corner. Well, away from the weather and well away from Ms. Carmichael." Kirsten suddenly appeared with a clipboard in hand. "And I'll make sure you have some help with your setup." She waved her hand to Landon, who was striding by. "This lovely lady needs some help moving her things."

"*She* gets help?" Ms. Carmichael said. "I'm the one who..." she trailed off, suddenly looking afraid and meek. "Never mind. Thank you for your help, Ms. Fox."

Emmy turned to see what had made her stop complaining. Her dad was glaring at Ms. Carmichael with a look of fury Emmy had never seen from him before.

## Chapter 7
# Security

"How's the setup going?" Pierce was standing behind Emmy. She was happy to see him. Never in her life had she been afraid of her dad, but the look of pure hatred he had given Penelope Carmichael left her shaken.

"Crazy craft ladies," she said under her breath. "I'm glad to see you, though. I thought you were out of town this week?"

"Things wrapped up with the case I was working on a lot faster than I thought they would. And I got a message from Kirsten about extra security for the bazaar. Do you know what that's about?"

Emmy shook her head. "She's trying to get me to put my grandmother's diamond star on the tree in the square. She says it will be a big draw."

"A big draw, alright, for every thief in the area. You told her no, right?"

"Madelyn said she has some kind of security thing worked out." Madelyn was Emmy's cousin's widow and the resident Sharp Island tech expert. Emmy walked with Pierce to the end of the row of booths.

Pierce watched the vendors and sighed. "We're doing the whole tourist thing again?"

"Yeah, Kirsten is some kind of machine. I think I need to find her off-switch."

"At least this time we aren't dealing with a ghost or a murderer." He leaned over one of the booths and rapped his knuckles. "Knock on wood."

"No, just an overbearing ex-con of a father," Emmy said quietly. She looked around, but her dad had disappeared.

"That bad, huh?" Pierce said.

"I don't know what I'm supposed to do with him. He's in my business, in my house, in the middle of everything I do. He can't seem to stay out of my work, and he thinks I'm still twelve. A twelve-year-old who doesn't know how to take care of herself. I miss my space already." She leaned against him and sighed. "I need to figure this out."

"Why don't you just tell him this isn't working?"

She pulled away. "Yes. I'm going to throw my father out of the door while I celebrate Christmas without him." She shook her head. "I'll make it work, somehow."

"Boundaries," Ramona joined them at the booth. She was wearing a knitted green sweater dress with bells knitted into the fabric. "You need to establish boundaries, and then you need to stick with them."

"Where did you get that dress?" Emmy asked.

"I saw it when that sweater lady was unpacking her things. She gave me a great deal on an advance sale." Ramona gave a little spin. "What do you think?"

"I think it's absolutely hideous."

The voice came from Madelyn. Emmy braced herself. Ramona was Madelyn's former mother-in-law. They were about as fun together as the two crazy craft ladies from the bazaar.

"Speaking of boundaries and the people who like to get on your last nerve," Ramona said.

"Doling out unsolicited advice again?" Madelyn said in a mock-sweet voice.

"Yes actually. I was using my vast experience in dealing with leeches to help Emmy remove a couple of bloodsuckers."

"We all know you're well acquainted with things that thrive in dark, slimy places," Madelyn said.

Emmy sighed. The last thing she needed was more bickering, but at least Madelyn's arrival had saved her from a lecture from Ramona that she wasn't in the mood for.

"Yes, unfortunately, you have been part of my life for the last twenty-three years," Ramona said. "What brings you out of your cave this time?"

Madelyn rolled her eyes toward Ramona before turning her attention to Pierce and Emmy. "Kirsten asked me to rig up some kind of security system for your star. I told her she was insane and that it couldn't be done, but I think I've figured out how to do it."

"Really?" Emmy asked.

"Fortunately, I don't have time for Madelyn's newest experiment. Think about what I said about boundaries, Emmy," Ramona walked away, leaving a faint tinkling behind her.

"How does it work?" Pierce looked skeptically at the mass of wires Madelyn had laid out.

"I'll show you. Everything had to tie into the main power to make sure there would be enough juice for the tree lighting and a way to make the whole place light up as soon as the star was put in place. I also had to find a way for our little Christmas Princess to put the star on top of the tree easily so she doesn't drop it."

"Christmas Princess?" Pierce turned to Emmy. "You re-instituted the pageant?"

"Yeah. It's happening tomorrow night. It's just a bunch of little girls in frilly dresses. We had to come up with a diplomatic way to decide who got to light the star," Emmy said.

"Right," Madelyn said. "Since we had to secure the star to the tree anyway, figuring out how to set up an alarm that would keep people from stealing the star seemed like the next logical step." She held up a thin, star-shaped harness of wire. "I came up with this. The harness fits the star exactly; once in place, it completes the circuit, transforming the square into a winter wonderland."

"How does that keep someone from stealing the star?" Pierce asked.

"Well, if the thirty-foot height isn't enough of a deterrent, we have this." Madelyn pulled the star out of the harness, and an ear-splitting whine filled the air.

"I think we get it!" Emmy yelled, holding her hands over her ears.

Madelyn turned off the alarm, but not before many of the vendors who were setting up their booths came to see what the racket was.

"What is that awful noise?" Ms. Carmichael seemed to have recovered from whatever had made her afraid.

"We're just testing out our new security system," Emmy said. "Hopefully, you won't hear it ever again."

"Security system? I wasn't aware this was a high-crime area. If I remember correctly, our contracts don't cover the theft of our goods. If it's something we should worry about-"

"You honestly think anyone is going to steal something as hideous as one of your sweaters?" Without looking, Emmy knew who the second vendor was. She also knew that both ladies were working up to another argument.

"This is not a high-crime area," Emmy broke in, trying to keep them from going at each other again. "We're just taking extra precautions because this star is a very valuable family heirloom." As soon as she said it, Emmy knew she'd made a mistake. The two women were eyeing the star with keen interest.

"From a purely sentimental standpoint," Emmy said. She laughed nervously. "It's been in my family for years and has been a part of the Sharp Island Christmas Celebration for a very long time. For that reason, it's priceless."

Estelle ventured closer. Something in her eyes glittered like one of her bedazzled sweaters. "It sure does sparkle, doesn't it?"

"It's lovely," Ms. Carmichael said. "But that doesn't answer my question. Are our booths insured against theft or not?"

"Did you see it in your contract?" Emmy's dad's voice boomed as he joined them.

"Well, no." Ms. Carmichael appeared to both shrink back and scrutinize Emmy's dad at the same time.

"Then the answer is no. Feel free to get your own insurance for the booth." He put his hand on the shoulder of the woman who had walked in with him. "My friend Nancy here knows a thing or two about insurance."

Emmy hadn't seen her dad or Pierce's mom come into the square. Seeing them together surprised her. Nancy had been her mom's oldest friend, and Emmy had just assumed that all of her mom's old friends disliked her dad. Brighton Redding certainly did. Maybe since they were both ex-cons, they had found some common ground.

"No, thank you." Ms. Carmichael still seemed afraid of him. "If I decide it's necessary, I have several agents I've worked with in the past." She turned on her heel and walked away.

"I don't doubt that woman has had several insurance agents. I'm guessing that none of them ever wanted to work with her twice," Nancy said.

Estelle laughed out loud. "Isn't that the truth?" She had obviously heard the remark, even if Ms. Carmichael missed it.

## Chapter 8
# Playing Santa

"Speaking of insurance and criminal elements..." Emmy's dad leaned against the booth. "I couldn't help but overhear your conversation with Madelyn. You aren't really planning to put the family star at the top of the tree in the square, are you?"

"I am," Emmy said, and for some reason the disapproving look he gave her made all the reservations she'd had about hanging the star fade away. She'd never been a defiant teenager, but as an adult, her dad's suggestions seemed to rub her the wrong way.

"Do you have any idea how valuable that star is?" her dad said.

"I do." Nancy volunteered. "I had it appraised over twenty years ago for an insurance policy your uncle was going to take out. It was worth a lot of money then. Now it would probably pay for a small boat, or at least a decent car."

"But I don't need a boat or a new car. I like having something that's been in the family for that many years. And I like being able to share it with the whole town. If the island were in crisis again, maybe I'd consider selling it, but things are actually going pretty well right now."

"The star doesn't belong to the island. It belongs to you. You need to learn to take care of your own interests for a change. Is that insurance policy still good?" Emmy's dad asked.

"Although that was actually one of my legitimate policies," Nancy gave Pierce a sideways glance. He didn't like it when his mom brought up the reason she had gone to prison. "That was a long time ago, so no."

"Maybe you should look at getting it insured again," her dad said.

"For once, I'm with your dad on this one," Pierce broke in. "Maybe not on the selling part of it, if the star is that important to you, but hanging it on top of a tree seems like asking for trouble."

Emmy didn't like the two of them ganging up on her; it just made her want to dig in her heels. "What else am I supposed to do with it? It's too big for a normal Christmas tree."

"If you really want to display it, you can wait until next year and hang it in the Town Hall, or some other place that's not completely out in the open," Nancy suggested.

"And leave the top of the tree bare this year?" Emmy asked.

"Maybe you could find something just as big, but cheaper," her dad said. Pierce nodded in agreement.

Emmy crossed her arms. "We don't have time to switch it out now. I trust the security system Madelyn put in, and I trust the people on the island. I've already decided."

"My island, my rules, huh?" Her dad looked disappointed in her. It was a look that used to melt her when she was a kid. Now it just made her angrier.

"Pretty much."

"I just hope you don't regret it," her dad said.

"I won't," Emmy said, but there was a pit in her stomach that made her think they might be right.

The Three Wise Guys were sitting together at a table in the White Sails Restaurant. Birdie, the former cook who had taken over the restaurant, had gotten it opened just in time for the Christmas carnival. Clark stood when Emmy walked in. "The famed Emerson Fox."

"The famed Clark Franklin." She answered back.

He held out a chair for her. "Please join us."

"Thank you. All those times I watched your show, I never imagined I'd be having tea with you."

Clark smiled magnanimously, "Always nice to meet a fan."

Emmy turned to Jay Gold. I've been watching your YouTube videos. You're hilarious, and your charity work is impressive. *Comedy for a Cure* seems to do a lot of good things."

Jay's dark eyes lit up. "Thanks. I founded it after my mom died of cancer. She's the only person who believed in me when I got into this crazy business. I would have never gotten this far without her support."

"Or gotten this far without your 'cancer isn't funny, but this is' videos going viral," the third man, Dennis, said. He had a note of jealousy in his voice.

"You're right. I guess, in a way, I owe that to her as well."

Dennis looked at Emmy expectantly. All she knew about him was that he had known her dad. She racked her brain, but that's all she could come up with. "How long ago did you and my dad work together?"

"Eight years ago, maybe? We didn't work together for very long. The company didn't last long after your dad left." There appeared to be some malice in his voice. Emmy guessed it was toward her father. The company had collapsed under the weight of the embezzlement scandal. Dennis had probably lost his job. He shook his head. "I'm glad to hear things worked out for your dad with the legal stuff. It can be a messy business when you deal with people's money."

"Very messy," Clark said, looking straight at Dennis.

"Yeah." Emmy changed the subject. Not just because of the tension she felt between them, but because this line of questioning was going down a path she didn't want to follow. "You quit your job to live your dream, I think that's fabulous," Emmy said.

"Pretty risky if you ask me," Clark said. "I got into this business when I was too stupid to know any better. I was just lucky that it paid off."

"It's not such a risk if you already have money tucked away for a rainy day, right?" Emmy said.

"Right," Dennis said. For a former investor, he seemed pretty uncomfortable talking about finances.

"Emmy, there you are." Kirsten walked into the restaurant with a tall, white-bearded man. "This is our Santa Claus, Nicholas Star." She stepped aside so Emmy could greet the man who stood beside her.

Nicholas was tall and burly with that "Northwest logger" look. He was wearing a red flannel shirt and worn jeans. His beard and hair were both white, but his face looked younger than the white hair implied.

Emmy stood. "Nice to meet you, Mr. Star."

He enveloped her hand in his. "Nick is fine, or if you prefer, St. Nick." He laughed. "Or Santa. I've kind of gotten as used to those names as the one I was born with. I've been in this business for a long time. As soon as the candles go out in the jack-o'-lanterns, I'm having my red suit cleaned."

Emmy doubted Nicholas Star was the name he was born with, but the man fit the role of Santa Claus, and with that much experience... "Well, we're happy to have you here."

"And I'm happy to spend a few days with you on the island. This is a beautiful place." He looked out the window at the gray clouds moving in. "As long as the weather holds. I hear everything will be outdoors. How is that going to work?"

"Beautifully. Wait until you see the Santa's Workshop my boyfr– I mean, our carpenter has put together." Kirsten said. "I'm sure you've never had such an amazing place to work before."

Emmy agreed with that. Landon had done a great job with all the carpentry work. Although they'd received a myriad of complaints from Penelope and Estelle, none of them had been about the construction of the booths.

"You'll be staying at my bed-and-breakfast, the Keeper's Cottage."

"Are you full up?" Nicholas asked.

"Between my place and the Cliffside Inn, we have plenty of space for tourists and any of the bazaar people who are staying for the entire week," Kirsten said.

"How bizarre are they?" Nicholas asked, another chuckle rising from his throat.

Emmy shook her head. "Most of them are pretty tame, but there are a couple."

"I get that. I've worked at a lot of craft fairs. There are these two ladies, rival ugly sweater sellers, who never stop fighting and complaining."

"Penelope and Estelle. Yeah, they're here," Emmy answered.

He rubbed his beard. "This should be fun. You didn't put them next to each other, did you?"

"Across the aisle," Kirsten said. "A mistake we rectified almost immediately."

"Well, at least it won't be a boring weekend." Nicholas reached for the to-go bag he'd ordered. "How far to the Keeper's Cottage? I'd like to get settled."

"I'll take you there now," Kirsten said.

As they walked away, Emmy's dad walked into the restaurant. "Who was that?"

"Jolly Old Saint Nick," Emmy said. "Nicholas Star, our Santa Claus for the weekend."

"There's something about him that seems familiar," Wayne said. He stroked his own white beard.

"Does it seem as if you were looking in a mirror?" Clark asked.

Her dad wrinkled his eyebrows, as if he didn't get it. "No. It just feels like I've seen him before."

## Chapter 9

# Christmas Princess

A row of little girls in frilly dresses sat in the green room of the town's historic theater. A crowd of mothers swarmed the contestants, doing hair and makeup, listening to last-minute instructions, and waiting for the show to start. The theater had sat vacant for years, but Landon and Kirsten had worked their magic to make it usable. It wasn't a full restoration. There wasn't time or money for that, but they'd done a good job getting it ready for tonight.

Emmy was wearing a long red gown, something Ginny had ordered in for her. Kirsten had insisted Emmy serve as a pageant judge. She reluctantly agreed. Emmy didn't like the idea of choosing a winner and possibly incurring the wrath of the other pageant moms when their darlings weren't chosen.

"Just in the 'Nick' of time!" Kirsten joked as Nicholas and The Three Wise Guys joined them backstage.

"Sorry I'm late." Estelle bustled in, carrying a large square box with sparkling silver wrapping paper and a bedazzled red bow.

"I can't wait to show you how it turned out." Estelle was almost giddy as she set the box on the table and glanced around. The little girls and their mothers were preoccupied with hair and makeup. "It's supposed to be a surprise," Estelle explained, lifting the lid off the box. Inside was a little tiara, bedazzled with red, green, and white jewels.

"Oh, it's beautiful!" Emmy exclaimed.

Estelle softened, glowing at the praise. "Ms. Loche asked me if I could make one for the pageant when I signed up for a booth for the bazaar. It turned out rather nice, didn't it? Of course, it would be much prettier if it were real."

"Well, it's just a little girl's Christmas pageant, not Miss Universe or anything like that," Kirsten said. "But you did a beautiful job." She turned to Nicholas. "It will be on the table backstage, ready for you to award it to our little princess."

Nicholas was in his Santa suit and looked much more jolly and relaxed than he had the first time Emmy had seen him. He appeared to be one of those people who felt most comfortable portraying someone else.

Kirsten cleared her throat and turned to the Three Wise Guys, all dressed in dark suits. "Thank you gentlemen for agreeing to help tonight. I need you to—"

"Equal airtime!" Penelope Carmichael's voice echoed from the back of the theater. "If she gets to show off her bling with that atrocious bit of a crown, I should get the chance to showcase some of my items as well."

Clark shrunk back toward the dark curtains at the edge of the stage as Ms. Carmichael strode to the front of the room.

"This isn't a presidential election. It's a little girl's Christmas pageant," Estelle shot back.

Ms. Carmichael stopped at the edge of the stage. "You're clearly showing favoritism toward one vendor over another. I demand the chance to show off my products, too."

Kirsten blew out an impatient breath. "Ms. Pearson doesn't even sell crowns in her booth. What would you suggest we have you do? It's too late for you to knit the stage curtains."

Ms. Carmichael held herself up indignantly. "It doesn't matter; in my judgement I should be part of this pageant. I deserve to-"

Emmy saw her escape. "That's it. You can be a judge. You can take my spot."

Ms. Carmichael looked taken aback. "A pageant judge?"

"Yes, I'm sure you'll be an exceptional judge," Emmy said.

"Being judgmental is one of her most prominent qualities," Dennis said, not quite under his breath.

Ms. Carmichael narrowed her eyes. "I am an excellent judge of character, and as for you—"

"It's settled then," Emmy said. "Ms. Carmichael is our new pageant judge."

For the first time, Ms. Carmichael looked hesitant. "I'm more than qualified to judge your competition–I know a thing or two about talent and beauty–but how does that showcase my sweaters?"

"I'll point out that lovely dress when I introduce you." Clark emerged from the edges of the stage and indicated the multicolored, crocheted sweater dress Penelope was wearing.

Ms. Carmichael's icy expression melted under his gaze. She flushed red. "Well, I guess the pageant could use a professional opinion."

"And," he said, turning to Estelle as the woman opened her mouth to protest, "I'll point out you crafted that lovely crown."

Kirsten looked flustered. "Very diplomatic of you, but–"

"It seems like the best solution for everyone involved, don't you think?" Clark's voice was satiny smooth. Ms. Carmichael appeared transfixed.

"I guess so. It's just that I'm not sure when you'll have the chance to make that announcement," Kirsten said.

"Don't worry, I can slip it in easily, between numbers, a kind of PSA of sorts. That reminds me, we'd better get to the sound check. Which microphone will I be using?" Clark said.

"Microphone?" Kirsten looked at him with confusion.

"Yes," Clark laughed. "I've been accused of being a loudmouth, but I don't think I can emcee without a microphone."

"Oh." Kirsten looked uncharacteristically flustered. "We asked Jay to emcee. You and Dennis will be judges." The youngest wise guy stepped forward and nodded uncomfortably. "I guess the message to your agent didn't get passed on correctly. We're going to have a bit of a younger crowd. The kids know him from his YouTube channel and social media posts, and they really relate to him. Your brand of comedy is a bit…"

"Dated?" Clark supplied. He let out a little guffaw, as if he didn't care, but he definitely looked put out. "I guess it's time to pass the rubber chicken of comedy onto the next generation." He turned and made a big show of straightening Jay's tie. Then he clapped him on the shoulders. "Well, my boy, make your elders proud. We'll just be sitting at the judge's table, masterminding your untimely demise. No bathroom jokes or farting noises created with your armpits, please. This is a classy competition."

Jay looked embarrassed, but he smiled. "Come on, Clark, that takes away at least half my repertoire."

"I know," Clark said, rolling his eyes. "I suppose we must give the crowds what they want."

As he moved to the stairs at the front of the stage, Emmy caught Ms. Carmichael staring daggers in Jay's direction. Clark offered her his arm. "My fair lady and fellow judge."

She giggled like a star-struck tween and let him escort her to the judge's table.

Emmy moved to a seat in the VIP section and sank into a chair beside Pierce. "Very diplomatic of *you*," he said as he put his arm around her. "Now you can enjoy the show without worrying about maternal backlash when someone's little angel doesn't win."

Emmy leaned into him and felt the tightness leave her stomach. Now that she wasn't a judge, she was actually looking forward to watching the pageant.

"We need to look into higher-end performers once we renovate this theater," Emmy's dad said as he sat heavily in the chair next to her. "Think of how much we could charge for one of these box seats if we brought in some real talent."

"I thought you weren't coming," Emmy said. "You said the pageant was kids' stuff."

"It is kids' stuff, but maybe I've reached the age where I'm looking forward to that part of life again." His eyes twinkled. "The way you used to talk about kids, I was sure I'd have a grandkid or two by now. If you'd married Collin–"

"If I'd married Collin, you wouldn't have any grandkids." Emmy's face flamed as Pierce raised his eyebrows at her. "He made it clear that raising children was a waste of time and resources."

Her dad patted her knee. "That's okay. I'm sure some guy will come along who'll make you think about having your own little dress-up doll." He nodded toward the stage. "I guarantee the moms are more invested in this than any of those kids."

There was a lot Emmy wanted to say to her dad, and a lot she wished he hadn't said, but Jay walked on stage to begin the pageant, so she just sat back and fumed. Pierce reached over and squeezed her hand. She wasn't sure if it was a gesture of comfort, solidarity, or something else. She wasn't sure how he felt about kids. It wasn't a discussion that had come up in their relationship.

The Christmas Princess Pageant went off nearly without a hitch. The little girls successfully made it through a gingerbread-themed song and dance number. They performed various talents, answered the judges' questions, and floated across the stage in knee socks, Mary Janes, and fluffy dresses.

The only discord came from the judge's table. Ms. Carmichael appeared to take her position as judge very seriously. She had a permanent appraising frown on her face and spent most of her time scribbling notes on the paper in front of her.

At the end of the pageant, the little girls stood holding hands in the center of the stage. The judges, ending with Ms. Carmichael, passed a white envelope to Emmy. She sealed it with a bit of red wax and embossed it with the Sharp Island crest, then took it to the front of the stage and handed it to Jay.

As she left the stage, Emmy noticed Ms. Carmichael glaring at Jay again. She realized he'd forgotten to introduce the judges entirely. They hadn't given Ms. Carmichael the promotional spot promised.

Jay appeared oblivious to her glare as he tore open the envelope with a dramatic flourish. He cleared his throat, flashed a winning smile, and then looked down at the results. He froze. The color drained from his face. It took a few breathless seconds for him to recover. He played it off as if it were part of the drama of announcing the winner, but something about the results had flustered him.

The applause overwhelmed his hesitation as they crowned six-year-old Bryn Lea Foster Island Christmas Princess.

After the crowning, Emmy took the microphone. She thanked Jay and the judges, and she ensured Estelle and Penelope received recognition. She forgot about the look on Jay's face and the glare Ms. Carmichael had given him until the pageant was over.

Bryn Lea's mom came up on stage and asked Emmy if she could have the envelope with her daughter's name on it for her scrapbook.

"Of course," Emmy said and went in search of the envelope. She found it lying in the garbage can backstage. Bryn Lea's name was intact on the top, but someone had shredded the bottom of the paper. Emmy pulled the pieces out of the garbage and fit them together.

The pieces spelled out another name at the bottom, but it wasn't the name of someone who was in the pageant. It was a name Emmy didn't recognize. The shredded words said:

*Candy Mason*

## Chapter 10

# Disturbing the Peace

E mmy hadn't slept well again. Despite the industrial pair of earplugs she'd bought, she could still hear her dad snoring. Her thoughts had been turning over in her head like a dryer full of sneakers, so she probably wouldn't have slept anyway. She was worried about all the things that could go wrong today. It was the morning of the tree lighting, and the jeweler hadn't finished cleaning and repairing the star yet.

Besides the stress associated with the lighting and the Christmas festivities, Emmy couldn't help but worry that something else was going on. Maybe her anxiety came because she was used to things never being exactly what they seemed on Sharp Island. Last night's pageant had confirmed that. Jay was the intended recipient of the note Ms.

Carmichael added to the bottom of the pageant results, but what did it mean? Why? And what was that woman's issue, anyway? Did she live to make other people's lives miserable? The message meant nothing to Emmy, but she knew it meant something to Jay. He'd disappeared right after the pageant, so Emmy didn't get the chance to talk to him.

"Big day today," her dad boomed as he sat at the table, ready for her to serve him breakfast. It had become their morning routine. Emmy hadn't figured out how to tell him they should take turns with the cooking, or that he could probably get by with cold cereal.

"Yeah." Emmy cracked an egg into a bowl so she could start an omelet. Her phone dinged. She looked at the text and sighed. "This isn't good."

"What isn't good, Pumpkin?" her dad asked without taking his eyes off his phone.

"I sent the star to the jeweler in Seattle to be cleaned and repaired. The man at the shop assured me he'd have it done early this morning. But now he's saying it will be this afternoon." She looked at the text. "He's saying something about the extra project taking longer than he thought. I don't know what he's talking about. I'd better call him." She moved to dial the number, but her dad stopped her.

"Maybe it's a sign that you shouldn't be using the star," he said.

Emmy was too stressed to be diplomatic. "If I don't have the star, nothing will work right with the lighting. If it's going to be in the afternoon, I won't have time to get everything done. Pierce was going to take the day off. Maybe he'd have time to—"

Her father covered her hand as she started to text Pierce. "If it's that important to you, I can pick up the star. I have a meeting in Seattle, anyway. After all, I'm the one who recommended Shay Jewelers."

"I don't think that's a good idea." Emmy bit her tongue. She didn't want her dad to think she didn't trust him with the star. Even if were true.

"Why not? I've been there dozens of times. It will free you up for everything else. Learning to delegate is a huge part of business. One you need to be better at."

"Right." Emmy thought about it for a second. She didn't really have any other choice. "Thank you. It would help me out a lot if you could get the star. They already have my credit card information. You just need to make sure you're on the three o'clock ferry so you don't miss the lighting."

"Dad's on it. I won't let you down."

Emmy hoped that was the truth.

The air outside was crisp. Miraculously, it wasn't raining. Emmy left her dad to get ready for his meeting in Seattle and hurried to put the finishing touches on the main tree in the square. Someone had brought in a lift, and the lights were hung. Madelyn's security system was in place. Emmy was going to add the big, colorful Christmas bulbs that had been stored behind the bookshop for too long. She was excited to decorate the tree and see the completed effect. She was even excited about the upcoming bazaar.

Landon met her in front of the big tree. "It looks pretty good, don't you think?"

Emmy hadn't talked to him much since he had voted to sell the island, then found out he wasn't actually a descendant of one of the island's founders and not entitled to a vote.

Emmy set the box of decorations in front of the tree. "It all looks great. You do excellent work."

"Thanks," Landon smiled. "Would you like me to help you get the rest of the boxes of ornaments?"

Kirsten took him by the hand. "Emmy has her own lackey. I need you over here."

"I guess that means I'm your lackey." Pierce carefully set another box next to the one she'd carried. "I can think of worse things to do on my day off than help you decorate the big tree." He looked around. "Where's your dad?"

"He had an appointment on the mainland with his parole officer. I didn't have to go with him this time." Emmy took a breath that felt strangely like freedom. It was the first day in a long time she hadn't had her dad shadowing her, asking questions, pointing out things she'd missed, or things he would have done differently.

Pierce didn't ask; they'd already had plenty of conversations about Emmy's dad.

She smiled. The sun was bright; everything was going great. She needed to fix her attitude. "But he'll be here tonight for the lighting. Despite everything, I'm glad to have him here for Christmas."

Piece put his arm around her. "Family makes you crazy sometimes, but it's nice to have them around. My mom will be here for Christmas, too."

"Maybe we can get them together so we can have some 'just us' time. They could compare prison stories," Emmy said.

"Yeah," Pierce said, but he flinched at the word 'prison.' His mom's criminal record was still a sore spot for him. She also knew he was protective of his mom and that he still didn't trust her dad.

They decorated to the sounds of the Victorian Carolers and the high school band from the mainland practicing their music for the lighting. Although they were in the middle of the town square, using a lift and a tall ladder, with people buzzing around them, Emmy could imagine they were in the living room of her house or his, maybe even theirs, listening to Christmas music and decorating a Christmas tree. She hadn't let her mind wander in that direction too much when it came to Pierce. After everything that happened with Collin, she wasn't eager to jump back into that level of commitment. Pierce had already proved he wasn't like Collin, but she was still wary.

They finished putting up the last of the giant bulbs, and Emmy stood back to admire the tree. It looked perfect to her, but Pierce got back on the ladder and adjusted some ornaments to a higher or lower branch. She smiled at how particular he was. That was just Pierce; Emmy didn't need to change that.

"Did you ever get that loose diamond fixed on the star?" Pierce asked as he climbed down from his last change.

"Yes. It's being cleaned and repaired by a jeweler on the mainland."

"You're still hanging it up tonight?"

"Yeah."

He shook his head, but he didn't remind her what a terrible idea he thought it was. On that point, at least, he and her dad were in violent agreement. "How are you going to get it back in time for the lighting tonight?"

"My dad is picking it up," Emmy said.

Pierce raised his eyebrows. "Are you sure that's a good idea?"

Emmy opened her mouth to protest, to defend her dad, but she knew he was right. "No. But I have to trust him sometime. He swore up and down that he'd guard it with his life. Then he went into some story about taking me to the lighting when I was a little girl. He said my eyes got huge when they put up the star. He said, 'That's when I knew you were a diamond girl.'"

"Are you?" Pierce asked.

"A diamond girl?" Emmy shrugged. She was trying to stay casual, but his question caused her heart to pound. "Probably not like Estelle. She blings everything in sight."

"But you've had diamonds before?"

She shrugged. "Dad got me a pair of diamond earrings for my sixteenth birthday and a real diamond necklace for graduation. I sold them both after he went to prison. That was kind of it as far as me and diamonds go."

"I know of at least one more," Pierce said softly.

"Right, there was the garish diamond engagement ring Collin gave me. It was so huge and showy I was afraid to wear it in public. Ginny used to joke that after a lifetime of wearing it, I'd have horrible arthritis just in that finger." Emmy stooped, realizing she had said too much.

"You didn't like the ring he gave you?" Pierce asked.

"The ring was okay. It was the guy who was the problem." Emmy rolled her eyes.

He smiled and reached for her hand, rubbing the spot where Collin's ring had once been. "Whether it was the diamond or the guy that was the problem. I like how things worked out."

"Me too." Emmy stood on her toes to kiss him.

"That was mine!" A familiar screech cut through the otherwise festive sounds around them.

"They're like toddlers. Overgrown, angry toddlers." She looked around. "And as usual, Kirsten is MIA."

"Would you like me to arrest both of them for disturbing the peace?" Pierce asked.

"Could you please?" Emmy asked.

"I'm actually off duty, but..."

Emmy let out a dramatic sigh. "I guess I can be diplomatic one more time."

"Just one?" Pierce's eyes sparkled.

"After that, I'm letting you throw them in jail."

"It's a deal," Pierce said.

Emmy walked toward the two ladies and arranged her face into a bright smile. "Hello ladies, is there a–"

"My stapler. She took my stapler," Penelope said.

"I did not take your stapler," Estelle turned to Emmy. She held up a sparkly pink stapler in the shape of a high heel. "As you can see, I have my own stapler."

"Not that one. An industrial one, like the one I was using to hang my lights."

"I don't need an industrial one. My lights have hooks that attach them to the side of my booth. See?" Estelle pointed out a row of diamond lights that indeed hooked nicely to her booth.

"What about over there?" Penelope pointed the knitting needle she had in her hand to the corner of Estelle's booth. "You used an industrial stapler to put up the hangers for your heavy sweaters. How do you explain that?" She crossed her arms over the bright green elf sweater she was wearing. "Solve that mystery for us, Ms. Fox."

"I borrowed one from that handsome carpenter," Estelle said triumphantly.

Landon walked by at that moment. He looked immediately guilty. "What did I do?"

Estelle batted her bejeweled eyelids. "You lent me your stapler."

"That's right, I did," Landon said. He reached into the tool bag slung over his shoulder and pulled out a silver industrial stapler. "Do you need it again?"

"No, honey, that's all we needed," Estelle said.

"But that's my stapler!" Penelope protested.

"Is it?" Landon dug deeper into his bag and pulled out an identical stapler. "I guess I picked this one up by mistake."

"No harm done. Just another misunderstanding." Emmy gave the two women her best annoyed glare. She wished she could believe that was the end of their bickering, but she knew it wouldn't be. With those two around, there was no chance of having a silent night.

## Chapter 11

# Lifeless at the Lighting

A sizable crowd of people filled the square. The morning's unpleasantness between Penelope and Estelle seemed to be forgotten in the gathering of excited children and the glow of the upcoming holidays. A steady stream of customers moved through the vendor area. There were long lines to visit Santa Claus and the petting zoo. The camel trainer had put a saddle on the camel and was charging people to have their picture taken while they sat on it. They weren't camel rides exactly, because the camel never even stood up. Balthazar the camel had been kneeling ever since they'd prodded him into his pen. The other animals were livelier.

Brynn Lea Foster sat on a little chair in the middle of the square. Her dark hair had been curled into ringlets under her tiara, and she was wearing a fluffy white coat and a sparkly dress for her one and only responsibility as Christmas Princess. The lift would carry her and Santa to the top of the tree to place the star. As soon as the star was in place, light would bathe the square, the band would play and the carolers would sing.

At least that was the way it was supposed to go.

Emmy was chatting and smiling—thanking everyone for coming. Inside, she was panicking. Everything was in place except for the star. The tree lighting was scheduled for seven o'clock. It was nearly five-thirty, and her dad hadn't shown up yet. Her mind raced. What would she do if he didn't come back with the star? Could she have her own father arrested? Could she send the police after him?

Pierce handed her a paper cup of tea that smelled of cedar and mint.

"Thank you. Now everything is perfect." But he saw through her tight smile.

"Your dad hasn't made it back yet, has he?"

"No."

She braced herself for the 'I told you so,' but he just squeezed her arm. "Do you know if the ferry was running on time?"

"I checked it twenty minutes ago, and yes, it arrived on time." Emmy said. "He's not answering his phone."

"It will all work out," Pierce said, pulling her into a hug.

The vendors were slowly closing up shop to move into the square with the islanders and tourists. Emmy scanned the crowd, hoping that maybe her dad had slipped in without her noticing. There were no men with white beards, not even the Santa Claus they'd hired.

The Victorian carolers sang their way toward the front of the crowd. Their melodic harmonies and period costumes added just the right ambiance to the evening. Emmy wondered which days Kirsten had booked them for and whether they could stay in a central location to perform. In front of Penelope's or Estelle's booths seemed like a good idea. Those two could use a reminder of what peace on earth really meant.

"What do we think, ladies?" Kirsten joined them at the edge of the square.

"Magical," Ginny said.

"You haven't seen magic yet," Kirsten said. "This is just getting started."

Emmy fought down waves of panic. "But my dad..."□

Kirsten pressed her headset to her ear. "He's here," she said to Emmy.

"He made it?" Emmy practically fainted with relief. She wanted to go run to the staging area near the vendor's booths to see the star personally and ask her dad what took him so long. But the crowd pressed around her, and there wasn't time.

"I told you it would be alright," Pierce said, reaching for her hand.

The carolers broke into an a cappella version of *Here Comes Santa Claus*. Bryn Lea's mother fluffed the little girl's dress and then her hair. The little princess stood waiting for her cue.

According to the script, Santa Claus was supposed to meet her at the lift, trade her tiara for the cutest little red hard hat available, and then hand her the gift-wrapped box that contained the diamond star. She would open it. Then they would both enter the lift, and the lift would take them up to place the star atop the tree.

The lights in the square dimmed. The music swelled. Kirsten nodded.

Bryn Lea flashed a toothy grin and stepped forward. Emmy waited for the "Ho ho ho," and the jingle of bells that would signal the arrival of Santa Claus.

The carolers paused. Bryn Lea was waiting; the crowd was waiting; the place where Santa Claus was supposed to enter the square remained empty. The little girl looked at her mother in confusion.

Kirsten touched her finger to her headphones. "What is happening?" She listened for a second. "Where is Santa Claus? What do you mean it's not the right box? Are you sure? No. Get them singing again. I don't know, do they know *Up on the Housetop*?"

Emmy leaned closer, wishing she had a headset. "What's going on?"

"No big deal. We'll figure it out." Kirsten's voice was calm, but there was frustration bordering on panic in her eyes.

"What's going on?" Emmy hissed again.

Kirsten pressed her hand to her headset. "Keep singing. No, have her wait."

"The star is missing," Pierce guessed.

"The star is missing?" Emmy said.

Kirsten didn't answer, but based on the look on her face, Emmy guessed Pierce was right.

"Has anyone seen my dad?" Emmy scanned the crowd. Her heart sank; trusting her dad had been a huge mistake. But if he'd stolen the star, why go to the trouble of coming back at all? He could have pawned it in Seattle and been on his way already.

He wouldn't have stolen the star, but he was missing. The carolers were looking at Kirsten for some kind of direction. They were on their third Santa Claus-themed song.

The only one left was *I Saw Mommy Kissing Santa Claus,* and no one wanted that. The crowd was getting restless. Brynn Lea looked as if she was about to burst into tears.

Emmy was getting close to that herself.

"Someone switched the box?" Kirsten said into the headset. "I don't care which of them made the box for the pageant, or if one is offended by whatever box we use; I just want that star in here ASAP!"

Emmy didn't know what any of that meant, but she had a feeling it had something to do with the two crazy craft ladies.

"We'll hash out who stole what from whom after this is over. Get the right box to Santa NOW!"

Emmy squeezed Pierce's hand. "Maybe I should go see what's–"

Clark, from The Three Wise Guys, walked to the lift at the front of the square as the chorus scrambled to come up with another song. Despite the panic, he moved slowly and confidently, waving to the crowd as he went. He made a big gesture of whispering in the little girl's ear, loud enough for the crowd to hear. "I hear you're missing a star."

"Santa was supposed to bring it to me," the little girl said with wide-eyed innocence.

"You are in luck, my dear," Clark said. "I have just the people you'll need if you're looking for a missing star." He took a low bow. "May I introduce you to my friend?"

Brynn Lea looked at him as if she wasn't sure, but nodded.

"Jay Gold."

Jay took the stage to enthusiastic applause.

After a minute, Dennis hurried onto the stage. Clark gave him a sharp look. "And our tardy friend, Dennis Mirr."

He spread his arms. "And I'm Clark, Clark Franklin Sense."

The three stood behind the little girl. "And together we are The Three Wise Guys."

"Wise Guys?" The little girl said. "Aren't the Wise Men supposed to be the ones who find the star?"

"I'm afraid there wasn't enough in the budget for them to make an appearance, so you're stuck with us," Jay said.

The crowd laughed, and Emmy felt some of the weight leave her shoulders.

"You said Santa was supposed to bring you the star?" Jay asked.

"Yes. I was supposed to stand right here and keep smiling, but he didn't come." The little girl looked at him like he could help her.

"He's probably just running a little late."

Clark jumped in. "I heard he had to pick up Rudolph from the hospital."

"The hospital?" The little girl said. It was hard to tell if she was acting with the men or if she was honestly worried about Santa Claus.

"Don't worry," Dennis said as he turned around. He was wearing a glowing red nose. "He was just getting a nose job."

The crowd groaned.

"Keep them going," Kirsten said. "Someone find the right box and get Santa out here!"

"Naw, that wasn't it at all, gentlemen," Clark said. "I heard there was an accident with some mistletoe."

"Mistletoe?" Jay asked. "What kind of accident do you have with mistletoe?"

"If any of us know what kind of accident mistletoe might cause, it would be you, pretty boy," Clark said. He leaned in conspiratorially into Dennis' ear. "I heard someone was kissing someone underneath the mistletoe."

"Your mama was kissing someone under the mistletoe," Jay said.

"Not you, you idiot. I heard it was some jolly guy in a red suit," Dennis said.

"You mean Santa Claus?" Bryn Lea said.

"Yeah, Santa Claus, that's who it was," Clark said.

"Who was he kissing?" Dennis said.

"Your mama!" Jay said again.

The three of them leaned together and broke into *I Saw Mommy Kissing Santa Claus.* After a few bars, the carolers joined in.

Emmy laughed despite the stress. The Three Wise Guys had done an excellent job of covering up the delay.

While they were singing, a very rosy-cheeked and out of breath Santa Claus appeared at the edge of the crowd. He had a white box with a big red bow on it in his hands. He was trying to compose himself.

"He's here!" The children in the crowd yelled.

The band started playing "Here Comes Santa Claus." The carolers and the crowd joined in.

The Three Wise Guys gave a low bow as a still red-faced Santa breezed past Emmy toward the center of the square, leaving behind the faint scent of peppermint.

"Ho ho ho," he croaked, still out of breath. "Sorry I'm late." He pushed the box toward Bryn Lea, a bit abruptly. "But I heard you and all the Sharp Islanders have been very good this year."

"Yes, Santa," it was the only line she had practiced. Bryn Lea opened the box, and her mouth opened in a big "Ooooh!" She lifted the diamond star out of a bed of tissue paper, and the crowd ooooh'd too.

Emmy breathed a sigh of relief. She still didn't know where her dad was, but at least the star was where it was supposed to be.

Santa helped the little girl into a red hard hat, and they stepped into the lift together. The crowd cheered as it rose in the air. Once it reached full height, the little girl lifted the star and placed it on the clips at the top of the tree. For one breathless moment nothing happened, then the whole square lit up with brilliant white lights.

The band and the Victorian Carolers burst into a round of *Do You See What I See?* The crowd cheered. Pierce leaned over and kissed Emmy. She basked in the glow of the lights. A wave of triumph washed over her.

"We need Dr. Gregory now!" The familiar voice behind her cut through the music and the crowd. Emmy's dad staggered to the edge of the light. Blood stained the front of his shirt. "She's been stabbed!"

# Chapter 12
# Body at the Bazaar

"D addy!" Emmy ran to him. He stepped back to keep from getting blood on her white coat.

"It's not mine, baby." He pointed back in the direction he had come from. Pierce took off in a run toward the vendor area.

Emmy was still looking for some kind of wound on her dad. "What happened? Whose blood is this?"

"Penelope's, the sweater lady. I found her slumped over in her booth. I thought maybe she'd just worn herself out and was sleeping on the job. When I got closer, I could see the blood underneath her table. I tried to stop the bleeding with one of her sweaters, but I think it's too late." He took a breath.

Emmy ran to the booth. Penelope Carmichael was sitting in the chair at the back of her booth. She was slumped forward, a knitting needle embedded in her throat. Pierce was standing beside her, his hand on her wrist.

"What's all the fuss about?" Estelle came from behind her booth. "Aren't you all supposed to be at the..."

She stared at Penelope's body. "Is she..."

Pierce looked up at all of them. "Yes. She's dead."

Kirsten came around the corner. She froze, a horrified look on her face. Behind them, the band still played, the carolers still sang, the lights still glowed, but everything had changed in a heartbeat. Emmy took Kirsten's headset from her and pressed it into her own ear.

"What's going on?" Landon's voice crackled over the headset.

"Find Dr. Gregory and Officer Peters. Send them to the vendor area. Do it quickly, but quietly."

"What's going on, Em?" Ginny's voice was next.

"I'll explain later. For now, tell the band to keep playing and then have The Three Wise Guys go on, but ask them to cut their show down to about fifteen minutes. Keep everyone on the other side of the square." Emmy was surprised at the calm in her voice. She turned to Pierce. "Will that work?"

"For now, yes. I don't suppose there's any way to detain everyone here, or get names." He stood and turned to Emmy. "Don't let anyone touch anything."

Estelle moved to the edge of the booth and sniffed. "Impaled by her own sword." She shook her head. "What a way to go, and amid so many fashion atrocities." She stepped back. "If she's dead, does that mean I can have the premium booth? I mean, after it's all cleaned up, of course."

Emmy stared at her, dumbfounded. The woman didn't appear in the least bit shocked by what had happened. There was no remorse, not even pretended remorse, for the woman lying dead on the ground in front of her.

"I don't believe we'll be going through with the bazaar after tonight. Or really any of it."

"You won't? Then I certainly hope you'll honor the 'unexpected disaster' clause in the contract."

"You'll all get full refunds," Emmy said.

Her dad stepped forward. "Now, wait a minute. I read the contract thoroughly, and it said that no refunds would be given after the first day. You had at least one good day of business. If we decide to cancel the bazaar, the most you'll get is a partial refund."

Emmy couldn't believe the two of them fighting over something so trivial with a dead woman between them.

"Again?" Officer Peters said as he came around the corner. "I had a feeling when Landon came and got me, but I can't believe there's been another murder. I guess anything is possible on this island. Maybe you should change the name from Sharp Island to Murder Island."

Emmy had a sinking feeling that the name might stick.

## Chapter 13

# Crafting a Murder

Ms. Carmichael's body was in the morgue, and the crowd had dispersed for the night. Pierce was searching the dead woman's booth, and Emmy was wearing gloves to help him bag up the evidence. He was speaking into a recorder as he cataloged the contents of the booth.

"A wide assortment of knitting and crochet needles, all sizes. No match to the one found in the victim's throat." Pierce dropped the items into separate bags.

"Several skeins of yarn in every color of the rainbow. A full cash box. Money doesn't appear to be a motive for the murder."

He counted and shook his head. "Eighty-seven knitted garments; fifty scarves and thirty-seven sweaters, including two that were used by Mr. Fox in what he claims was an attempt to stop the bleeding."

He stopped the recording when he saw the look on Emmy's face. "I have to say it that way."

"Guilty until proven innocent?" Emmy said.

"I'm sorry," Pierce said. "But I have to look at all suspects. Just like you did before."

"Right," Emmy said. She'd suspected Pierce's family members before. She wished she could be sure that her father wasn't involved, but she'd suspected him of murder once herself.

"Maybe you should head home. It's late and you've had a very long day. You don't need to sit here while I bag up yet another..." he held up a bag of fuzzy balls with a questioning look.

"Those are called pom-poms," Emmy supplied.

"Right." He turned on the recorder. "Eighteen bags of pom-poms in assorted colors and sizes."

"Some with sparkles," Emmy said, but there was no humor in her voice. She should take Pierce's advice and go home, but she'd finally convinced her dad to go back to her apartment. She wasn't in a hurry to rehash with him everything that had gone wrong with the tree lighting tonight.

"Speaking of sparkles." Pierce opened a flat, opaque box. At the bottom was an assortment of crystals and sequins.

"Very pretty, but..." Emmy examined the gems inside the box. "Not really her style. Estelle goes for the bling more than Penelope."

"Do you think she stole this box from her rival's booth?" Pierce asked.

"It hardly seems worth stealing. There aren't that many here." She shook the box. "Only about a dozen left. But it's a big box. Maybe there used to be more." She remembered what she'd heard over the radio. "I wouldn't put it past Ms. Carmichael to have stolen this and thrown most of the gems away."

"I wouldn't put much past either of them," Pierce said.

"Even murder?" Emmy asked.

He set his mouth into a firm line. "That remains to be seen."

The thought hung in the air while they continued to sift through the booth.

Pierce held up a box of assorted shapes. "What would you call these?"

"Felted holiday shapes," Emmy said.

"Felt holiday shapes?" he asked.

"No, felted–they're covered in felt, but she used a needle to make them look fluffier."

Pierce shook his head as he added the shapes to the growing pile of evidence.

"If I leave, how are you going to identify the random bits and bobs of craft supplies scattered around this booth?"

"Which semester was it that you majored in arts and crafts?" Pierce asked.

"Clothing and textiles," she corrected him, "but that was only one class. Needlework, sewing, all of it takes patience I lack. But I was a devoted Girl Scout for nearly two weeks one summer. Most of my craftiness comes from that." She picked up a blue and white object. "For example, do you know what this is?"

"Easy. A glue gun. Remember, I was a Cub Scout once too." He bagged up the glue gun. "I got what felt like a third-degree burn with one of these at day camp."

"Yeah, why do they let kids use these things anyway?" Emmy picked up a colorful box. She shook it. "Want to play 'Name the Craft Item'?"

He took the box and shook it. "Based on the smell, potpourri, I would guess this is full of some kind of mint potpourri."

Emmy took it from him. "Mint isn't usually used in potpourri, especially not this much mint. It smells boozy to me." She peered inside. It was full of different colors of lace, but something had spilled all over it. She sniffed deeper. Besides mint, the lace reeked of alcohol.

"Peppermint schnapps," she guessed.

Pierce confirmed her suspicion when he found a broken bottle under the table. He held it up. There were only a few drops of the minty alcohol inside. "This is pretty potent stuff."

"And yet still festive," Emmy said.

The peppermint tickled something in her memory. When Nicholas Star finally put in his appearance, he smelled like peppermint. It wasn't necessarily an unusual smell to come from someone playing Santa Claus, but considering what they had just found, it might be something that tied him to the scene of the crime.

"When you're done there, I want you to look at something." Madelyn stood at the corner of the booth long after everyone else had gone home.

"Go. I've got this," Pierce said.

"What's this about?" Emmy asked as they walked away.

Madelyn didn't answer, so Emmy followed her to the square where the tree still glowed ethereal white in the gathering fog. Madelyn gazed up at the star at the top of the tree. "I didn't want to say anything in front of Pierce in case I was wrong, but..." she shook her head. "I don't think that's the right star."

Emmy looked at her as if she were crazy. "What do you mean?"

"I mean, I calibrated the hooks on either side of the star to fit perfectly. Seating it in the space I built automatically triggered the connection, lighting the tree and everything around it."

"And it did, right?"

Madelyn sighed. "Actually, no. I rigged a backup. If the lights didn't come on immediately, I was prepared to throw a switch. That's what I did."

Emmy paused, trying to figure out what all this meant. "Could it have changed in size when the jeweler fixed the loose diamond?"

"Not that much," Madelyn said.

"So you think someone switched out the diamond star for something less valuable?"

"I'm not sure. It could have been that the clips weren't exactly right, or that the little girl didn't get it quite seated exactly on the hooks. But..."

"But you think my dad may have switched out the star when he took it to the jeweler?" Emmy said. "That's why you didn't say anything in front of Pierce, because you wanted to give me the chance to find out for sure first."

"Besides your dad, you, Pierce, Ramona, and I are the only ones who have seen the real star up close for years. I thought you could look and see what you thought. The lights are due to go off in about ten minutes."

"Why do I think this is going to involve me going up in a little white bucket?" Emmy asked.

"Good guess."

The lift had been discreetly parked behind the Christmas village after the lighting. Madelyn walked over and started it up.

"Do you know how to work that thing?" Emmy asked.

"Easy," Madelyn said.

"For you," Emmy replied. As she watched Madelyn maneuver the lift into place, she wondered how Madelyn had ever let herself be pigeonholed into managing a clothing shop for so long when her talents clearly lay in anything tech or equipment-oriented.

The bucket stopped just in front of the tree. Madelyn handed Emmy a hard hat and then donned one herself. They strapped in, and Madelyn pulled the bar that would make the lift rise. "Hang on."

"To what?" Emmy asked. She didn't have a particular fear of heights, but after being in the rafters of the burnt-out Town Hall with a killer, she had kind of lost her taste for them.

They reached the top of the tree just as the lights flickered out. Madelyn pointed to the way the star was seated in the clips. "It doesn't look quite right, but I guess I could have made a mistake with the dimensions."

"What about the alarm?" Emmy asked, imagining the whole town coming running to the square if it got triggered.

"I turned it off." Madelyn pulled the star off the clip and handed it to Emmy. They both looked at it under the light of Madelyn's high-powered flashlight.

"What do you think?" Madelyn asked.

The crystals lining all five points sparkled in the light, but Emmy could tell the depth of the sparkle wasn't there. She turned it over in her hands, but she knew it was a fake.

"And?" Madelyn studied her face.

"It's not the same star. At least we don't have to worry about it being stolen." Emmy sighed and seated it back on the hooks at the top of the tree. Her stomach felt sick.

"Because it already was," Madelyn said. "What are you going to say to Pierce?"

"I don't know," Emmy said. "The bigger question is, what am I going to say to my dad?"

"I'm sorry," Madelyn said.

Something stuck to the side of the fake star caught Emmy's attention. It was a long, satiny bit of yarn, snagged on the edge of one of the crystals. Gently, she untangled it from the star. It didn't look like something off of Bryn Lea's dress or Santa Claus' coat. It looked like a piece of yarn from one of Penelope Carmichael's sweaters.

## Chapter 14

# Nosey Notebook

M s. Carmichael's room at the inn had only been hers for a couple of nights. In that short time, she'd filled it with handcrafted items—a knitted blanket at the foot of the bed, a tea cozy on top of the electric kettle by the sink, scarves and hats placed on all four posts of the four-poster bed.

Pierce pushed through a pile of sweaters. "After everything we'd bagged up at her booth in the bazaar, I never imagined there could have been more."

"She was a very prolific knitter," Emmy observed.

Pierce moved to a knitted laptop bag beside the little desk in the room. He plugged the laptop into the wall and booted it up. While he waited, Emmy searched through the bag.

It contained a pair of knitting needles, three rolls of yarn–red, green, and white—and a small book with a leather clasp.

"There's a password on it," Pierce observed.

Emmy opened the little book. She flipped to a page labeled "passwords." Under "laptop," she found the word "Improvaganza."

Pierce typed it in and an opened spreadsheet appeared on the screen. "It worked. That book is an IT security person's nightmare. At least we don't have to ship all her electronics off and wait for the tech lab to go through it."

"Interesting password," Emmy said. "Improvaganza was the name of the show that Clark Franklin was on before he got his big break on *Comedy Train*."

"This is also interesting," Pierce said. Emmy leaned closer to the screen. "It looks like her profit sheet from her sweater business." He studied the columns. "If this is all from sweater sales, she did pretty well for herself."

"I wonder who stands to inherit from her sweater fortune?" Emmy asked.

"We're still trying to find some kind of next of kin for her. It doesn't look like she had any family. If she has a will, the money will probably go to some home for stray cats."

"That's sad," Emmy said. "I wonder if she lived her life alone. Maybe that's why she was so demanding all the time."

"Or she lived alone because she was so demanding all the time." Pierce opened Penelope's email and read some of the subject lines out loud. "Would you please reconsider your last review? Thanks for ruining my business. We aim to keep our customers happy. Please tell us what we could do better. We will not be issuing a refund. Following your poor treatment of our employees... You are no longer welcome in our..."

"Sounds like a bunch of responses to critical reviews," Emmy said. "She struck me as the kind of woman who was always complaining about the food or the service or whatever, a real 'Can I see your manager?' type."

"Yeah, she probably made a few enemies. Lucky for us, they're narrowed down to the few who we know were in the vendor's area just before the tree lighting."

"No chance someone from the outside snuck in?" Emmy asked.

"According to Dr. Gregory's initial assessment, she bled out pretty quickly. Someone else coming in isn't likely. We can narrow the suspects down to the people who were in the vendor's area during the hour before the lighting."

"We have to figure out who from that group had a reason to want her dead," Emmy said. "Do any of them own a restaurant or a small business?"

"Other than Estelle and that rivalry, no. The other vendors left the area and went to the lighting." He hesitated for a long moment. "But I know of at least one person who knew Ms. Carmichael outside of the island."

The tone in his voice made Emmy think whatever he was about to say she wouldn't like. "There was an incoming message on her phone, asking her to call the Walla Walla Penitentiary."

"The Walla Walla penitentiary?" The familiar name left a bitter taste in Emmy's mouth. "Why did they want to talk to Ms. Carmichael?"

"Probably because she was a key witness in an embezzlement trial and the person she helped put in jail was due to be paroled."

Emmy remembered what Ms. Carmichael had said about Emmy's dad being familiar to her. She turned to face Pierce. "Let me guess, the trial that put my dad in jail?"

"Yeah, turns out she was a temp receptionist for the firm your dad worked for. More than that, she was *the* receptionist from your dad's old firm."

"You mean the person who found the discrepancies in my dad's accounts?" Emmy said. "My dad would have told me if he knew her, right?" But like so many other things, Emmy wasn't sure. She remembered how afraid Ms. Carmichael had looked after meeting her dad.

"What I want to know is, if the penitentiary told her your dad was likely heading for Sharp Island, why would she have come here?"

"You don't think it's a coincidence she ended up on the island?" Emmy asked.

"No," Pierce said. "I don't know why she would choose to come here after the warning, especially since this is a relatively small craft fair." He indicated the spreadsheet on the computer in front of him. "These numbers and locations tell me she's used to going to much bigger venues."

Emmy thought for a minute. "If she knew my dad, then she probably knew Dennis, too. I wonder if there's a connection with him?"

"Dennis?" Pierce asked.

"Dennis Mirr, from the Three Wise Guys. He worked at the same company as my dad. They recognized each other when Dennis got off the ferry."

"That's something we might want to look into. Any idea how long Dennis was at the firm with your dad?"

"Not very long. No one stayed at that firm long after the scandal. It shut down. Dennis and Ms. Carmichael probably both lost their jobs. Maybe she came to confront him about that, or put in some kind of complaint, or..." Emmy trailed off. "I wonder if she had a connection to Clark Franklin, too. She had to have a reason to use the name of his show for her password."

"Good point. We should ask him about it." Pierce said.

"So that's two who have a connection." Emmy thought for a moment. And then there's Jay."

"Jay?" Pierce asked.

"Ms. Carmichael wrote a name at the bottom of the results for the pageant. It was a name that shook Jay up enough that he tore it into little pieces. I found it in the trash can after the pageant."

"Interesting. Do you know what the name was?"

"Candy Mason," I think.

Pierce wrote the name down in the notebook he kept with him. "Sounds like a threat to me."

Emmy nodded. "Two and possibly three of our wise guys had some connection with Ms. Carmichael. And we know of at least one other person who had a problem with her."

"Estelle?" Pierce said.

"Yeah, but it's probably not someone she was only casually acquainted with. If I remember my criminal psychology class right, the killer was someone who had some kind of personal relationship—someone who had a grudge. The killer didn't take anything. It was a quick death, and a pretty brazen one. If anything had gone wrong, Penelope would have cried out, and someone would have heard her."

"I couldn't have summed that up better myself." Pierce was smiling at her with something like pride.

Emmy ducked her head. She hadn't meant to go off like that, as if she knew more than Pierce. Obviously, he had studied more about criminal psychology than she had. To cover her embarrassment, she looked around the room. Something was wedged between the mattresses. Emmy pulled it out. It was another notebook. The label on this one read, "Observations."

She flipped through the pages, reading a passage here and there. "Mrs. Carmichael was a regular Harriet the Spy."

"Harriet who?" Pierce asked.

*"Harriet the Spy.* It's a book I read as a kid. This little girl spies on everyone and writes things down in her notebook." Emmy flipped to the back of the notebook and read a few pages.

> *"The woman who sells roasted nuts is cheating her customers. Her sign says, 'Ten dollars a pound,' but I checked her scale when she stepped out of the booth. It weighs heavy."*

"You don't have anyone selling roasted nuts here," Pierce pointed out.

"I think this was from a previous craft fair." Emmy turned to a more recent entry.

> *That bling lady is here. I thought my previous threat to expose her would have kept her away, but here she is, pretending to be a Queen of Diamonds when she's actually the Queen of Counterfeits, passing her bedazzled sweaters off as a craft when all she has is a glue gun and a box of rhinestones. Let's hope the customers here see through her garish creations.*

Pierce raised his eyebrows. "Another threat? I wonder what Ms. Carmichael meant by exposing Estelle."

"No idea." Emmy flipped to the next page to see if there was more, but Penelope's poison pen had found another target.

> *The Santa they've chosen is as shifty as they come. Ex-con, if I ever saw one. He was talking to Estelle earlier today. They looked like they were up to no good.*

"Does she have something bad to say about everyone?" Pierce asked.

Emmy skimmed the page and flipped to the next one, and the next one. It took a couple of pages to find anything positive.

> *He's here! I was afraid that after all, he'd back out. I don't dare speak or even write his name, but I'm sure he'll talk to me. This time will be different. No crazy stunts, just an invitation to go out for drinks. I slipped him a note at*

*the pageant, but I didn't get a response. Think, Penelope. How do we pull this one off? How do we get him alone so we can discuss the legal matters?*

"Any clue who she was talking about?" Pierce asked.

"Maybe Jay, but the note she passed him wasn't a friendly one." Emmy's mind was spinning. Could Penelope have been talking about her dad? Who else would she have *legal matters* with that needed to be discussed?

"Does she mention anyone else?"

Emmy skimmed the entries. "She thinks Kirsten is insane. I'm a pushover–ouch–you're hot but uptight, and basically everyone else is a crook or a liar." Emmy read a few more passages. "This one stands out."

*Being here is a risk, but hopefully worth it. I don't imagine W would recognize me, although I'll never forget him. My biggest triumph in life was taking him down. D is here too, weasley thing that he is. I could never pin anything on him, but I'll be watching. Something familiar about that young comedian. He comes off as a boy scout, but there's something off about his charity. Comedy for a Cure? He has a racket, believe me. I'll get to the bottom of it before the week is up.*

"So she came here even though my dad was here. Something was worth taking the 'risk.' She thinks Dennis is crooked and Jay, too. No mention of Clark, though."

"Unless he's 'he who must not be named,'" Pierce pointed out.

"I guess that would explain the password." Emmy turned to the next page.

"Someone ripped out the next few pages," she said.

"How do you know that?" Pierce took the notebook from her.

"There's the impression of writing on the next page, a lot of writing, not just one page's worth."

He examined the page. "You're right, good call."

"I'll have my office go through this and check into the claims about Jay's charity, look up the name you gave me, and do a thorough background check on Nicholas and pretty much everyone else."

"What do you want me to do?" Emmy asked.

"I would say stay out of it if I thought it would do any good." He sighed. "Start by talking to your dad, and then go from there."

"I'm not going to interrogate my own father," Emmy said.

"I'm not asking you to. But you're more likely to get details and catch him in a lie than I am."

"That sounds like an interrogation to me," Emmy muttered. "Do you think my dad did this?"

"I can't exclude any suspects right now," Pierce said. "Whatever you do, be careful. Whoever killed Penelope Carmichael knew what they were doing. I'm worried that we're dealing with a career criminal this time."

Emmy didn't dare ask if he thought her dad fit into that category.

## Chapter 15

# Accidents Happen

"Despite Mr. Fox's dramatic entrance, most people didn't see him come in. Good thing, a bloody man who looked like Santa Claus would have traumatized every kid in the square. Luckily, the crowd was focused on the lights and the show."

Kirsten was speaking from the end of the long table in the bookshop. It was serving as the venue for the Founder's Council since the Town Hall had burned down during the island's first (and probably last) masquerade ball.

They'd shut down the bazaar and all of the Sunday activities and called an emergency meeting that included not just the Founder's Council—herself, the Hamiltons,

Stan Rhinehart, Brighton Redding, and Kirsten–but most of the business owners on the island. Her dad had also insisted on coming. Emmy hadn't had the energy to stop him.

"I think we all agree that we should cancel the rest of the weekend," Emmy said.

"Canceled?" Kirsten sounded surprised. "I spoke to the vendors, and they want to continue. It's only a few more days. We can keep the murder on the down low and just move forward with our plans."

"Is that even possible? Can we really continue with all the holiday plans after someone was stabbed in one of the booths?" Mrs. Hamilton turned to Pierce, who'd recently joined the council as a member of the Hamilton family.

"We can't cancel it now," Brighton jumped in. "I have twenty-five vessels and thousands of tiny lights lined up for the harbor parade Sunday night."

"And I just took delivery of enough food to cover the guests who have reservations for the duration of the festival. Most of it is perishable, and we're not likely to see another influx of visitors before spring," Stan, the owner of the Cliffside Inn, said.

"I did the same for the Cottage," Kirsten said. "And I know the shops in town have already planned and purchased food and merchandise for the weekend."

"I was just getting things back to normal at the restaurant, or at least what passes for normal these days," Birdie said. The former chef had taken over the White Sails restaurant after the last owner, had ended up dead in the fish tank.

Emmy turned to Pierce. "Could we do it? Could we keep as much information about the murder as we can from leaking out until the weekend is over?"

"It wouldn't be my first choice," Pierce said.

"Are we sure it was a homicide?" Kirsten asked. "Could Ms. Carmichael have tripped and accidentally stabbed herself in the neck with her knitting needle? It seems like kind of odd choice for a murder weapon."

Dr. Gregory passed his hand across his face. "I suppose it's possible. But evidence showed someone may have moved her body after they stabbed her. Most of the blood was on the floor beneath her booth, not on the table she slumped over."□

"So someone propped her up with her back to the crowd to make it look like she was still alive," Emmy said.

"Or maybe after she climbed back up after she fell on the needle," Kirsten continued hopefully.

"Again, possible, but not likely. "The wound in her neck would have caused her to bleed out quickly," Dr. Gregory said.□

Emmy was feeling lightheaded, the way she always did when people were talking about blood.

"Why didn't anyone hear anything?" Pierce asked.

"The neck wound also prevented her from crying out. The killer probably knew that would happen," Dr. Gregory said.

"If there is a killer," Kirsten said.

Pierce and Dr. Gregory exchanged a glance. Finally, Pierce spoke up. "With all the plans and preparation this thing took, we should probably see it through."

Emmy looked at him, surprised. This attitude was a huge departure from how he had felt before about town celebrations interfering with his investigation.

He nodded to acknowledge her surprise. "In some ways, it might be an advantage this time. It would give me a reason to keep the key suspects in this case from leaving the island, at least for a few days. We might wrap this whole thing up pretty quickly. The crowd was in the square watching the tree lighting. Based on the estimated time of death and how fast Ms. Carmichael bled out, there were only a few people who were close enough to have killed her."

"And who might they be?" Emmy's dad spoke up.

"I'd rather not get into that here," Pierce said.

"You can say it. I discovered the body. I'm an ex-convict. I'm your chief suspect," Mr. Fox said. There was a challenge in his words, in his stance, and in his entire demeanor. □

"Fair," Pierce nodded. "But you weren't the only one with the opportunity to kill Ms. Carmichael."

"That woman, Estella or Estelle or whatever, was right there after it happened. She never left her booth, so she must have seen something." Emmy's dad pointed out. "And she didn't seem too broken up over the other crazy sweater lady getting stabbed."

"The Three Wise Guys were hanging out in the vendor's area while we were searching for the star," Madelyn said. "I'm not sure at what point they jumped in to save the show."

"What happened with the star, anyway?" Emmy asked.

"It was a misunderstanding," her dad said. "There were two gift boxes, and no one told me which one I was supposed to use. Then there was an argument between those two women."

"What kind of argument?" Pierce asked.

"Something about a box of missing gems?" Mr. Fox said.

Pierce and Emmy exchanged a glance. They'd guessed right about the box of bling being stolen.

"Jolly Old St. Nick was there for a while and then MIA when it was time for him to go on," Ginny added.

"He probably just got a little lost on the way. If you ask me, our Jolly Old Elf was a bit too jolly. When he was at the tea shop earlier today, I saw him add something to his tea that was not on the menu." Ms. Lee extended her thumb and pinky in a drinking gesture.

"He wasn't the only one," Ginny said. "I saw the recently deceased take a couple of nips from a bottle she kept under the table in her stall."

"So she was drunk?" Kirsten looked almost happy. "So maybe this was an accident. Who's to say she didn't get a little tipsy, trip in her stall and impale herself with one of her knitting needles?"

Pierce shook his head. "We don't have the pathology results back yet, but I doubt she was drunk." Emmy knew he didn't believe that was what had happened anymore than she did.

"What are the odds we can call this an accident that's under investigation until this weekend is over?" Kirsten said.

"I guess it's possible." Pierce didn't look convinced.

"Of course it's possible. In fact, that's probably what actually happened. And until we know that for sure, we can just keep this unfortunate incident quiet," Kirsten said firmly.

Emmy looked over at the council and the shop owners around her. This wasn't necessarily something that they would need to vote on, but she asked anyway. "Moving forward or closing things down?" She asked.

"Moving forward," the majority said.

She turned to Pierce with the question in her eyes.

"Moving forward, I guess," he said.

"Moving forward," Emmy repeated. She hoped they weren't making a deadly mistake.

## Chapter 16
# Disaster

"To say that was a disaster is an understatement," Emmy's dad said when they got home from the Founders' meeting.

Emmy looked at him with an expression that she hoped conveyed how tired she was and how the last thing she wanted to do was hear him tell her everything that had gone wrong.

It didn't work.

"To begin with, you should have reined those two ladies in a long time ago, or thrown one or both of them out. Maybe you could have added a 'public disturbance' clause in the contract."

Emmy tried to keep it light. "We could have added a Santa Claus to their contract and they still would have found something to fight about."

He looked at her seriously. "Emmy, this isn't a joke. The fate of your business, I mean your island, may rest on this." He moved to her laptop. "It's too late to salvage this disaster, but I put together a plan for any further events you might decide to have."

"Wait, you hacked into my laptop?" She asked.

"I obviously don't have one of my own. Besides, it wasn't hard to figure out that your password was your mother's birthday. I've used that one myself a few times. In fact, it was so obvious that I changed it for you."

"You changed my password?" Emmy asked.

"Can we stick to the important points? Please, sit where you can see all of this," he gestured to the couch next to him and set the laptop on the coffee table in front of her. "You're really lowballing your business potential by renting out booths to cheap crafts and trinkets. You should really go for more high-end items. This is a privately owned island and you are a multi-millionaire."

"On paper, I'm a multi-millionaire," Emmy said. "Everything I have is tied up in this island."

"That's something we'll be addressing later. One mess at a time."

Emmy stared at him, dumbfounded.

He pulled up a spreadsheet. "If I were you, I'd bill this Christmas festival or bizarre festival or whatever you're calling it as something else, something with more class, something that would attract some of Seattle's elite. I want you to be thinking bigger, beyond these little touristy things and to something that will draw in a nicer crowd–a yacht club to replace Redding's run-down ship business, fine dining instead of fast food, and quaint cafes. The patisserie has potential, but Anjuli needs to sell everything at a higher price point."

"What if I like the island the way it is?"

He patted her leg. "You're just letting your fear get in the way of what this could be. If we work together, you won't have to work so hard or worry so much. Just provide the capital, and I'll make things happen for you. Before you know it, you'll be spending your days on luxury cruises to real, tropical islands, or touring Europe while Dad takes care of everything."

"What if I don't want any of that? What if I like being here? What if I like being in charge? I've brought the island back from the brink of disaster twice now and—"

"You mean you've brought the island to the brink of disaster twice now. You were very fortunate that someone figured out what Khonico was doing before you went bankrupt and lost the island."

"I figured out what Khonico was doing. Pierce and I did. I figured out who killed Uncle Edward. With the help of the town, we salvaged Sharp Island's reputation. We already have people booked for next fall, and did you see the turnout at the tree lighting tonight? No, I guess you didn't, because you were too busy stealing my great-great-grandmother's star."

She stopped, out of breath. She hadn't meant to blurt that out, but there it was.

He stared at her, but she couldn't read his expression. The accusation shocked him. She wasn't sure if it was because he didn't think she was smart enough to figure it out, or because he hadn't been the one to steal the star.

When he finally spoke, it was with measured control in his voice—an undercurrent of pity mixed with anger and disappointment. It was the way he'd spoken to her when she was a little girl. Actually, it was the way he'd always spoken to her.

"Someone stole the star?" He asked. "When? I saw it way on top of the tree, even though I told you it was a terrible idea to put it on public display. Don't tell me it was stolen right under your boyfriend's nose."

"The star that was hung in the tree was a fake. A very good fake, but a fake."

He narrowed his eyes. "You're sure about that?"

"Yes." She took a breath. "What did you do with the original star? Did you pawn it off? How did you get the jeweler to make such a believable fake so quickly?"

He shut the laptop and stood up. "Emmy. I know it's been a long day for you—everything that went wrong with the tree lighting and then the murder. I don't blame you for being confused and out of sorts. The star that was hung in the tree is the one I picked up from the jeweler's. They repaired the loose diamonds, they cleaned it, they took excellent care of it, as did I." His tone elevated as he continued talking. "If you're looking for someone who might want to take your star and kill the ugly sweater lady, I'd suggest Estelle the Bling Queen. She's obsessed with sparkly things. Besides, she's the one who brought about the box confusion."

"Box confusion?" Emmy asked.

"Your assistant Kirsten had one all laid out for me to put the star in, but Estelle decided we needed a different one, a sparklier one or something. She took the original box and swapped it for the one she'd made for the pageant. She could have switched the stars in the confusion and stabbed Ms. Carmichael while everyone else was focused on the lighting. She was the only one who never left the vendor's area."

Emmy could tell he was trying to distract her. "That doesn't matter, because the estimated time of death was just under an hour before they found her body. Anyone who was in the vendor's area at that time could have done it."

"Even me?" he asked.

Emmy let out a long breath. "I'm not saying you're a murderer."

"No, just a jewel thief."

"I'm not sure I even know who you are," Emmy said.

A hurt look passed over his face. Emmy regretted the entire conversation immediately. She sighed. "So you put the right star in the original box?"

He folded his arms. "I brought your star back safe and sound, even though I still think you should sell it and everything associated with this island and the Sharp family. Look at all the stress and pressure this has put you under. It wasn't fair for Edward to entrap you with this island."

"I'm not entrapped by this island. Sharp Island is my home. I belong here like I never belonged anywhere."

He shook his head. "Sweetheart. You're too young and sweet and naive to see it, but you're in prison here every bit as much as I was. The sooner you sell your portion of the island for a hefty profit, the sooner you can get on with your life."

"Dad, I don't–"

He held up his hand. "Don't worry, I'm here now, and I'll help you navigate this disaster."

## Chapter 17
# Ornamental Suspects

"Where to start?" Emmy opened a box of homemade Christmas ornaments on the table in front of her. She was at Pierce's apartment. She needed her space after the fight with her dad, so she told him she was going to help Pierce decorate his tree.

It wasn't entirely a lie. The little pine tree she and Pierce had cut from the woods outside of town was set up in the corner of the room, but for now it was naked except for a pitiful string of white lights.

"Okay." Emmy pulled out a little Santa ornament. "Who was in the vendor's stalls at the time Ms. Carmichael was killed?"

"Emmy," Pierce's voice had a note of warning in it. "I thought we were here to spend some quality time together decorating my Christmas tree."

She rolled her eyes. "We both know I'm not going to let this go. We might as well work together."

He sighed in resignation and then moved closer to the figures on the coffee table. He took the Santa Claus figure from her. "Like your dad said, Nicholas Star was the person most obviously missing from where he was supposed to be. When he finally arrived, he smelled of peppermint. Either he snuck in a last-minute candy cane to make sure his breath was fresh, or he had a bit of peppermint schnapps on the way through."

"While that was probably not the best thing for him to do, as he was on his way to take a little girl up thirty feet in a lift, it doesn't make him a murderer."

"Right, but there was the bottle of schnapps under Ms. Carmichael's table when we searched it, so it puts him firmly at the scene of the crime."

"But what is his motive? He was looking for a drink, and she surprised him?" Emmy asked.

"I'm not sure yet. I need to do some checks into all of their backgrounds. Good chance Nicholas Star is not his real name, though."

"Right. Speaking of stage names." Emmy pulled out three wise men figures from the box. "Larry, Curly and Moe, or Clark, Dennis and Jay were also near the booths before the lighting. What do we know about them?"

"Well, we know Clark Franklin has been in the comedy business for years."

"And we know Dennis worked with my dad at one point," Emmy added.

"What exactly was their association?"

Emmy could tell by Pierce's tone that he was wondering if Dennis had been involved in the part of her dad's business that had sent him to jail. "Dennis was part of the firm my dad worked for. My dad said he was a rising star–pardon the pun–in his firm. But Dennis acted as if he didn't know the outcome of my dad's scandal."

"There might still be something there," Pierce said. "Is that something you could talk to your dad about or?–"

Emmy hesitated. She hadn't mentioned the fake star, or her fight with her dad, or her suspicions about what he might have done, but if they were going to be working on this together, she couldn't keep secrets from him.

"Actually, I'm not talking about much of anything with my dad right now," Emmy said.

"Did he leave?" Pierce asked.

"If only," Emmy said under her breath.

"What was that?" Pierce asked.

"Nothing." She picked up a little crocheted angel ornament with a crooked halo. "I got in a fight with my dad when we came home from the meeting because... because he has all these ideas about how Sharp Island is supposed to be run, and he thinks he can do it all better than I can and... and because the star at the lighting was a fake."

Pierce stared at her. "The star on the tree is a fake?"

She nodded. "Madelyn figured it out because it's slightly smaller than the original. The clips don't quite fit it right. She had me go up and look. It's not the same star."

"So you think your dad switched it out when he went to have the star repaired?" Pierce asked.

"Probably. I mean, who else had access to it?"

Pierce sat back. "Actually, in the confusion of the wrong box and the missing Santa in the vendor area, there were probably a few people who might have had access to make the switch. Remember the bedazzled lady?"

"Estelle?" Emmy asked.

"She did a great job on that crown. She might have been able to put together a believable fake, or someone else could have. The way I heard it, the star was sitting unattended for much longer than it should have been. It's possible that someone killed Ms. Carmichael because she saw them take the star."

"So you don't think my dad took it?" Emmy asked.

"I didn't say that. He's still the most likely suspect, at least for that part of it, but he may not be the only suspect." He looked over the ornaments in front of them.

Emmy picked them up one by one and surrounded the angel ornament in the center that ironically represented Penelope Carmichael. "Nicholas, Estelle, Dennis, Clark, Jay, and my dad. Everyone here had access to the star and to Ms. Carmichael before she died."

"Are you sure you want to do this? If your dad is a suspect, maybe you should..."

Emmy thought for a minute. "I need to know, one way or another, who he really is."

"Okay." He picked up a wooden star ornament and slid it into the middle of the table. "I don't want anyone else to know the star is a fake. It might help us figure out who the murderer is."

"Good idea." Emmy sighed, looking over the pieces. "The accident line is only going to last for so long. We need to talk to these people and get some answers soon."

"We?" Pierce asked. "You know I've already questioned all of them, and I have their official statements."

Emmy covered his hand with hers. "We both know that sometimes it's what's not on the official statement that counts."

# Chapter 18
# Premium Space

E mmy didn't have to go looking for Estelle. The vendor found her nearly as soon as she stepped into the Town Square early Monday morning. Estelle was already at the bazaar, even though it wasn't scheduled to open until the afternoon. □

"Ms. Fox. I hate to be a bother, unlike some previous vendors, but I was wondering about that premium space? The one that was recently vacated?"

Emmy looked at her in dumbfounded amazement. "You mean Ms. Carmichael's space, the space that's vacant because she died?"

"As a matter of fact, yes. I mean, she won't be needing it." Estelle looked at Emmy and waved her hand dismissively. "I know you think I'm being insensitive, or rude, or disrespectful to the dead, or whatever, but this is my job. The holiday season is my bread and butter, and I took a chance on your little bazaar. I'd like to see it pay out. Business is business, and there's no use crying over spilt milk."

"Except in this case, someone spilt blood, not milk," Emmy said grimly.

"Of course, of course." Estelle waved her hand again. "It was a tragic accident, but we can't let it derail our goals."

"You're sure it was an accident?" Emmy asked, seeing a way to get into her questions. "Did you see what happened?"

Estelle seemed to backtrack. "I was just parroting what your handsome boyfriend has been spreading around and what your illustrious Founder's Council decreed."

"So you don't think it was an accident?" Emmy asked.

"I didn't say that either." She appeared flustered. "I don't know what happened to that woman. I was in my booth for the entire night. You know, my back booth, around the corner, out of sight of the other booths and most of the customers?"

Emmy ignored the hint that they had treated Estelle unfairly. "So you didn't see or hear anything?"

"I heard a lot of bustling around looking for that pretty star. Two of the three idiots talking about where the third one was and then trying to decide if they should intervene in whatever disaster was happening in the square. I heard something that sounded like glass breaking." She paused for a second. "Ms. Carmichael was speaking to someone. I'm not sure who. I heard something like, 'I know what you did. Don't think I won't—'"

"Don't think I won't what?" Emmy asked.

"I don't know. I didn't hear anything after that."

"Did she stop talking suddenly?" Emmy asked.

"Maybe. How was I supposed to know? The crowd was really loud, and I was way over in this corner. Besides, I was trying to figure out what had happened to my box of bling. I always keep it in the back of my booth, in the top tote. It comes in handy if something comes loose or if I have downtime to work on a project."

"The one you accused Ms. Carmichael of stealing from you? I heard the two of you got into another argument. How is that possible if you never left your booth?"

Estelle waved her hand again. "I did leave the booth, but that was ages before she died. I'm still convinced she stole it."

"What exactly was in the box? A bunch of sequins and other sparkly things? In a plastic tote?" Emmys asked.

Estelle's eyes lit up. "Yes, have you seen it?"

"We bagged it up as evidence last night. It was in Ms. Carmichael's booth."

"I knew she'd taken it. When can I get it back? I'm in the middle of creating my most beautiful sweater yet. An ode to your lovely Christmas star. There will be at least one hundred individual gems of varying sizes."

An idea struck Emmy. "How many fake gems did you have in the box?"

"At least a couple hundred."

"I have bad news for you. The box we found last night only had about twelve gems left in it."

"Really?" Estelle looked at her in disbelief. It took her a second to regain her composure. "That sneaky little...I wonder what she did with them. You didn't find them on her body, did you?"

"No. What gems went missing? Were they different colors or?–"

"All clear rhinestones and crystals, not the cheap kind either, so if there's any way to get them back—"

"If they show up, I'm sure Pierce will let you know," Emmy said. "So when was the argument, and when exactly did you last see Ms. Carmichael?"

Estelle pursed her lips. "When everyone moved to the square for the tree lighting, I saw my chance to get some work done, so I pulled out my project. When I reached for my box of gems, it was gone. I knew immediately who had taken it. It was that nosey, vindictive, jealous woman."

"And you confronted her?"

"Of course I did, and of course she denied it. We had a bit of a spat. I could see she wasn't going to admit that she'd taken them. I went to find your boyfriend or that other officer, but there's never a cop around when you need one. I figured I could bring it up later, so I went back to my booth."

"And you didn't leave your booth again until—"

"Until that man started yelling about a stabbing."

"What time would you say your fight with Ms. Carmichael was?"

"I know pretty close to exactly. It was 5:30 when I realized the gems were missing. I was thinking I had two hours of quiet time to work on my sweater, since I didn't care to go to the lighting."

"So you saw Ms. Carmichael about 5:30? What time did you hear her voice?"

"That I'm a little less clear on, but I would say it was about six-fifteen, give or take."

"And you have no idea who she was talking to?" Emmy asked.

"No."

"Man or woman?"

"Definitely a man." She leaned forward. "If I were to guess, I would say it was that third comedian, not the handsome one or the famous one."

"You mean Dennis?"

"That's the one. Penelope didn't trust him."

"How do you know that?" Emmy asked.

"Observation. She has this notebook that she takes with her everywhere. I've seen her writing things in it every time we do a show like this. After Dennis walked by she started scribbling something in it."

"And that means she didn't trust him?"

Estelle nodded. "That woman wrote nothing good about anyone in that notebook. I'm sure there are pages and pages in it about me."

"You've seen the book. You know what she wrote?"

"No, I only know how she looked when she wrote in it, that 'gotcha' glare she had. I've had the misfortune of being associated with her for the last four years, as we've ended up at the same craft fairs repeatedly. Forget the sweater business. That woman was a professional tattletale."□

Emmy considered what Estelle was saying. The women were enemies and rivals, but Estelle might have known Penelope Carmichael better than anyone there. Still, if she knew about Penelope's notebook, maybe other people did too. Maybe she wrote something in the notebook that someone didn't like, and they killed her for it. That would explain the torn-out pages.

"What do you know about the boxes for the lighting being switched?" Emmy asked.

Estelle waved her hand. "Your friend Kirsten needed a wrapped gift box for the lighting. The one she'd prepared had gone missing, but I knew I had the perfect one. A star with that many sparkles deserves a box that does too. I was happy to help."

"You just happened to have a box that was ready to go and that was big enough to fit the star that went on top of the tree? Different from the box you used at the pageant?"

Estelle's glittered eyes went wide in an expression of innocent surprise. "Why, yes. I do all my own gift-wrapping. It saves a lot of time to have the boxes ready in advance. Some of my sweaters are quite bulky."

"I guess that makes sense. I heard Ms. Carmichael made one for the star, too."

"Her and her equal air time." Estelle rolled her eyes. "Yes, she came up with a box that was absolutely hideous. I don't know why she ever thought anyone would use that one."

"So, was your box used for the lighting?"

"No. Sadly, they found the one they were supposed to use. Mine was much nicer, but I guess good taste runs pretty thin around here." She sniffed. "Now, about my booth space. I'd like to move in before the crowds arrive this afternoon, provided someone cleans it up, of course."

Emmy shook her head. "I'll check with Detective Hamilton. Don't move anything yet."

## Chapter 19

# Chit Chat Interrogation

T he Three Wise Guys were staying at the Cliffside Inn Bed and Breakfast. Emmy went to see them under the guise of thanking them for saving the tree lighting. When she got there, she only found Clark at the table. He was reading something on his phone, and there was a pile of Stella's famous waffles and bacon in front of him.

"Good morning," she said. "Are you by yourself?"

"Until you showed up, yes." Clark stood and pulled out the chair opposite him for her.

"Where are the rest of your troupe?" Emmy asked, sitting across from him.

"Jay is predictably still in bed. If the sun hits him before noon, he glows or sparkles in the sunlight—something that makes young women swoon. Dennis said he had some business to attend to this morning, so I guess I'm the only one here for you to question."

"Question?" Emmy tried to sound innocent. "I actually came to thank you for saving the show the other night. If it weren't for your quick thinking, it would have been a disaster."

"You're welcome. But aren't disasters that end in murder kind of your specialty?" He asked.

"Why would you say that?"

"I never take a job without researching it first. You and this whole island intrigue me. That's why I answered Ms. Loche's ad for entertainers. And that's why I could guess that your visit this morning was more than a social one."

"I am very grateful for your quick thinking," Emmy said again.

"I'm sure you are. And I appreciate that. But don't you really want to know where we all were just before we went on stage? Don't you want to know what we may have seen or heard as it related to the woman who accidentally had a knitting needle shoved through her jugular?"

The way he made light of it made her uncomfortable, but she decided if Clark could level with her, she could level with him. "Okay, where were you just before you saved the day?"

"Watching your event coordinator and her bumbling boyfriend search for a bow-wrapped box that wasn't there one moment and then reappeared almost magically the next moment."

"Why would you say that?" Emmy asked.

"They turned things upside down, looked at every flat surface and every place it could be. And as I understand it, once Jolly Old St. Nicholas showed up, the box magically reappeared."

"Where did it reappear?" Emmy asked.

"All I can give you is a secondhand account. I was on the stage with my fellow village idiots when the box appeared, but from what I've heard, it was on the front table of Ms. Carmichael's booth."

"But Ms. Carmichael was already dead by that point, or..." Emmy hesitated. "At least she may have been dying. When was the last time you saw or heard her?"

"Let me see," Clark thoughtfully drained his coffee cup. "She and Estelle had been at it again. Estelle was looking for supplies and she had gone over and accused Ms. Carmichael. Then I think Estelle went back to her own booth to sulk because no one was there to complain to.

"After that, I paid little attention. A mob of my devoted fans accosted me, and I was forced to sign autographs." He raised his eyebrows. "You don't look like you believe me, Ms. Fox."

Emmy blushed, "I believe you, I just..."

He laughed. "No, you don't believe I have that many fans left. You may be right. But there was one highly devoted woman there, and she took my attention away from everything else in the vendor's booth while she gushed shamelessly for a few minutes."

"Do you know who she was? Did you get her name?" Emmy asked.

"Unfortunately, I didn't catch the name of my alibi-establishing fan club of one. But perhaps you can use your super-sleuthing powers to ferret her out for me. She was an older woman, small with dark hair. After she left, I saw your little princess sweating in the wings, wondering when Santa Claus would arrive. I decided to give her and everyone else a break. I turned to round up my boys. Dennis was nowhere to be found, so I waved Jay over and started for the stage. Dennis must have gotten there just then because he followed us on stage. Just as we got there, I heard glass breaking and someone swore."

"Do you know who that was?" Emmy asked.

"Just that it was a man," Clark said

"Do you know where Dennis had been?" Emmy asked.

"I didn't get the chance to ask him, and it slipped my mind until just now."

"Any chance Dennis said anything to you about knowing Ms. Carmichael before?" Emmy asked.

"He said they'd worked together briefly."

"Did he say if he had a grudge against her or..."

Clark looked shocked. "No. Not Dennis. He's too, I don't know. I guess the word would be ordinary. Besides, what conceivable motive would he have for killing a woman he barely knew?"

"Right," Emmy said. "What happened next?"

"At that point, we were all onstage, so the entire crowd could vouch for our where-abouts. Soon after, as you know, Mr. Claus finally made his appearance. We finished our bit, stood back for the tree lighting—spectacular by the way—and the next thing I knew, Mr. Fox was coming in covered in blood and yelling about someone being stabbed."

"Did you have a good view of Ms. Carmichael's booth?" Emmy asked.

"Yes, but I wasn't paying attention to what was going on there. My attention was primarily on the stage. I've done improv enough to know when a show needs a rescue. I was just waiting for the right moment to jump in." He stood. "Forgive my manners. Would you like something to eat? I've already eaten, but..."

"I'm fine. Thank you." Emmy was impressed by how polite and straightforward he was. For the years of fame behind him, Clark Franklin seemed pretty grounded. "Who did you see enter Ms. Carmichael's booth?"

"Pretty much everyone."

"Everyone?" Emmy asked.

"Everyone who was around. Let's see. First there was the other crazy sweater lady and the fight. Then Mr. Fox was there for a bit. I'm not sure why. Jay was there briefly. He told me he was looking for an ugly sweater to buy so he could wear it on his YouTube channel. He must not have found one he liked, because he came back empty-handed. We've already established that Santa Claus was missing, and my friend Dennis walked on stage just after Jay and I did. Up to that point, we hadn't seen him."

"Did you go into Ms. Carmichael's booth for any reason?" Emmy asked.

He looked thoughtful, stroked his chin, and then said, "Why yes, I did. I'd caught my jacket on a loose nail in one of the booths, and I was looking for a needle and thread."

"And did she have one?"

"I didn't get the chance to ask. About then, the woman I told you about showed up. Then I realized that your show was in trouble, so I headed over to see if I could help."

"So you didn't talk to Ms. Carmichael at all?"

He looks thoughtful again. "No, I don't believe I did."

"And you never fixed the tear in your coat?" She asked.

He laughed. "Did you notice it?"

"No. I was too busy being grateful for the save you made."

"You're very welcome. Oh, our business tycoon has returned."

Chapter 20

# Chapter 20: Comedic Motives

E mmy looked up to see Dennis, his cell phone in his hand. "No. I said to sell those and get as many shares of what we talked about before. Yes, I understand the risks. I'm not a moron. Just do it." He hung up the phone as he sat down.

"Business? This early in the morning?" Clark said.

"I thought you'd given all of that up," Emmy replied.

Dennis looked at her with a start. It took him a second to regain his composure, as if he were worried about what she'd overheard. Finally, he smiled. "I still dabble. It's a kind of game now. Especially since the money means practically nothing."

"Moneybags here should talk." Clark poured syrup over his waffles. "Some of us still have to work for a living."

Emmy was surprised. "You must have made a fortune with the rights from *Comedy Train*. I still see it all over the internet."

Clark wrinkled his nose as if the bacon from the buffet had gone bad. "You'd think so, wouldn't you? Except I signed that contract when I was too young to know any better. My agent was a complete hack and so I got practically nothing. Why do you think I'm here doing two-bit comedy instead of retired in a luxury flat in Chelsea?"

His demeanor had changed so quickly that Emmy instinctively moved back.

"At least you can say you were something once," Dennis grumbled. "At least you chased your dreams. Some of us had to wait a lifetime to make their dreams a reality."

"Your time will come, my friend." He patted Dennis' hand. "Just stick with me and keep reaching for the stars."

Emmy wondered at the way he had said the word "stars." Was there some kind of hidden meaning behind it? Or was she reading too much into everything.

"At any rate, it's your turn to answer our hostess' questions. We wouldn't want to lose it all over a murder charge. I've played in prisons before. Talk about tough crowds."

"Murder?" Dennis said. "I thought the going theory was an accident. Penelope tripped and impaled herself, right?"

"Penelope?" Jay asked. "When did you and Ms. Carmichael become so chummy?"

Dennis shook his head. "We're not. I haven't seen her for years. Penelope Carmichael used to be the receptionist at our firm. At first, I didn't recognize the face, but I definitely recognized the attitude. She was always in everyone else's business." He turned to look at Emmy. "Especially in your dad's business. She was constantly going to his office. If she weren't so horrible, I would have guessed they were having an affair."

Emmy's stomach got tight. Besides the fact that Penelope had been the whistle-blower on her dad's embezzlement, she wondered what their relationship had been when they worked together. "What do you remember about her from those days?"

"It was a long time ago." Dennis acted as if he wished he hadn't brought it up. "But I remember she was quite clumsy back then, so it could have been an accident. She fell on her knitting needle under her table, so no one noticed her until it was too late to help her."

"Ah, but you don't have all the facts straight, my friend. They did not find Ms. Carmichael under her table. She was sitting in her chair." Clark nodded toward Emmy, as if he had made an important connection.

Dennis looked from Clark to Emmy. "She was in her chair?" He took a breath. "So it wasn't an accident."

"I didn't say it wasn't. We have to look at every angle," Emmy said. "I mean, Pierce has to look at every angle."

Clark smiled. "Oh, don't discount your part in all of this. What is it, five murders under your belt now?"

Dennis looked at her with something like fear. "Five murders?"

Clark laughed. "Emerson hasn't committed any murders. She's solved them. She's a regular Hercule Poirot, or is it Miss Marple?"

"More like Nancy Drew," Jay walked in carrying an enormous stack of waffles, topped with at least half a dozen strips of bacon. He wore plaid Christmas pajama pants, a tight black t-shirt that said, "Comedy for a Cure," and his dark hair stuck out all over. He obviously hadn't shaved or showered. He wasn't even wearing shoes. He had on a pair of Pokemon slippers–Snorlax, Emmy observed.

"Nice of you to roll out of bed and join us," Clark said.

"Not much gets me up before eight–" He glanced at his watch. "Before nine o'clock, but the smell of breakfast was killing me."

"Stella's cooking has that effect on people," Emmy said.

"So, Ms. Drew, what brings you here this morning?" Jay squeezed into the place next to Emmy.

"Interrogations disguised as morning chit-chat," Clark said.

"I'm not, I mean…"

"Don't worry, dear. We'd all like to figure out what happened to poor Ms. Carmichael." Clark put his napkin on his plate. "If you're done with me, I'd like to take a little walk. It's actually turning into a nice day."

"No problem," Emmy said. She wasn't sure she'd gotten anything useful from Clark, but this would be easier one-on-one.

Clark stood. "Be nice to the boys, Emmy. If you find out that one of them is a murderer, could you wait to unmask him until after our last show on Saturday night? A good comedian is hard to come by."

"I think it should be part of the show," Jay broke in. "Think of the free publicity that would bring if we solved a murder on stage."

"Maybe not the kind of publicity the island needs right now, though," Emmy said. After the last unplanned production on the island, she was pretty sure she didn't want any more publicity like that.

Jay licked syrup off his fingers. "There's no such thing as bad publicity."

"Our young friend here is all about the publicity," Clark said.

"One of us has to be. We can't all get by on ancient reruns," Jay said over a mouthful of bacon.

"Ouch. And on that note, the old man makes his exit." Clark bowed and walked toward the front door.

Dennis' phone rang. He glanced down at the number. "Sorry. I'll have to take my turn later. This is important." He hurried out of earshot before he answered the phone.

"And then there was one," Jay said. He took another piece of bacon off the stack of waffles and, while he was chewing, asked, "So, what did you need to ask us all?"

It struck Emmy how good-looking he was, unshaved and disheveled as he was. If anything, it made him more appealing.

"What made you decide to go into comedy?" It wasn't the question she had come prepared to ask.

"You mean, what is my 'motive' for going into comedy?" Jay asked.

Emmy laughed, even though it wasn't that funny.

"I dunno." Jay shoveled a bite of waffle into his mouth and chewed thoughtfully. "I mean, I was always the funny one at school, the class clown and all of that, but really I think it was my immense desire to become rich and famous that led me to this career path."

"Rich and famous?" Emmy asked. "How is that working out for you?"

He wiped his hands on his pajama bottoms and pulled out his phone. "Not bad, not bad at all." He pulled up a social media site. There was an impressive number of followers attached to his name.

"Wow," Emmy said appreciatively. "How did you get so many?"

"I should say 'years of hard work,' but really I did it the new-fashioned way. I had a series of videos go viral. Honestly, it's what got me this gig. Clark saw it and called me."

"Your *Comedy for a Cure* videos, right?" Emmy said.

"Yep. First, it was just about raising money to help pay some medical bills for my mom, but it got bigger and bigger. Then I realized it was my ticket to fame and fortune."

"Fame and fortune? Your mom's cancer was the way for you to be successful?"

He reached across the table and picked up the syrup bottle. "It's a joke, Emmy. A bit of dark humor, maybe, but laughter is the best cure for anything. My mom used to say that." For a minute, he concentrated on his breakfast. "After she passed away, I decided to honor her memory by continuing with the charity."

"That's really great," Emmy said.

"It's a decent shtick." He shrugged. Emmy couldn't tell if he was still joking, if he was sincere about the charity, embarrassed, or honestly more focused on the "rich and famous" part.

"But you didn't come here to get my life's story, or at least not the whole thing. What do you need to know about the night of Ms. Carmichael's tragic accident?"

"Basically, everything you remember about that night."

Jay leaned back and took another piece of bacon between his fingers. "Chaos, mostly. I like chaos; I can turn it into comedy gold if I tell the story right. Everyone was running around, trying to find that star, trying to find Santa Claus, and those two old ladies were going at it, as usual."

"And what were you doing?" Emmy asked.

"Just taking it all in. But then we had our own mystery to solve."

"What mystery was that?"

"Dennis was AWOL. That's not unusual. He says he wants to be a comedian, but he's still glued to his phone and married to his investments. Clark and I were trying to decide whether we could do the set without him. He showed up just in time to save the show."

"When was the last time you saw Ms. Carmichael?"

He added syrup to the next waffle layer on his plate. "After she and Estelle departed to their respective corners, it got quiet. I'm sure they were just gearing up for round two. I remembered I was going to do an 'ugly sweater' bit on my YouTube channel, so I walked over to see if Ms. Carmichael had anything I could buy for that."

"Did you find something?" Emmy asked.

"Actually, yes. There was this amazing sweater that looked like it had Clark's face knitted into it. It was so perfect I would have paid almost anything Ms. Carmichael asked for it."

"So you bought the sweater?"

"No, unfortunately. Ms. Carmichael wasn't in her booth. I figured she'd gone to the lighting with everyone else. I was going to go back and buy the sweater as soon as it was all over." Jay leaned forward. "Hey, you don't know what happened to that sweater, do you?"

Emmy mentally went back through the piles of sweaters she and Pierce had bagged up. There weren't any sweaters that looked like they had a face on them, Clark's or otherwise. "No."

"Weird. I wonder what happened to it. There wasn't anyone else around to buy it."

"That is weird," Emmy said. "What else do you remember? Did you hear anything?"

"Like what?" Jay asked.

"If I told you what you should have heard, it might influence what you thought you heard," Emmy answered.

"I'm not sure that makes sense, but okay." He set down his fork and leaned back. "A little while after I left her booth, Ms. Carmichael was arguing with someone."

"Do you know who it was?" Emmy asked.

Jay looked uncomfortable. "I didn't get a good look at him. I don't like to stare when there's a fight going on, but it looked like either Mr. Fox or the guy who is playing Santa Claus."

Emmy sucked in a breath. "What makes you think that?"

"I saw an older guy with a white beard and kind of a gut, but I didn't see his face."

"Did you hear what Ms. Carmichael was so mad about?" Emmy asked.

Jay thoughtfully chewed on another piece of bacon. "Actually, now that you bring it up, what she said was kind of interesting, considering what happened later."

"What did she say?" Emmy asked.

"She said, 'What are you doing here?' And I didn't hear what the guy said after that, but she said, 'That's all in the past, don't think you can threaten me.' It was quiet for a minute. He may have said something that I couldn't hear. Then she shouted, 'I saw what you did. Don't think I won't tell her what you really are!'"

Emmy swallowed hard. Ms. Carmichael must have been talking to her dad. She must have finally recognized him.

"Did you hear anything else?" Emmy asked.

"I left for a few minutes after that."

"Left, where?"

"Your friend, the cute one, asked me for some help with some decorations that had fallen down."

"Ginny?"

"Yeah, that's her, Ginny." Something sparked in Jay's expression. "Anyway, when I came back, Ms. Carmichael was sitting in her booth. I went to see if she'd let me buy the sweater. She had her back to me and she was, how do I put this gently, 'uncharacteristically quiet.' I asked if she was okay."

Emmy held her breath, wondering if Ms. Carmichael could already have been dead. "Did she answer?"

"She said everything was fine."

"Everything was fine?" That didn't sound like Ms. Carmichael to Emmy. With her, there was always something to complain about. "Did you go into the booth?"

"No, I was standing just outside. I asked about the sweater and she said it wasn't for sale."

"But you're sure it was her who answered?" Emmy asked.

"Yeah. It was her booth. It was a woman's voice," Jay said. "Why?"

"Just thinking," Emmy said. "Then what happened?"

"Your friend Ginny called me again. The decorations still weren't staying up. We had to re-staple them." He fidgeted with his napkin. "Do you know if she's dating anyone?"

Emmy looked at him in surprise. She didn't expect the question. Jay was very good-looking and Ginny was single. She was distracted by the idea that they would look great together.

"Never mind. Forget I asked." Jay was actually blushing.

Emmy shook her head and worked to refocus her thoughts. "That's all you remember?"

"Sorry, not much to go on." He cut the last bit of his waffle into a few pieces, swirled them around in his syrup, and then put it all into his mouth at once.

She waited for him to finish chewing. "So you can't tell me for sure whether the man in Ms. Carmichael's booth was our Santa Claus, or Mr. Fox?"

"Old guy with the white beard?" He laughed for a second. "Sorry, I guess this time of year, that doesn't narrow things down. I'm not sure. Everyone had been looking for Santa, and he showed up soon after that, so maybe he was the one in the booth."

"So Dennis and Nicholas and my dad were all missing about the same time?" Emmy asked.

"Your dad? The other guy with the white beard is your dad?" Jay looked surprised. "I guess I didn't connect the two Foxes. Interesting."

"What is interesting?" Emmy asked.

He made a face. "It's not really for me to say...and I hope you don't take offense to this, but..." he hesitated.

"But what? I promise there isn't much you can tell me about my dad that would offend me now."

"Okay. Dennis told us all that Wayne Fox was the biggest con man he'd ever known. He said, " If that diamond-studded star ends up missing, you all know who to blame.""

Emmy sat quietly for a minute. Despite what she'd said, the words stung. Even if she half-believed them herself. It also meant that Dennis had lied to her and her dad. He must have known about the outcome of the company scandal all along.

Jay stood up, his plate empty except for a puddle of syrup. "Funny thing about that, though; I didn't know the star had real diamonds in it until he said that. I would have never guessed it was that valuable."

Emmy stood and put her hand on his arm. She couldn't let him leave without asking one more question. "One more thing. I saw that Ms. Carmichael wrote something on the pageant results. A name? You seemed upset about it. Why?"

He avoided her eyes. "I was just confused. There were two names. I didn't know which one was supposed to be the winner. It took me a second to realize the second one wasn't one of the girls in the pageant."

"So you don't know who the second name was?"

"No. I'd never seen that name before in my life."

Emmy knew he was lying.

## Chapter 21
# Financial Motives

Emmy walked along the edge of the water, watching the waves smash against the rocks. The wind had picked up, and it looked like it was going to rain soon. Her discussion with Clark and Jay had given her more questions than answers. She needed some fresh air before she went back to her office.

She was sure her dad was there. Before their fight, he'd been asking for all the financial records for the island, and she'd agreed to let him see her quarterly reports. She knew he was trying to help in his own way. He wanted to be in the middle of things. He wanted to be useful. But the more he interfered, the more Emmy worried about what his motivation was in all of this. She was afraid he was positioning himself to take control of her life, the island, everything. He controlled her whole life until he went to jail. Even from there–

"I told you to be patient." The voice, muddled by the wind, was coming from above her. Someone was at the edge of one of the rocky ledges. They probably didn't realize she was on the beach, or they didn't realize how well the sound carried from the cliffs to the beach below.

She moved closer to the cliff, so she was more concealed and could hear better.

"I gave you a chance," a second voice said. "And you keep promising big returns. So far, I'm just getting the runaround."

"These things take time. It's like a good comedy routine. You have to keep working at it and trying new things. You don't always get the laugh on the first try."

It took Emmy a minute to recognize the voices. The first voice was Clark, and the second one was Dennis.

"You don't need to tell me how comedy is supposed to work. I've been in the funny business for most of my life. You were supposed to take care of everything else for me. I gave you your big break in all of this. I'm not sure I understood how big a risk it was."

"You can't play it safe and expect to get the returns you're after," Dennis said.

"Yeah, but at what cost in the meantime?" Clark said. "I need some proof that you're as good as you say you are."

"Don't worry. This whole thing will be wrapped up soon. I'll get it all together for you as soon as this gig is done. I can't be everywhere at once."

"Yeah, so far you have a knack for being in the wrong place."

There was less confidence in Dennis' voice when he said, "You didn't tell that cop or the woman where I was just before the show, did you? I mean, it was all legitimate. It just looks bad, considering the circumstances."

"I haven't said anything. But if things don't start moving along soon, I might remember a few details I forgot to mention."

"Is that a threat?" Dennis asked, but the waver in his voice made Emmy realize he just took it that way.

"Just a little insurance on my investments," Clark said.

They must have turned around and headed back, because although Emmy knew they were still speaking, she couldn't make out what they were saying.

It sounded like Clark had tied up some of his money with Dennis. Maybe in exchange for giving Dennis a start in his career in comedy. Dennis was being evasive. With that and the other phone call she'd overheard, she guessed the money he had invested wasn't doing well.

One detail from their conversation stood out to her. Where had Dennis been just before the lighting?

## Chapter 22
# Testosterone Tuesday

The Pirate's Cove was crowded. It took Emmy a minute to realize it was Tuesday, or as the men in town put it, Testosterone Tuesday, the night when they all gathered to watch sports and drink. Not that they didn't do that on the other nights of the week, but this particular gathering was in answer to the women's meetings that were usually held on (Women's) Wednesday.

It felt awkward to be one of only four women in the bar, especially since two of the four were servers. The woman in the corner she didn't recognize, but the man sitting across from her was the person she had come to see.

Even out of costume, Nicholos Starr looked like Santa Claus. He was wearing another flannel shirt, a green plaid this time, and a pair of jeans. The smell of peppermint permeated the air as she got closer to the table. She stopped when she realized who the woman was. It was the sparkle that bounced off her sweater even in the dim bar light that gave her away. Estelle was sitting across from Nicholas Starr. They leaned together, engaged in conversation.

In a heartbeat, Emmy decided that instead of talking to Nicholas, she'd listen. She took a table to the side of them, in another dark corner, where she could overhear their conversation.

"It sounds like they're going to keep the festival going, despite everything. Cover the whole thing up." Nicholas's voice was full of worry.

"Good thing for both of us, isn't it? If they closed things down, we'd both be out of a lot of money," Estelle answered.

"Yeah, I guess so. It just makes me nervous. Police officers around, taking a special interest in what's going on." Nicholas took a long swig of whatever was in his glass.

"It's not like you're going to get another gig this late in the season, especially not with your record," Estelle said. "As it was, I had to stretch your credentials a bit when I talked you up with that event planner."

"And I appreciate all of that. I"m just not sure sticking around is the safest thing to do right now, for either of us. Sooner or later he'll recognize me and then the whole thing will be over."

"Impossible. Your own mother wouldn't recognize you now. Besides, it's not like he doesn't have his own things to hide. If he comes after us, all we have to do is trot out one of the skeletons that he keeps in his closet, and I can guarantee he'll be as silent as night."

"Yeah, you're probably right. But I can't shake the feeling that someone saw the whole thing and—"

"No one saw anything. It will be okay as long as you don't get nervous and screw things up. I've never seen bling like that, and I'm not leaving without my share of it," Estelle said. "Besides, the one we really need to worry about is—"

"Emmy! Did you come to join us, or are you poking around for clues again?" Landon strode over from the bar and slid into the booth across from her, as if he had just noticed she was there.

The conversation at the next table went silent. Landon had a knack for turning up at the wrong time and messing things up. She didn't know what Kirsten saw in him except she liked a fixer-upper.

Landon and half the men in the bar were watching her, waiting for an explanation of why she was here in the bar, sitting in a dark corner by herself on Testosterone Tuesday.

Her mind raced as she tried to come up with a good excuse. "You caught me. My TV isn't working, and I wanted to make sure I caught the big..." Her eyes searched the bar for the nearest TV. The only one she could find had a curling competition on it. "The big curling competition."

Landon followed her gaze. "You like curling?"

"Yeah. It's one of those oddball things I got into in college," Emmy said.

"Great!" Landon directed her toward the front of the room. "There's not a whole heck of a lot on tonight, so we'd love an explanation of how the game works."

Emmy wasn't sure whether Landon was trying to call her out in front of the men at the bar, or if he was genuinely interested in curling. Whatever his motivation, he had ruined any chance she might have had of hearing more from the pair in the booth. They probably slipped out as soon as Landon said her name.

A voice behind her spoke up. "I know curling. Used to play a little myself back in Montreal."

It was Nicholas. His voice was much stronger than it had been when he was talking to Estelle. He strode to the front of the room. "What do you want to know?"

Emmy turned to Nicholas with a grateful expression. For whatever reason, he had saved her from the embarrassment of admitting she understood nothing about what was going on with the sport on the TV.

"What is your favorite team?" Nicholas asked. There was no hint of the nervous man from the back table or of the jolly elf who had been at the tree lighting.

"Um..." Emmy felt her face go red. "It's kind of a new thing."

Nicholas looked suspicious. "Didn't you just say it was one of your weird college obsessions?"

"I just... I don't... I like all of them," she stammered. She glanced up at the screen, hoping there would be some hint of who was playing, how they were playing, and what curling was. A commercial appeared on the screen, and Emmy saw a way to save her dignity.

"We can talk after I get out of the restroom. I'm going to go now, so I don't miss any of the game."

"Match," Nicholas corrected her.

"Right, match." Emmy excused herself. She wondered how long she could hide in the bathroom before someone came looking for her. Hopefully, it would be long enough to read the full Wikipedia article on curling and memorize a few player statistics.

She briefly considered making an unceremonious exit out of the small window in the bathroom, but this was her chance to talk to Nicholas. Pierce's questioning hadn't yielded much, but if she could get Nicholas to let his guard down a bit, she might get more out of him. Maybe her feigned interest in curling would give them some common ground.

The match was in full swing when Emmy emerged from the bathroom with a rudimentary knowledge of curling. Whatever Nicholas had said to them about the sport had obviously created some interest. As Emmy walked in, one stone knocked into another stone in the center of the circle. Emmy tried to remember if that was a good thing or a bad thing. The answer came when all the men jumped to their feet and started high-fiving each other.

Emmy quickly thought back to what she had read, but her mind was blank. She spoke up anyway. "That was a great counter. I don't think the other team is going to recover from that."

"Not likely," Brighton Redding said.

Emmy scanned the crowd of men, but the white-bearded Nicholas was gone.

"Our not-so-jolly friend appears to have given you the slip," Brighton said. "Seems a pretty slippery character all around."

"Yeah." Emmy slumped onto the bar stool next to him. Another cheer rose from the men. Emmy was too discouraged to keep up her act. "So you're all into curling now?"

"Nicholas explained a bit while you were... indisposed. And as you pointed out, it's the only thing on." He gestured with his drink to the men around the room. "Get enough beer in these guys and they'll holler for a hamster race."

Emmy laughed. It was the most Brighton had said directly to her since she'd accused him of killing her mother. They had been in the same Founder's Council meetings often enough, but they hadn't had anything that resembled friendly conversation.

"Your dad staying with you now?" Brighton asked, without turning to face her.

"For now," Emmy said.

"I guess it would be futile to tell you to watch your back with him around," Brighton said.

"Nicholas or my dad?"

"Both."

"I've held my own against two murderers. I think I can deal with my own father." Emmy knew she should have said more to defend her dad, but she wasn't sure that was reasonable, and she was too defeated to get into an argument with Brighton tonight.

"Sometimes family is worse than the bad guys. They know how to get under your skin. Just make sure your loyalty isn't to the wrong person."

Emmy turned to him. "Who else am I supposed to be loyal to? We already figured out that he didn't kill my mom."

Brighton flinched at the mention of Emmy's mother, the woman he had loved for years before she married Emmy's dad. "I know. I'm not worried about Mags anymore. Nothing I can do for her. But you..." He shook his head. "Just be careful about where your trust lies, Emerson. Even considering the season, there are too many white-bearded men around this town, and at least one of them means trouble."

## Chapter 23
# Women's Wednesday

E mmy stepped inside the Cliffside Inn and shook the rain off her jacket before hanging it up. The mild weather had turned cold and rainy. The crowds for the bazaar had been sparse, and most of the vendors had packed up early. It was just the kind of evening that she would have liked to sit in front of the fire in the bookshop and read. She'd forced herself out once she heard what the group had planned for Women's Wednesday.

A fire glowed in the great room. An enormous Christmas tree decorated with antique ornaments rose to the second-story balcony. Women were holding wine glasses and chatting around the fire. Stella had pushed the tables together in the dining area to accommodate tonight's activities.

Ginny and Ramona were on a couch next to the Christmas tree. Ramona was wearing a garish emerald green jacket studded with bedazzled Christmas lights. It appeared she was an equal-opportunity shopper when it came to handcrafted, ugly Christmas wear. Mrs. Hamilton, Pierce's mom, Ms. Lee, and Anjuli were on the other side of the room, snacking off a Christmas-themed charcuterie board. Kirsten was at the front of the table talking to the person she had invited to lead the group in a "bling" craft night–Estelle.

Based on previous conversations, Emmy thought the women's group had only gotten together for things like hatchet throwing or archery, but apparently they did arts and crafts too.

Estelle was being evasive since she'd moved into the premium booth. Emmy thought a nice evening of crafting was the perfect casual setting to strike up a conversation with her. Emmy wanted to know what her connection to Nicholas Star might be, what the big secret was, and whether the bling they wanted to get a piece of was the Sharp family star.

Emmy walked to the front of the table where Estelle was laying out craft supplies. She had another box of assorted fake gems with her. It was much fuller than the other one. Besides the clear crystals, it had sparkly things of every shape and color.

Estelle was talking to Kirsten as they set up for the crafts. "I'm glad you went through with the bazaar. No sense letting that woman mess things up for everyone." Estelle said it as if she were talking about a spoiled kid who had thrown a tantrum and ruined a party, not a woman who had died–most likely been murdered–with her own knitting needle at her own craft booth.

Kirsten caught Emmy's eye and gave her a quick, annoyed glance. Kirsten was endlessly pleasant and businesslike, but it looked like Estelle's callousness had gotten to her too.

"Hopefully everything else goes smoothly," Estelle added as she laid out an assortment of plain sweaters in white, red, and green–ready to be bedazzled. "That tree lighting with the missing Santa could have been a complete disaster. The Three Wise Men really saved the day."

"Wise Guys," Emmy said, taking a seat near the head of the table.

"Wise Guys?" Estelle looked at her blankly. She looked at least as confused about how Emmy ended up beside her as she did with the remark about the comedy troupe's name.

"The comedy troupe calls themselves 'The Three Wise Guys,'" Emmy said.

"Oh, of course," Estelle said. "It's a funny play on words. Anyway, they really saved the day when Nicholas missed his cue."

"Do you know where he was?" Emmy asked.

"Probably breathing into a paper bag," Estelle answered. "Nicholas has terrible stage fright. He loves being Santa, but it terrifies him every time."

"So you knew Nicholas before this week?" Emmy asked. Again, it was something she already knew the answer to, but she wanted to gauge Estelle's reaction.

"Yes and no. He's been doing the Santa thing for years, and I've been doing the Christmas bazaar circuit for years. Our paths have crossed a few times."

"That's what you said when you recommended him," Kirsten broke in.

"You were the one who recommended Nicholas?" Emmy asked.

"Kirsten asked if any of us knew a good Santa Claus who might be available on short notice. I took a chance and called him. I don't know him very well, but I know he is a good Santa."

"How long have you been doing this?" Emmy asked.

"The Christmas bazaar circuit? About ten years. Since my husband left, I found out my whole life was a lie, and I needed to come up with something to support myself."

"It sounds like there's a story there," Emmy prompted.

"A long, boring and mostly tragic one," Estelle said.

"I'd love to hear it," Emmy said.

Estelle shook her head. "My life story can't be that interesting to you. Besides, I need to get this party started." She turned to the group, drinking wine by the fireplace. "Ladies, are you ready to bling these things?"

Emmy worked on a white sweater with a red bedazzled poinsettia in the middle. She'd taken a seat next to Estelle, hoping for more conversation, but Estelle kept getting up to help other people around the table and otherwise avoided her.

The women blinged the sweaters. The wine and conversation flowed freely. It wasn't until Ramona reached for a new bit of bling from the container in the middle of the table that something seemed off. She looked at it for a second, dropped it, and then crawled under the table to retrieve it. She was under the table for long enough that Emmy worried that she'd hurt her back and wasn't able to get back up.

Emmy joined her under the table. "Ramona, what's going on?"

"This," Ramona held up the bit of bling she'd gone to retrieve.

"Right," Emmy said. "Another rhinestone for your bedazzled blazer."

"This is no rhinestone." Ramona handed the piece to Emmy. "I know a diamond when I see it, but just in case, I checked." She held up a small compact from her purse. The mirror had a long scratch down the middle. "This is the real deal."

"Where did you find it?" Emmy asked.

"In the box with the rest of the bling. No idea how it got there."

"Why would Estelle have a diamond in the box with her rhinestones?" Emmy asked.

"Maybe she didn't know it was there," Ramona suggested.

"Or maybe it got mixed up with the rhinestones when she made the switch."

"You're saying you think Estelle stole the star?"

"Why not? She had the craft know-how to make the fake star and an abundance of sparkly things to create it."

"What are you two doing under here?" Ginny poked her head under the table.

"Digging for diamonds," Ramona said. She slipped the diamond into her pocket. "I'll just keep this safe until we get the chance to have it checked out."

Chapter 24

# Mostly Tragic

E mmy lingered with the excuse of helping clean up after everyone else left. When the room had cleared, she went over to talk to Estelle.

"Did you get everything moved into the new booth?" she asked.

"Yes, it's definitely a premium booth—great for traffic, good lighting to show off the bling, and the blood left on the floor is minimal." Estelle said it with such a deadpan face that Emmy had to do a double take.

"I'm kidding," Estelle said. "The booth is perfectly fine. I threw down a rug."

Emmy's stomach churned; she had a feeling Estelle wasn't kidding about the rug. She couldn't think of a smooth way to steer the conversation to the dead woman, so she just asked. "How long did you know Ms. Carmichael?"

"Know her?" Estelle sniffed. "I didn't really know her. Like Nicholas, our paths had crossed at different craft fairs. She was hard to miss. Penelope Carmichael always had something to complain about. The 'competing vendor, breach of contract' thing came up at about every show where we ran into each other."

"I heard you had a fight with her just before the tree lighting."

Estelle laughed. "It wasn't a fight. It was a heated discussion about her being a dirty rotten thief."

"Are you sure she was the one who took your box of fake gems?" Emmy said.

"Since you found it at her booth, and a chunk of the jewels were missing, yes."

"What did she say when you confronted her?"

"She said she hadn't seen it, but she was obviously lying. There was so much chaos going on that I couldn't find anyone to help me."

"So you gave up on your fight with Ms. Carmichael?" Emmy asked.

"Yeah. I figured it wasn't worth it at that point. I decided I could take my gems back another time, like when Ms. Carmichael went to watch the tree lighting."

"So you didn't plan to go to the tree lighting?" Emmy asked.

"No. That woman had stolen from me once. I wasn't going to desert my booth and let it happen again."

"But Ms. Carmichael didn't go to the tree lighting, either."

"I know. She was annoyingly present in her booth. I kept my eye on her, and she never moved."

"If you kept your eye on her, did you see anyone go inside the booth?"

"She had a few visitors. The older handsome, funny guy, the younger handsome, funny guy, that guy who looked like Santa." She closed her eyes as if she were trying to picture the moment. "Hmmm, the actual Santa, Nicholas, just before he finally found his way to where he was supposed to be. I think he was hoping to get her to give him a swig of the drink she had under her table for a bit of liquid courage."

"He knew she had alcohol in her booth?"

"We all did. She'd bragged earlier that she was planning on drinks at her booth with a special visitor."

"Do you know who that special visitor was, or if they showed up?" Emmy asked.

"No. I think that was supposed to have happened after the lighting. Unless he was one of the people who came through before."

"At what point did you notice anything was wrong?" Emmy asked.

"You mean, when did I notice she was dead? I didn't. I was working on blinging a Christmas project. It had gotten quiet, so I looked up and couldn't see her at the booth anymore."

"If you thought she had left, why didn't you get up to retrieve your box of bling?" Emmy asked.

"I started to, but when I stood up, I saw her legs under the table. I figured she had either rested her head or was bent over something she was knitting. Either way, she was still there, so I couldn't go get the box. Then I spotted that nice-looking police officer at the edge of the crowd for the lighting and I went to tell him about Ms. Carmichael stealing my gems."

"You mean Pierce," Emmy said, but she couldn't remember Pierce talking to Estelle before the tree was lit.

"Is he the young cop or the old cop?" Estelle asked with interest.

"The young one," Emmy answered.

"Then no. He's much too young for me. I went over to speak to the older police officer, but before I got there, all the lights came on. I was so mesmerized by that star that I forgot what I was doing." She leaned toward Emmy with a conspiratorial whisper. "It's all real, isn't it?" Her eyes glowed with some kind of mania. "I know diamonds. I used to own quite a few of them. There's something about the real deal that makes the room, or in this case, the entire square, light up."

Emmy didn't know how to answer Estelle. If she meant the star from the tree lighting, then the answer was no. The diamonds weren't real. By that point, someone had already exchanged the star for the rhinestone one. The glow in Estelle's eyes made Emmy wonder if Estelle knew the star had real diamonds on it. Maybe because she'd stolen it and replaced it with a fake one. □

"I was quite wealthy at one point," Estelle continued. "I got married my freshman year of college to a very rich man. I had a big house, lots of jewelry, a pack of sweet little French bulldogs, and a room full of pretty clothes."

"You mentioned you found out your whole life was a lie," Emmy prompted.

"Yes," Estelle shook her head as she gathered up the craft supplies. "Turns out my beloved husband had a couple of side pieces and a thriving and very illegal side business selling diamonds. All of that I could have dealt with, but instead of taking me when he fled the country, he took side piece number two.

"His criminal activities left me with nothing. I lost the house, the car, and all my jewelry. I had to let go of all of my sweet Frenchies except for my favorite. She passed away about three years ago."

"Was your ex-husband ever caught?" Emmy asked. The connection with the diamond smuggler and the missing diamonds intrigued her.

"Technically, we're still married. He never gave me the dignity of a divorce, although I could have petitioned for it. He escaped capture, and lucky for him, I never caught up with him either. I've been stuck living this semi-nomadic existence, peddling my handicrafts to strangers on street corners—destitute, with no skills beyond this." She gestured to the sweaters on the table. "I didn't finish college. I already had a rich husband. What was the point of continuing?"

Emmy recalled a similar conversation with her ex-fiance's mother.

"You don't know where he is now?" she asked.

Estelle seemed to hesitate for a moment. "No. I haven't heard a word from him in over ten years." She stood. "If you'll excuse me, I need to get some sleep before the bazaar opens again tomorrow. If I were looking for someone with a reason to kill Ms. Carmichael, I'd look at the head of that comedy group–Mr. Franklin Sense."

"Wait, why would you say that?" Emmy asked.

"You'll have to talk to him, but I understand the two of them have a long and sordid history."

## Chapter 25

# Ugly Sweater

"Clark?" Emmy stood at the door to Clark's suite at the Cliffside Inn. The door was ajar, but the comedian was nowhere to be seen. Emmy hesitated only a moment and then pushed the door the rest of the way open. "Clark, are you here?" She called again.

She stopped. An older woman's voice and then a man's voice came from inside the room.

"Hello?"

She heard laughter, but it was more than two people laughing. It was... she walked over to the television set, realizing what she had heard was a laugh track. A sketch from *Comedy*

*Train* was on the TV playing to an empty room. She paused for a moment, watching. She remembered this particular skit. It was one of Clark's most popular roles, that of Granny Flossie, an old woman who was obsessed with knitting. The character would sit in her rocking chair, knit, and spin humorous "yarns" about her family.

Ironic. Emmy hadn't thought of that connection before.

Although on-screen Clark was dressed in a gray wig, a floral day dress, and a knitted sweater, he looked much younger.

The old woman Clark was portraying on the screen scolded the younger man, brandishing one of her knitting needles. "Mark my words, that's the best yarn I've ever spun."

Emmy laughed out loud. Clark, as an old woman, was hilarious.

"I've always liked this episode." The voice from the back of the room startled Emmy.

Emmy backed toward the door, embarrassed. "Me too. Granny Flossie is one of my favorite characters on this show."

"Hasn't aged well though," Clark chuckled mirthlessly. "I guess my old characters aren't the only ones who haven't aged well in my life."

"Sorry. The door was open," Emmy said,

"Yes, the lock on it doesn't seem to hold well."

"I'm sorry about that. I can get Landon to look at it. It's not very safe if it doesn't lock."

"Are you saying you're concerned about my safety?" He shook his head and then answered his own question. "I guess there is a murderer on the loose." He gestured to the little table and chairs in the corner. "Since you're here, would you like some tea?"

"Thank you." She moved to the table while he went to turn on an electric kettle.

There was a tea cozy on it that looked very similar to the one Ms. Carmichael had in her room. For a second, he looked surprised. He removed it gingerly, and with an expression of distaste. He set it aside and turned on the kettle.

Unlike Penelope's room, Clark's was neat and clean and utterly devoid of anything that would stand out. Other than the tea cozy, only one object looked out of place. There was something balled up in the far corner, underneath the bed. Emmy wanted to see what it was, but she couldn't just climb under the bed with Clark watching. It was just out of reach of her chair, but if she got down on her knees...

Clark turned to face her as she bent down. "What kind of tea would you like? Kirsten put an assortment from the tea shop in my welcome basket. I have Sugar Plum Fairy, Ice Castle Delight, and Melted Snowman."

"I haven't tried Ice Castle Delight yet," Emmy said.

"Sounds good to me." He walked over and set two paper hot cups on the table in front of her and put a tea bag in each. "Ms. Lee's shop reminds me of my home in England: very nostalgic. Sugar? Cream?" he asked.

The electric kettle whistled. He turned to take it off the heat. Emmy pushed her empty cup off the table.

"Oh, shoot!" She said, dropping to her knees to retrieve it.

Once she was on the floor, she slid under the bed and pulled out the balled-up object. It was a hand-knitted sweater, just like the ones Ms. Carmichael sold in her shop. She turned it over. Knitted into the front of the sweater was a striking likeness of Clark. It was the one Jay had seen. That meant Clark had taken it. It smelled of peppermint and there was a brown spot on the collar.

"It's hideous, isn't it?"

Emmy started. Clark was on the floor next to her.

"I'm sorry, I didn't..." The look of fear on his face stopped her. "Where did you get that sweater?"

He stood and offered her his hand. "It's okay. I guess she can't do me any harm anymore. I might as well tell you the truth. If you were so worried about the safety of your guests and performers, maybe you should have done some background checks on some of the vendors." He nodded at the sweater.

"Penelope Carmichael has stalked me for years, leaving sweaters and knitted scarves in my dressing rooms or trailers on set, even in my house, on my bed. I'm sure the tea cozy was her work as well, though I hadn't noticed it until just this minute." He sank into the chair across from her. "At first it was flattering, but she was relentless. She had this idea that we were meant to be together. That... I don't know, because she saw me on TV, she had some right to me, or that we had some connection."

Emmy nodded. "When you saw her at the pageant, I saw a look of terror on your face. You recognized her immediately, right?"

"Of course I did. I've seen that face in my nightmares for years now. She was at nearly every show I did in the early days, at my book signing, and my first and third weddings."

"I'm sorry I put you in an awkward position at the pageant. If I had known..."

"But you didn't." There was a hint of annoyance, maybe even anger, in his voice.

"You handled it beautifully," Emmy said, trying to cover up her mistake.

"I didn't feel like it was in good form to ruin your pageant, although technically, Ms. Carmichael wasn't supposed to get within two hundred feet of me."

"Did she say anything to you at the pageant?" Emmy asked.

"No, but she slipped me a note, asking me to meet up with her before the tree lighting."

"She gave Jay a note too," Emmy said.

"Jay?" Clark looked surprised. Then he shook his head. "Even my stalkers like him better than me."

"Where is the note now?" Emmy asked.

He went to the small desk in the suite, opened a drawer, and handed her a piece of paper. A knitted pattern was on the edges of the page, and a cat playing with a ball of yarn adorned the bottom corner. "I kept it. I thought about turning it over to the detective, as proof she was violating her restraining order again, but when she died, it felt wrong to hand it over."

"It didn't occur to you that it might have been evidence?" Emmy asked.

"Evidence of what?" Clark looked at her blankly.

"Evidence of..." Emmy stopped herself before she said "motive," because the note would show that Clark had a motive for killing Ms.Carmichael. If he couldn't figure that out by himself, she wouldn't help him. "Evidence of what Ms. Carmichael was doing before she died," Emmy finished.

She took the note and read it:

*Dearest Clark,*

*Once again, fate has knit our paths together! When I heard that you'd started a Christmas-themed comedy troupe, I knew it would lead you right to me, and, wonder of wonder, it has. Just in the nick of time, I'd say. It's not something I want to put in writing, but I'm afraid you're in danger that you aren't aware of yet. An associate is not what they seem to be. Please meet me after your show tonight to discuss this matter. I'll have a bottle of your favorite beverage for us to share, a brand new sweater (my best yet) to keep you cozy, and information that might be the difference between life and death for you.*

*Please be discreet about this. I scoured my contract and I see nothing about fraternizing with the talent here, but we can't be too careful. Also, if the above unnamed party should get wind of what I know, it could spell disaster for both of us.*

*On pins and (knitting) needles!*

*Yours ever,*

*Penelope Carmichael*

Clark hovered over her shoulder, jumping in when she had just barely read the last line. "You see? She was threatening me. Disaster, life and death, she'd finally become one of those crazed fans."

"It sounded like she was warning you about someone else."

"You have to read between the lines. The entire message was a veiled threat."

"If that's true, then why was she the one who ended up dead?" Emmy asked. "I take it you never met with her?"

"I never intended to meet with her, but there wasn't the opportunity to do it, anyway. She was dead before I had a chance."

"Then how did you end up with the sweater?" Emmy asked.

He opened his mouth, but no answer came out.

"Estelle told me she saw you at Ms. Carmichael's booth before she died."

Finally, he nodded. "Jay had said something about a sweater with my face on it in her booth. I knew that meant she was up to her old tricks. I saw it just lying there, so I took it."

"Before or after she died?"

"Before," he said, but he didn't sound very sure. "She was at the booth, but she had her back to me. I didn't want to risk a confrontation, so I grabbed it quickly and walked away before she woke up."

"How did it get blood on it?" Emmy asked.

Clark looked at the stain she was pointing out and turned pale. "Are you sure that's blood?" He reached for the sweater. "I might have left a bit of chocolate on the table where I set it down."

She held it out of his reach. She doubted that Clark had just left a bar of chocolate lying around his otherwise spotless room. "I'm sure Pierce will want to have it tested."

"Of course." Clark nodded.

Emmy gestured to the note. "Do you know what she's talking about, the associate who isn't what they seem to be?"

"No, but she's always going on about something that she thinks I need to know. Like when she told me that my second wife was cheating on me with one of my co-stars, or when she said the studio wasn't honoring their contract with me."

"Was your wife cheating and did the studio breach their contract?" Emmy asked.

"Well, yes." He looked slightly defeated. "But imagine how much she would have to dig into my private life to find out that information."

"Yeah, that would take a lot of snooping, something Ms. Carmichael seemed to excel at, but if she was right before, maybe someone is not what they seem. Any idea who that might be?"

Clark stared at her blankly. "I have no idea."

Emmy looked thoughtful. "It might be a good idea to find out."

## Chapter 26
# Not Quite True

E mmy sat in the office next to her dad, across from the woman who had been assigned as his parole officer. She was tall with broad shoulders, with a short, no-nonsense haircut. She looked like someone who might have been a drill sergeant. Her name was Officer Hearst, and she always made Emmy feel like she should sit up taller and square her shoulders.

"So, Mr. Fox, how are things going on the assignments I gave you at our last meeting?" Officer Hearst said.

"All done," he said confidently.

"Really?" Officer Hearst looked at him skeptically. "You have a permanent place to live and a steady job?"

"Yes."

Emmy resisted the urge to speak up. They hadn't talked about her dad living with her permanently, and as far as she knew, he hadn't so much as done a computer search for "available jobs."

"Impressive," Office Hearst said, but she sounded skeptical. "Of course, I'm going to need documentation of both."

"The address is easy," Mr. Fox said. "I'm living with my daughter in her apartment on Sharp Island. We've decided to split rent and expenses."

Again, this was news to Emmy, but she didn't have the courage to contradict him.

"That's good to hear; so few of my parolees have the family support that you have."

"Oh, we're supporting each other. It's a mutually beneficial arrangement."

"Sounds good." The parole officer sounded enthusiastic, but she gave Emmy a sympathetic and understanding smile before she moved on. "And the job?"

"I'll be taking over as CFO of Sharp Island. That paperwork isn't all signed yet, but we can have that taken care of within a week or so, right, Emerson?"

Emmy stared at him, dumbfounded and utterly unable to hide her shock. The confident smile didn't so much as fade from his face. Either he was a better liar than she'd ever imagined (probably true) or he honestly thought she was going to hand over complete financial control of the island to him. Even if she wanted to do that, she couldn't without a full vote of the Founder's Council.

Emmy took a deep breath, but she couldn't bring herself to call her dad a liar in front of his parole officer. "There are still a lot of details to be worked out, and we're in the middle of some big holiday events on the island. It might take longer than a week or so to sort out what Dad's role might look like."

"That's fair," Officer Hearst said. "Considering your background, I would imagine you'd be well suited for a job like that, as long as you don't slip back into old habits." She turned to Emmy. "If I were you and your town council, I would work in a lot of checks and balances and a substantial probationary period."

Mr. Fox smiled at Emmy. "She trusts me. She knows I would never do anything that might put her reputation at Sharp Island at risk."

"That's very admirable, Mr. Fox. You appear to be doing much better than a lot of my parolees." She shuffled through some papers on her desk. As she did, she half-uncovered a picture. Emmy got just a quick glance before the parole officer pushed it back into another file, but she was almost positive she'd seen the face before.

"The only other question I have has to do with the murder that recently took place on the island. I understand you were in the vicinity and were questioned about it?"

"Oh, that's all cleared up, at least as far as I'm concerned. There is still some question about whether it was actually a murder or just a tragic accident. At any rate, I have an ironclad alibi. I was helping get things set for the tree lighting when the murder took place."

"Excellent." Office Hearst handed Mr. Fox a pile of papers. "When everything is set for your new job, fill these out and get them back to me as soon as you can."

She reached across the table and shook first Mr. Fox's hand and then Emmy's. She made eye contact with Emmy before she let go. "Let me know if you have any problems or concerns." Emmy sensed a warning in the woman's sharp gray eyes.

## Chapter 27
# Cash or Credit

"How about we go by Anthony's, my treat?" Emmy said as they left the meeting. She was hoping for a quiet table and a friendly atmosphere so they could talk seriously about all the half truths and outright lies he'd told the parole officer. The problem was that Emmy was pretty sure her father believed most of them.

"It sounds good, but I'm going to pay. I may not have the money I once had, but I can still take my baby girl out for dinner."

Emmy bit her tongue against telling him he never really had any money. For half her life, he'd lived on the inheritance money he'd stolen from her, and for the other half he'd lived on money he'd stolen from other people. "Please let me pay. We have a lot to talk about."

Her dad smiled. "Oh, you mean what I said about the job?"

"The job, the shared apartment, the alibi..."□

"Don't worry about it, Em. I know you've been hoping I'd take over things on the island, but you weren't sure how to ask."

His audacity struck Emmy dumb. Finally she managed, "I don't think you–"

"The financial part, at least. I know you're not ready to let go of all of it. I'll leave events like this Christmas thing to you and Kirsten—with my input, of course. The budget and the contracts will all need to be decided well in advance, as well as the entertainment and vendors. I won't be giving Kirsten so much free rein in the future."

Again, the audacity. Not only was he assuming he already had the position, he's made up. He assumed he had the power to manage Kirsten's position, too. "Dad, you know I can't make the decision to give you any kind of position without a vote of the council."

"Convincing the rest of the council to put me in charge of the business aspects of this won't be a problem. Even my parole officer thinks it's a good idea. You won't find anyone with my background who's willing to take on the mess that is Sharp Island's finances. I was looking through your accounts and I can see a lot of ways to cut costs and capitalize on the island's resources. My vast knowledge of business is just what Sharp Island needs to turn things around."

Emmy opened her mouth to say something. She wasn't sure what, but he kept talking. "And the apartment? It just makes sense for us to share it for now, at least until some nice guy scoops you up. At that point, you might be ready for some space of your own."

Now he seemed to have forgotten that the apartment was her own space. At least it had been right up to the point when he had taken it over.

"And on the subject of a nice guy. I have a few contacts from the old days who have sons who might—"

She stared at him. There seemed to be no end to his assumptions about her life. "I have a boyfriend, and I'm happy with the way things are now."

"Of course you are. That's because you don't have my ambition. Your mother was the same way. She liked things to stay the same. She never learned how to aim higher."

"Is that how she got stuck with you?" Emmy said, not quite under her breath.

"What was that?" her dad said.

"I said, take Fifth Avenue so we don't get stuck in traffic." She was fuming, but she'd never been good at standing up to him. They drove in silence until they got to the restaurant. He ordered, as was his usual, the most expensive thing on the menu. Emmy didn't say anything about that either.

She let her frustrations settle until their food came. "I can check in with the council and see what kind of position you could have on the island. We might not have exactly the position you have in mind, but I could see what they say." Emmy dreaded that conversation nearly as much as she dreaded the one she was about to have with her dad. Pierce had said interrogation, and maybe it was time to go into more depth about what had happened and where he had been the night of the tree lighting, especially since he had lied to the parole officer about having an ironclad alibi.

"I'm worried about the alibi you gave the parole officer. You told her you were helping set up for the lighting."

He took a sip of the wine he'd ordered. "And I was helping. I went all the way to Seattle to retrieve your star for you."

"But after you brought the star in you were gone for a long time. I don't want her to catch you in a..." she hesitated, "misunderstanding. Maybe you should tell me everything that was going on when Ms. Carmichael was killed."

He cut into his steak. "You mean where was I and what was I doing? I already talked to Officer Hamilton about this."

"I'd still like to hear it." Emmy hesitated. "There are some other things that happened that night that I'm trying to work out as well."

"Okay." He took another sip of wine and leaned back. "When I got to the jeweler, they still hadn't finished with your star. I had to wait for nearly an hour, and I almost missed the ferry. That's why I was so late getting back."

"But if you had made the ferry, you would have gotten in at 5:30, whether you were running late before or not."

"True, true." He nodded. "I guess it was the box that messed up my timing, and really, everyone else's."

"The box?" Emmy asked.

"Yes. When the original box went missing, your friend Kirsten had asked the sparkle lady if they could use one of hers. I guess that rubbed Penelope the wrong way, especially considering that Estelle had made the crown for the pageant, because she came up with a box, too. Both were sitting on the table when I arrived. One was a red box covered with knitting and a green bow on the top."

"And the other box?" Emmy asked.

"As you can guess, it was a white box covered in rhinestones with a big silver bow. Like the one from the pageant."

"So which one did you put it in?" Emmy asked.

"Neither. It was already in a box from the jeweler's. A plain white box. I left it in that box, next to the others."

"Kirsten was working out some last-minute disaster with the band, and you were hobnobbing with the people in town. I realized I had left my coat in the apartment and it was only going to get colder, so I went to retrieve it."

"So you just left the star on the table unattended?" She shook her head in disbelief. That didn't sound like the man who didn't want her to put the star at the top of a thirty-foot tree with a high-tech security system.

He shook his head at her and took another sip of the wine. "Of course not. Your friend Landon said he was on guard duty, so I left it with him."

"Did you see the fight between the two sweater ladies?" Emmy asked. "It wouldn't have taken you that long to get to and from the apartment."

"No, fortunately I missed that. I ran into Dennis on the way and we had a chat about some investments he's gotten himself into."

"So Dennis was with you? For how long?"

"Ten, fifteen minutes, maybe. He wanted my advice on some funds that weren't doing as well as he'd hoped. His phone kept going off the entire time, but he was ignoring it."

"The other guys in the troupe were looking for him," Emmy said.

"I guess so. When he finally answered it, I could hear Clark's voice yelling at him through the phone."

"What was he yelling about? Dennis being late?"

"I rarely eavesdrop." Wayne took another bite of his steak. "But it sounded like it wasn't about Dennis being late at all, more like Clark had asked Dennis to do something for him, something that Dennis had taken too long to do. At any rate, Dennis looked pretty embarrassed about it, so I walked away."

"And then you went straight back to the apartment to get your coat?" Emmy asked. She was adding the time in her head. Her dad had completely missed the lighting. He had arrived just in time to find Ms. Carmichael's body.

"No, I decided to grab something to eat at the patisserie since I knew the lighting would probably go late, but when I got there, Anjuli had already closed in favor of selling from her booth. I saw that the Big S was open. Fast food is not usually my thing, but I was hungry. I stopped by for a burger. You know how slow they can be there, and there was only one girl at the counter, one who looked like she was miffed that she had to work while the rest of the town was at the lighting. I got my burger and my coat. By the time I got back, the star was in place, the tree was lit, and then I found that Carmichael woman dead."

"So where is your ironclad alibi?" Emmy asked.

"The girl working at the Big S, of course. She saw me at about 6:30. The lighting was set to happen at 7:00. There was no way I could have eaten my burger, gone back to the apartment to retrieve my coat and made it back to the lighting in time."

"But the lighting got started fifteen minutes late, and Dr. Gregory said Ms. Carmichael was likely stabbed at about 6:50."

Her dad put his fork and knife down and looked directly into Emmy's eyes. "Are you saying I killed her?"

"No. All I'm saying is that isn't exactly an ironclad alibi, and it has nothing to do with you helping at the tree lighting."

"But you think your boyfriend suspects me? Is that it?"

"No, he didn't say, he just…" Emmy sighed. "He has to cover all his bases. And it doesn't look good if you're telling your parole officer things that aren't true, like your alibi or the job thing being all settled."

"Getting mixed up in it would only be a problem if I'd actually killed her, which I didn't, and the job thing, well, we both know I'm the best person to take that over."

"But are you? You have a record of embezzling money. I'm not sure I can convince the Founder's Council to turn over control of the island's finances to a felon."

"That's how you see me?" Mr. Fox looked hurt. "As a felon?"

"You are a felon. You spent the last three years in prison. You can't expect me to just forget that and move on."

He narrowed his eyes. "I'm still your father. I'm still the man who raised you and did everything possible to make sure you had the life you wanted to live." The more he said, the louder his voice got. People were staring at them.

Emmy lowered her voice. "Was it the life I wanted to live, or the life you wanted me to live?"

"What is that supposed to mean? You were a child. You didn't have any idea what kind of life you wanted to live. As your parent, it was up to me to provide the best life possible."

"What about now?" Emmy asked. "I'm not a child anymore. Did it ever occur to you that you and I might have completely different ideas about what my life should be like? Did it ever occur to you that I might have been happy with the way my life was going before you showed up, unannounced and uninvited?"

He threw down his napkin and stood. "Well, I don't want to mess up the perfect life you have planned for yourself, one that apparently doesn't involve helping the man who sacrificed everything for you." He snapped his fingers at the server. "Check, please."

"I'll take care of it," Emmy said.

But her father intercepted the check as it came to the table. He opened his wallet.

"Dad, let me at least pay for dinner."

He threw a wad of bills on the table. "I said I would take care of it." He turned and stalked away from the table.

Emmy sat, stunned for a second, then the server came by. He looked down at the money her father had left. "Were you paying by cash or card?"

Emmy picked up the money. There was at least three hundred dollars there, way more than the meal would cost. Her dad had done that all the time when she was growing up, just left a bunch of money on the table to show he had plenty to burn. But now he didn't; as far as Emmy knew, he had less than a hundred dollars to his name.

Where had he come up with so much cash?

"Miss?" the server asked again.

Emmy pulled out her card. "Credit, please."

She gathered up the money and stuck it in her purse. Wherever it had come from, her dad needed it more than she did.

Unless he'd already found a way to make more money.

## Chapter 28

# Questioning Santa

The man in the red suit looked anything but jolly when Emmy finally caught up with him before he began his shift at the Christmas village. He was sitting behind the "Santa's Workshop" part of the Christmas village, nursing a cup of coffee that smelled distinctly minty.

"Hi Nicholas, do you have a minute?" Emmy asked, pulling up a barrel next to her to sit down on.

"Actually, I'm supposed to be in place, in..." He looked around for a clock.

"About fifteen minutes, just enough time for a chat," Emmy said.

"About what?"

"About what you saw and where you were the night of the tree lighting."

He took a long drink. "I already told that police detective everything I knew. The last time I saw that woman was when I stopped by to see if she knew where the box we were supposed to use was. She wasn't in her booth, so I looked around a little. There was what looked like a gift box under the table, so I picked it up. Ms. Carmichael found me in her booth. She yelled, and it surprised me. I dropped the package and something broke. Whatever was in the box must have been something pepperminty, because I spilled it all over myself."

Emmy nodded. His explanation fit what they'd found in the booth. It also explained why Jay said he had heard Ms. Carmichael yelling at Nicholas. What it didn't explain was what she was yelling.

"Have you ever met Ms. Carmichael before?" Emmy asked.

He visibly squirmed and looked as if he were ready to bolt. "I've seen her at events like this before, if that's what you mean."

"Not exactly. I was more interested in whether she knew you from somewhere besides Christmas events."

"Where else would I have seen her?" He was looking everywhere but in her eyes.

Beating around the bush was getting her nowhere. "Someone said they heard Ms. Carmichael say she knew who you were and that she would tell everyone. Do you know what she meant by that?"

He was getting ready to run. Emmy sensed it. His leg shook, but he didn't leave. "She didn't say anything to me. Whoever told you that had me mixed up with someone else. Maybe that other guy with the beard. I heard he has a record."

Emmy nodded. She didn't know for sure that Ms. Carmichael had been talking tp Nicholas. She could have been talking to her dad. But if she was talking to her dad and not Nicholas, what had she seen him do?

"I guess that's a fair point. Except she said she yelled at you. What did she say when she saw you in her booth?"

For a second, Nicholas looked like a reindeer caught in the headlights of an oncoming snowplow. "She...she just yelled, 'Get out of here!'"

"She didn't say anything else?"

"No, or I don't know. I was pretty nervous to go on and...I don't like being yelled at."

Emmy nodded, trying to look sympathetic. "I heard you get nervous before you have to do the Santa thing. But I saw you after the tree lighting, and you seemed to have it all together. Is there anything you do to keep yourself calm?"

She caught his quick glance at his coffee mug. She was sure there was more than just coffee in it. He didn't answer, so she pressed the point. "Where did you go before the lighting? Some place to calm down?"

Again, he gave her a look like a caged animal. It took him a minute before he spoke. "Estelle asked me to go back to her room to see if she had left her box of bling there. She couldn't find it. She was sure that the other lady had taken them, but she wanted me to make sure."

"And that's why you were late?" Emmy asked. He nodded and took another long sip of the coffee. She was sure he was lying about where he had been, and likely about what Ms. Carmichael had said to him when she found him in her booth. "Estelle didn't tell me she'd sent you on that errand. Do you know what she was working on that she needed so many of her jewels for?"

He shook his head but answered. "She's making a special sweater. One with a lot of sparkles. It's supposed to be—" He stopped suddenly, like he'd said too much.

"It's supposed to be what?" Emmy asked.

He hesitated. "It's supposed to be something special."

Emmy thought of the real diamond Ramona had found in the box. "Something special, like the diamonds on it were real? Or at least some of them?"

Now Nicholas looked terrified. He shook his head furiously. "No. Estelle doesn't use real diamonds anymore, not like in the old days." Again, he looked as if he'd said too much.

"The old days?" Emmy asked.

"I mean, when she had a rich husband and all of that. She said she used to have lots of diamonds."

"Did you know Estelle before the bazaar?"

That question seemed to put him more at ease. "Yeah, we've known each other for a long time. She got me this job. She said it didn't matter that I was—"

"Santa, Nicholas, you have five minutes. I need you to get into position!" Kirsten was calling from the front of the building.

"That you were what?" Emmy asked.

He pulled his Santa hat on, still shaking his head. The bells at the end of the hat jingled, but the expression on his face wasn't jolly at all. He swallowed the rest of the coffee in a couple of gulps. "I need to get going."

Emmy put her hand on his arm. "If there's something you need to tell me. It's okay, I'll understand. I might even be able to help."

Something flashed in his eyes. He opened his mouth. For a second, Emmy thought he would start talking and tell her everything. Then his phone rang. He pulled it out, looked at the caller ID, and then silenced it.

Emmy caught a glimpse of the lock screen on his phone before he shoved it back into his pocket. It was a man holding a little girl on the beach. The picture looked old, maybe taken fifteen or twenty years ago. It took her a second to realize that the man in the picture was Nicholas. He was much younger and clean-shaven. She wondered who the little girl was.

"She's adorable," Emmy said.

Nicholas' face softened. "She's the best thing that ever happened to me. I really let her down."

Emmy sensed the anguish behind that statement. "I know what that's like. Maybe if you tell me the story, I can help you."

His eyes shone. For the second time, she thought Nicholas was going to spill all of his secrets.

"Now, Nick!" Kirsten yelled. "We've got a queue of kids across the square."

"Maybe we can talk later?" Emmy said.

He gave a quick nod and then turned to go through the door in the back of the set that led to Santa's workshop. Emmy watched his whole demeanor shift from nervous and shifty to jolly. It made her think Nicholas might be a better actor than he let on.

She walked away, but something about the picture on his phone had stirred up a memory. She stopped, realizing that the man in the screen saver and the man in the picture on the parole officer's desk were the same person.

They were both Nicholas.

Even though he was working off-island, Pierce picked up on the first ring. "Hey Em, how are things going in Christmas Town?"

"No one has ended up dead for a couple of days," she answered. She wondered when dark humor had become her thing.

"That's encouraging. Have you found out anything interesting about our latest case?" It made Emmy smile when Pierce used the word 'our' to describe the case he was working on.

"Actually, yes. Do you have a way of finding out the caseload for a parole officer? Like not by name, but maybe by mugshot?"

"Probably. Who's the parole officer?"

"Barbara Lystad," Emmy said.

"Isn't that your dad's parole officer?" Pierce asked.

"Yeah. I think there might be someone else on the island who shares that connection. Our own St. Nick."

"Interesting. He insisted Nicholas Star was his real name. He even had a driver's license to prove it. Nothing came up in his background check. If he faked all of it, it was a good fake. I'll let you know what I find. We can talk at my apartment before the boat parade tonight."

"Perfect. I'll bring food."

"What about your dad?" Pierce asked.

"I'm not sure if he's going tonight or not. We're not speaking again."

"What is it this time?"

"I told him I wanted the chance to live my own life."

"How dare you."

"I know, right?" Emmy hesitated. Right or not, she felt guilty about fighting with her dad and guilty about talking to Pierce about it, but the money he'd used at the restaurant got her thinking. Maybe he had switched the star. She wasn't ready to talk to Pierce about it, though. "Thanks for checking with the parole officer. If I'm right and he really is a felon, we need to know now."

She hung up the phone. When she turned around, Nicholas was standing in front of her. There's no way he didn't overhear her conversation with Pierce. She just didn't know how much he'd overheard.

"I forgot my bag of candy canes." He shouldered the felt bag he'd left next to his stool. He started for the back door to Santa's workshop and then stopped. "If you're looking for someone who had something on Ms. Carmichael, I'd check with your dad. I heard him tell one of those Wise Guys that if he ever got the chance, he'd take her down."

"Take her down?" Emmy repeated in disbelief.

"Yeah. He knows more about all of this than he's letting on."

Nicholas' eyebrows were nearly covering his dark eyes. Another change had come over him.

Emmy felt as though she were staring into the eyes of a very dangerous man.

## Chapter 29
# Missing Claus

The ornaments had never made it to the tree. They were still sitting on Pierce's coffee table. Emmy had been arranging and rearranging them for almost an hour. She had a key to his apartment, and she didn't want to deal with another fight with her dad.

The door opening behind her made her jump.

"Hey," Pierce said. "Sorry I'm so late."

Emmy took a breath. She'd been jumpy ever since she saw the look Nicholas had given her. She watched him the whole time he was playing Santa, but again, he seemed to be a different person—the jolliest and kindest Santa she'd ever seen.

"No worries, dinner is—"

"Done?" Pierce said, rushing to the kitchen.

Emmy smelled smoke. She'd gotten so distracted that she had forgotten about it. Her forgetfulness and the number of burnt offerings she'd made in her culinary classes had led her to drop that major and any dreams of becoming a professional chef.

"Shoot, sorry." Emmy looked at the chicken pot pie—one of Pierce's favorites. The crust was dark brown, and smoke mixed with the steam poured from the neat slits she'd made on the top.

"It's a tad over-baked," Pierce said in a mock British accent, imitating one of Emmy's favorite cooking shows.

"Sorry," Emmy said again.

"No worries." Pierce set it on top of the oven. "I was in the mood for pizza anyway."

He put in a quick order to the White Sails. Birdie had just added a fantastic stone-fired pizza to her menu, something Artie never would have tolerated.

After Pierce ordered the pizza, he sat down next to her. He gestured to the ornaments. "What are we looking at?"

"That depends," Emmy said. "What did you find out about the parole officer's list?"

"I have it right here." He moved aside two figures and opened his laptop on the coffee table in front of them. He pulled up a screen of pictures. "She just sent me this. I didn't have a chance to look befo—"

"That's him," Emmy pointed to a thin, clean-shaven man with the same eyes as Nicholas.

"Are you sure?" Pierce zoomed in on the picture.

"I'm sure." Emmy shivered. The man in the picture wore the same expression as the man who had confronted her behind Santa's workshop.

Pierce clicked on the picture, and the man's rap sheet came up.

"Nicholas Carson," he read out loud. "Convicted of diamond smuggling."

"Diamonds," Emmy leaned closer to the screen. In a way, this all made her feel better. If Nicholas were a diamond thief, it was less likely her dad was the one who had stolen the star.

"Yep, and look at this: 'known associates, Kenneth Pearson.'"

"Estelle's husband. So they knew each other before."

"Looks like it."

"So, now what?" Emmy said.

"Well, we have a known jewel thief and some missing diamonds, and we have a murder. I'd say we have our guy. But we need proof."

"And we need to fire him as Santa, like, now. We can't have him around a bunch of kids." Emmy shook her head. "The irony is that Kirsten wanted to have my dad be Santa, but I said no because he's a felon, and then we hired a felon anyway."

"When is the next time he plays Santa?" Pierce asked.

"We have the lighted Christmas parade in a couple of hours. He's on the main ship at the end of the parade."

Pierce stood. "I'd better bring him in for questioning now."

The doorbell rang, signaling that their pizza had arrived. "Sorry about dinner."

"No worries. I'll grab a slice on my way out."

"I need to call Kirsten. She won't be happy that she has to find another Santa on such short notice."

Emmy dialed Kirsten's number while Pierce paid for the pizza. She picked up on the first ring.

"I was just about to call you." Kirsten sounded breathless. "We have a problem."

"Yeah, that's what I was calling you about. We need to find a new Santa."

"How did you know?" Kirsten sounded shocked. "He's been missing since his last shift this afternoon."

"Missing?" Emmy said. She turned and looked at Pierce.

He set the pizza box down. "We'll be right there."

---

"We both need a night off," Pierce said as they hurried to the dock by Brighton's shipyard. It was the staging area for the lighted boat parade.

"No kidding," Emmy said. She had been looking forward to relaxing with Pierce and watching the boats. The lighted boat parade was another Sharp Island tradition that hadn't happened for a long time.

"Beautiful night for this," Brighton Redding intercepted her at the dock. For once, he appeared happy.

"It looks great." Emmy scanned the crowd. She didn't see Kirsten, and she hoped not to run into her dad. Brighton and her father were old enemies and rivals for her mom's affection. They hadn't crossed paths yet. She didn't want to be there when that happened.

"It does." Brighton's eyes twinkled. "Your mom always loved the boat parade. I'm happy to see you revive that tradition. If I recall correctly, you liked it quite a bit when you were a little girl."

"I wish I could remember that," Emmy said. Sometimes she felt as though there were some hazy memories of her mom, of the island, of all of it. She'd avoided asking her dad about those days, but maybe it would be good for both of them if they talked about it.

"I do, too." He looked at her with eyes that could have been mistaken for misty. "Good thing there's time to make new memories." He touched his cap. "I'd better make sure everything is ready to begin."

"Thanks again," she called after him.

Pierce gripped her hand tighter, reminding her they had more important things to do than talk. □

The parade began while they searched for Kirsten. They backtracked along the parade route, watching it in fast forward. It looked like everyone from Sharp Island who owned a boat (just about the entire island) had gone all out. The parade featured lighted pirate ships, Christmas trees, fantasy boats, even a Nativity scene, followed by the Three Wise Guys on their own boat, dressed in elaborate costumes, sitting on a giant lighted camel.

"I'm surprised Kirsten didn't decorate the real camel and add him to the mix," Pierce said.

"They probably couldn't get him to move from his spot in the petting zoo," Emmy said. "I prefer the reindeer. They're a bit more lively."

Brighton's biggest ship pulled away from the dock just as they arrived. It was a remake of the Christmas village in town, all made of lights. Santa sat on a big red chair on an elevated platform.

"I wonder where Kirsten came up with a new Santa on such short notice," Pierce said.

The man playing Santa looked right at Emmy and gave her a big "Ho, ho, ho."

"Oh no," Emmy said, recognizing him immediately.

"What's wrong?" Pierce turned to face her.

"I should have known she would ask him. That Santa is my dad."

"Nicholas went AWOL just before we all headed to the boat parade," Kirsten explained over a cup of hot tea. Crowds filled the tea shop after the parade. "Your dad was nice enough to fill in. Since there were no kids involved, I didn't think it was a big deal."

"It wouldn't be, except we really need to find Nicholas. It turns out he is also a felon and a jewel thief."

"Oh," Kirsten took a long sip of her Muddy Snowman, a mix that Emmy thought was more hot cocoa than actual tea. "Do you think he could have stolen the star and maybe...?"

"That's exactly what we think. That's why Pierce and Officer Peters are out looking for him now." Emmy glanced at her phone. Pierce had told her to go inside, that he would call her as soon as he found Nicholas.

"When was the last time you saw him?" Emmy asked.

"He disappeared right after his shift. He gave a big "ho, ho, ho" and waved to the kids and then walked through the back door of his workshop. I'd told all the performers to meet us at the staging area behind the boat shop, but he never showed. We found his suit in the alley behind the Christmas village. Your dad was there, and he was willing to fill in, so it seemed like the best option."

"I guess it was your only option." Emmy took a long sip of Wintergreen, a minty tea with a hint of pine. "I just wish we knew where Nicholas was."

"Well, the ferry won't run for another twenty minutes, so unless he has a boat, he's got to be somewhere on this island."

"There were plenty of boats in the parade, but they were all pretty conspicuous and maybe too small to take him all the way to the mainland. Officer Peters is making sure there are no stowaways on the ferry." Emmy set her teacup down. "Speaking of missing people, any idea where my dad is right now?"

"Emmy!" A bearded man in a red suit burst through the doors of the tea shop.

"Dad!" Emmy jumped up.

He looked frantic, but moved closer before he spoke again.

"Where is Pierce?" He looked up. The entire coffee shop was staring at the disheveled Santa, his half-unbuttoned coat not quite hiding the red stains on the shirt underneath.

Emmy met him at the door. "He's looking for Nicholas."

Her dad swallowed hard. "I found him."

# Chapter 30
# Killer Candy

"I was on my way back to our apartment," Emmy's dad said as they examined the dead man in the alleyway behind the town square.

"You found the body?" Officer Peters asked. "Again?"

"Yeah." Her dad looked grim.

Emmy didn't know whether to hug him or scream at him. Guilty or innocent, he had a knack for showing up in the wrong place at the wrong time.

"Same kind of wound," Pierce was saying. "Some kind of puncture wound to the neck. Too big to be a knitting needle this time. I'm not sure what it might have been."

Emmy avoided looking at the body: the sight of blood still made her nauseous, and Pierce couldn't stand the sight or sound of someone throwing up. Instead, she was looking at what was near the body. The smell of candy canes permeated the air. The green bag she'd seen Nicholas carrying was mostly empty and sat at his feet.

"A candy cane?" she thought out loud.

"What are you saying, Emerson?" Her dad asked.

She picked up one of the candy canes that had spilled out of the bag. They were long and fairly thick. Kirsten hadn't skimped. She'd bought the good ones. Maybe too good.

She held up the candy cane. "What about one of these?"

Pierce looked at her as if she were crazy.

"Haven't you ever sucked on a candy cane until it had a sharp point on the end?"

"It is possible," Officer Peters said. "Also a pretty clever way to get rid of the murder weapon."

"Except if you did it that way, the murderer's DNA would be all over the wound." Pierce said.

"I guess so." Emmy examined the candy in front of her. "Maybe it's worth looking at. I'm sure there are other ways to get a sharp point on a candy cane. And like Ms. Carmichael, a sharp point through the throat like this would make it impossible for him to yell."

"Now this is interesting," Officer Peters said. He produced something small that sparkled from the dead man's pocket.

"Another diamond?" Emmy asked.

"It looks like it."

"Good thing this is the last day of the Christmas Festival," Kirsten said.

"Yeah, it will be pretty hard to call this one an accident." Pierce looked down at the body again. "But I don't want to let any of the key players leave the island yet." He stood. "Speaking of key players, any idea where Estelle is? I think we need to start this round with her."

Estelle was locking down her vendor's booth when Emmy and Pierce arrived.

"So another one bites the dust, huh?" She sat in her chair and indicated the two chairs across from her.

"So you've heard," Pierce said.

"When bodies go down, rumors will fly." Estelle folded a soft red sweater with a half-bedazzled Santa Claus in the middle.

Emmy studied the woman; she had never met anyone as cynical about murder as Estelle.

"Well, let's have it. 'Where was I when Nicholas Star disappeared?' That's an easy one. I was in my booth. I had a line of customers, any of whom could vouch for my whereabouts."

"How do you know what time Nicholas disappeared?" Emmy asked.

"Again, rumors fly. Also, a couple of those Wise Guys were looking for him. The old one and the young one, I think. Maybe you should talk to them."

"We will," Pierce said. "But first, we want to talk to the person who knew Nicholas Star as Nicholas Carson."

Estelle patted the folded sweater. "I was wondering when that might come up. Yes. The man in red was one of my husband's business associates. Ironically, one I actually liked. When I ran into him a few weeks ago, he was out of jail, but down on his luck and trying to find a job. I'd just heard your little town needed a Santa, so I recommended him."

"But you knew he was an ex-con and therefore wouldn't be able to get a job, especially not one working with kids."

"Yeah." Estelle didn't look like that thought bothered her at all. "He said he had the right connections to come up with a clean slate. I didn't question it."

"So you recommended Nicholas out of the goodness of your heart?" Pierce said.

"Yep. As you know, I'm very soft-hearted," Estelle said without a hint of irony.

"If he could get a new identity so easily, why not get a regular job?" Emmy asked.

"I'm not sure if you noticed it, but Nicholas wasn't the brightest bulb on the tree. When he worked for my ex, he had a couple of very specific skills. Beyond that, he's mostly useless. Being Santa requires a white beard, a beer belly, and a few 'ho ho hos.' That bit he could do."

Emmy considered the change in Nicholas' face when he heard her talking about him. She didn't buy that he was as stupid as he pretended to be. She doubted Estelle believed that either.

"What specific skills did Nicholas have when he worked with your husband?" Pierce asked.

"He had an eye for diamonds; specifically, he had an eye for knowing at a glance what was valuable and what was worthless. He could tell a fake from a real diamond at a hundred paces. And he could break into just about anything."

Pierce nodded. "Interesting. And are you sure that's not the specific skill set you brought him here for?"

Estelle spread her hands out to indicate the packed-up sweaters in front of her. "Honey, this is as close as I get to diamonds these days."

Emmy and Pierce exchanged a glance. So far, they'd kept the missing star a secret, but with two murders, maybe it was time to bring that part of this into the light.

"So you didn't bring him here to find out if the Sharp Island Christmas Star was the real thing?" Emmy asked.

"I knew it!" Estelle's eyes lit up with the mania that Emmy had seen before. "I knew the diamonds on the star were real as soon as I saw it."

"Except the star you saw was not the real thing. Someone switched it before it went up at the lighting," Emmy said.

"But the one you had in the square, when that horrible alarm went off, that one was real, right?" Estelle sounded so sure. Emmy exchanged a glance with Pierce. If Estelle had known it was real all along...

"What did Nicholas say about it?" Pierce asked.

Estelle looked defiant. "We didn't talk about the star. Mostly, he just went on and on about how stressed he was. He was convinced that his cover had been blown, and that someone was out to get him."

"Do you know of any reason he should have been afraid?" Emmy was hoping for a confession, something that would ease her fears about her dad's involvement.

"Not that I can see. Nicky was always paranoid."

"Was there anyone in particular that he talked to or seemed worried about just before he died?" Pierce asked.

Estelle looked thoughtful. "At first, it was that woman, Ms. Carmichael. He said she made him nervous, that she was always watching him, like she knew who he was and she was holding it over him."

"You mean like blackmail?" Pierce asked.

"Not that I wouldn't put it past Penelope Carmichael to blackmail anyone. You've seen her little notebook, but I don't think it went that far. I think it was more of a look she gave him. I'd seen that look from her too, like she was just waiting for the right moment to reveal all your secrets."

"You said at first he was afraid of Ms. Carmichael. Who was he afraid of just before he died?" Emmy asked.

Estelle sat for a long time, as if she were trying to decide whether to speak up. She was quieter than they'd ever seen her.

"He seemed afraid of your dad, Wayne Fox. I think they had met when they were both in prison. When I first told him about the gig on the island, he acted like he already knew all about Sharp Island. He said one of his buddies from the inside had talked about it. The buddy had even mentioned a diamond-studded star. I didn't know who he was talking about until I overheard the argument."

"The argument?" Emmy asked.

"Yeah. A few hours before he started his last shift, I heard an argument between Nicky and Wayne Fox. It sounded like Wayne had threatened to expose him. They had the same probation officer or something. Wayne knew Nicky was breaking parole.

"Nicky stood up to him. He said, 'I'm not the only one with something to hide. If I'm going back to prison, then I'm not going alone.'"

"Is that all he said?" Pierce asked.

"That's all I *heard*," Estelle said.

Emmy caught the emphasis. "Did you see anything?"

"Yes," Estelle said. "I him slip Nicky something."

"What?" Emmy asked.

"If I were to guess, I'd say it was a diamond. Some kind of payment to keep Nicky quiet. But maybe your dad didn't think that would be enough. Maybe he was looking for a more permanent solution."

Emmy looked at Pierce. Had Nicholas backed her dad into a corner? Maybe they'd worked together to steal the star. If he had taken the star and Nicholas knew it, how far would her father go to protect himself?

Emmy shook her head. She couldn't believe her dad was a murderer, but a diamond thief...

He had money again. Where did it come from? She remembered the jeweler had mentioned a side project when she'd asked how soon the star would be ready. What was the side project? She wanted to believe the best of her father, but that was getting harder and harder.

She needed to know whether the star he had picked up was the real one. There was only one way to find out.

"Shay Jewelers," the voice on the other end of the line said. Shay Jewelers was the place Emmy had taken the star to be cleaned and repaired.

"Hi, this is Emerson Fox. You recently did a clearing and a reset for me on a family heirloom."

"Yes, of course. The beautiful diamond-studded Christmas star. Very impressive."

"Thank you." Emmy took a breath. She wasn't sure she wanted to know the answer to the next question, but she couldn't keep wondering. "You had mentioned a side project, but I didn't see it on the bill. Could you tell me what that was?"

"Let me look through the jeweler's notes." There were a few moments of silence, while Emmy's heart pounded in her ears.

"Yes, it's right here. Your father paid cash for that piece. That's why it doesn't appear on your invoice."

"And what was the other piece?" Emmy asked, but she was afraid she already knew.

"A replica of the original star."

## Chapter 31

# Keeping it Safe

"How are you doing, sweetheart?" Emmy's dad was on the couch when she came in. "I put on a pot of tea."

"Tea?" Emmy asked. As far as she could remember, her dad had never put on a pot of tea in his life. Why would he choose now to make tea?

"Yeah. Funny how addictive that stuff Ms. Lee makes is. She calls this one Snowflake Serenade. I swear it tastes like there are ice crystals in the hot tea. I'm not sure how she does that."

The kettle whistled.

Her dad got up and poured a couple of mugs of tea and then sat down beside her. "How did the interview with Estelle go? Did you get a confession?"

Emmy wrapped her hands around the mug, even though it was nearly too hot to hold. "No, but I found out something important. Something about you."

Her dad took a long drink from his mug, a drink that made her think he hadn't filled his cup with tea. "I knew Nicholas. I'm sorry, I should have told you. But I know what it's like to come back from jail and try to make a new start. He was trying to make an honest living, even if he wasn't very honest about it. He'd left behind a daughter, someone he wanted to get back to. When we were in prison together, he talked about her all the time, about how he just wanted her to be proud of him again. I understood that."

Emmy was watching him closely. He looked as despondent as he had when he first came to the island. But was that all an act so he could get her to trust him? She couldn't, not anymore. "Estelle said she heard him threaten to expose you."

"Expose me for what?" Her dad looked genuinely confused. "He's the one who was in danger of being exposed. All of my secrets are out in the open. If she heard us arguing, it was because I told him he'd never win his daughter's trust by telling lies and evading his parole officer. I told him he needed to come clean."

Emmy's anger seethed under the surface. She gripped the mug so tightly that it shook in her hands. Her dad claimed he'd tried to convince Nicholas to come clean for the sake of his daughter, but here he was lying to her. "Estelle also said she saw you slip him something. She thought it was a diamond."

"Where would I have gotten a loose diamond?" He asked, but he was no longer looking her in the eye.

She set the mug down to keep herself from throwing it at him. "I know you switched the star before the lighting."

Her dad drained his mug and then set it down. "I was hoping you wouldn't find out about that."

The calm, matter-of-fact tone in his voice made her even angrier. She'd wanted to believe that he'd changed, that he would never do anything to hurt her, but then he stole something that was valuable to her in more ways than just money.

She couldn't stay calm any longer. "How could you? I trusted you. Even though everything and everyone was telling me I shouldn't, I—"

"Hold on baby, I did it for your own good."

"My own good? It's always about you doing things for my own good! But it's never actually for me. It's all for you! What is your excuse this time? You sold the diamonds so you could take care of me, because you don't trust me to take care of myself?" Emmy tried to keep the hot, angry tears from spilling over.

Something dawned in his eyes. "You think I had a decoy star made so I could sell the diamonds? You think I stole the star?"

"Isn't that what you just said?" Emmy asked.

"I had the fake star made to keep it safe. I told you it was a bad idea to leave something so valuable out in the open like that, but you wouldn't listen. There wasn't time to renew the insurance policy, so I went behind your back to keep it safe. I was planning on switching the star back after the bazaar was over."

It took a minute for what he was saying to sink in. "Wait, you still have the star?"

"Yes. That's why I didn't go straight to the town square when I got off the ferry. I wanted to put it in a safe place here in the apartment. It's been here all along. You really think I'd sell your great-grandmother's star?"

Emmy didn't know how to answer that question.

"Despite everything, you don't trust me," her dad finished. He sounded defeated. "What else? Do you think I killed Ms. Carmichael? Or Nicholas?"

Emmy looked him directly in his eyes. "No. I don't think you killed anyone."

He let out a long breath. "That makes me feel a little better." He stood. "Now let's go get your star so you don't have to worry about that part of it anymore." He headed to his bedroom. "I bought a safe when I was in Seattle and hid it in the back of my closet." He moved his clothes aside to reveal a black safe. He spun the dials and then pulled the door open. "See. The star has been here the whole time."

But the safe was empty.

## Chapter 32

# Trust and Lies

"So you're saying the star wasn't stolen before, but now it is?" Pierce stared into the open safe.

"I left it here the night of the tree lighting. I set the combination and made sure the door was closed." Wayne Fox looked miserable. More miserable than Emmy had seen him since he got out of jail. For the first time, the bravado was gone. He acted as if the star being stolen was the biggest thing he had done to let her down.

"Are you sure it was here?" Pierce asked.

"Yes."

"Did anyone follow you back to the apartment?" Pierce asked.

"Not that I saw." He was thoughtful for a few minutes. "I talked to both Dennis and Nicholas on my way out of the town square. I suppose one of them could have followed me here."

"They were both missing just before the tree lighting," Emmy said. "Either of them would have had time to steal the star and get back when they did: late, but still in time to put in an appearance."

"I'm sorry, honey." Her dad's voice was uncharacteristically humble. "I keep trying to help, to make things easier for you, or protect what's important to you. It seems like whatever I do, I make things worse."

"It's okay, Dad." Emmy couldn't stop herself from giving him a hug. "Your heart was in the right place."

"I'm sorry, but I can't be that nice about the whole thing." Pierce's blue eyes crackled, as if they had fire and ice in them. Emmy had never seen him look so angry. "What do we have besides your word that the star was ever in the safe, or that it made it back to the island at all?"

"Pierce, I—"

He held up his hand. "Emmy, I get that you want to believe your dad is innocent, but the evidence is stacking up against him. He's lied in the past, and I think he's lying now." Pierce turned to face Mr. Fox. "You say you hid the star to protect Emmy? Well, you aren't the only one who wants to protect her. I think it's time someone started protecting her from you."

"No one needs to protect my daughter from me." Mr. Fox's voice rose. "I wouldn't ever do anything to hurt her."

"You mean like embezzling money from your company and abandoning her to fend for herself while you were in jail?"

Mr. Fox hung his head. "I can't change what happened in the past. I can only try to make it better. Ever since I came here, I've been trying to make it better."

"Instead, you've made everything worse." Pierce shook his head. "You've come into some money lately, and I've been in contact with a pawnshop in Anacortes. A man fitting your description recently pawned some loose diamonds."

Her dad blanched. Emmy looked from Pierce to her dad in disbelief. Pierce hadn't mentioned the pawn shop. He must have been trying to protect her from the truth.

Her dad's face blanched. "Those were diamonds I'd inherited from my grandmother. I left them in a safe deposit box while I was in jail." He turned to Emmy, his eyes pleading.

"I'm sorry. I'd always intended to save them for you, but I was tired of being a leech. I sold them, so I'd have some money to pay my own way. You can check where the diamonds came from."

"I did, and unfortunately, both the diamonds from the star and any you may have inherited were too old to have been cataloged or engraved with a serial code."

"Right," Mr. Fox paused for a minute. "But the jeweler who cleaned the star had to have notes on the cut or clarity of the diamonds."

"Minimal," Pierce said. "Not enough to rule out the idea that the diamonds you pawned weren't the diamonds in the star."

"Is that where the diamond you gave Nicholas came from?" Emmy asked.

"It was one of my grandmother's that I hadn't pawned yet. It was payment for his assessment of the other ones."

Pierce still looked skeptical. "You paid him a whole diamond?"

"It was a small one. Look, I know you don't get it, but Nicky was really trying to turn things around for his daughter. If giving him that little diamond kept him from sliding back into his old ways and ending up back in prison, then it was worth it."

"All of that could be true," Pierce said. "Or it could be another one of your lies."

"Since Nicky is dead, you'll have to take my word for it."

"Or I could arrest you now, at least for the theft of the star. Emmy didn't give you permission to take it anywhere but to the jewelers and then back again."

Emmy had been silently listening to the heated exchange between the two men she loved most. She wasn't sure whether her dad was telling the truth or if Pierce was right and she was being naive. Either way, she couldn't be the reason he went back to prison.

"No. I won't press charges."

Her dad and Pierce stopped arguing and turned back to face her.

"Are you sure?" Pierce asked.

"Baby, thank you, I–"

Emmy held up her hand. "It doesn't mean I believe your story, and it doesn't mean I trust you. And it doesn't exclude you from the murder investigation."

For once, her father was speechless.

Emmy took a breath. "But as far as that goes. I'm going to do whatever it takes to clear your name."

## Chapter 33
# Breaking and Entering

Dennis was the slipperiest member of the Wise Guys. He was always on the phone or rushing off to take a call. It was like he'd really never left the world of an investment banker, even though he said he had.

Emmy tracked him down to the cliffs above the beach. He was walking by himself. A misty rain fell, and the wind beat the waves against the shore below. As usual, he had his phone glued to his ear. The sound of the wind and the waves drowned out whatever he was saying, and he quickly ended the conversation when he saw Emmy.

"Hello, Emerson," he said. His voice was cheerful, but strain was written on his face.

"Hi Mr. Mirr," she said.

"It's Gobel, actually. Mirr is barely a stage name. One I'll be getting rid of soon."

"What brings you out here on a day like this?" Emmy asked.

"The need for privacy," he said, then quickly added, "Not from you. I've just been living in close quarters with Clark and Jay for too long, and I needed to check on some investments."

"I get the need for privacy," Emmy said. "I'd gotten kind of used to living by myself before my dad got out of jail."

"That situation would make anyone uncomfortable," Dennis agreed.

"You knew about my dad's conviction, even though you acted like you didn't when I first met you."

"Of course I knew, but I didn't think it was the right time to bring it up in front of you."

"But you did bring it up," Emmy said. "You asked him how that little scandal turned out. You invited him to give more details."

"I guess I did. I was curious about his take on it. When he chose to lie about it, I didn't think confronting him was the right move."

"Fair point," Emmy said. She gestured toward his phone. "I thought you had given all of that up."

He sighed. "Turns out it's hard to walk away from real life. Turns out you still need money to survive, and comedy doesn't exactly pay the bills. Not even for someone like Clark, who 'made it big'." Dennis put the words in air quotes, and his voice had an edge of bitterness to it.

"So, Clark is in financial trouble and he asked you to help him out?" Emmy knew it was a pretty bold and nosy question, but she'd already guessed the answer based on the notes from Ms. Carmichael's notebook. She watched for Dennis' reaction.

"He was in financial trouble long before I joined him. I agreed to help him with his finances if he helped me get my start in comedy. What he doesn't get is that a financial portfolio takes years to build. I can't turn his finances around in a few weeks, especially not when he continues to spend like he's still got a million in the bank."

"I'm guessing it's been hard for you to rein him in," Emmy said.

"Babysitting Clark and Jay was not what I had in mind when I joined this group."

"And yet you were the one who was missing just before it was time to go onstage the night of the lighting," Emmy said.

"Yeah, funny how that made me look like the irresponsible one when I was doing everything I could to straighten up the mess they'd both gotten themselves into."

"What kind of mess?" Emmy asked.

"It's not for me to say."

Dennis appeared leery of her questions, so Emmy backed off. "My dad said he talked to you a bit before the lighting?"

He huffed. "Shows you how desperate I was. I actually asked a felon for investment advice. No offense."

Emmy tried not to let his last remark bother her. After all, he was right. Her dad was a felon. "How long did you two talk?"

"Ten minutes at the most; he seemed to be in a bit of a hurry, but he actually gave some good advice."

"On the investments?" Emmy asked.

"No. In general. He said exchanging favors like that with a man like Clark was a bad idea and that I should cut ties as soon as possible."

"And have you?" Emmy asked.

Dennis nodded. "I was trying to figure out the best way to tell Clark that I'm done with the show and with being his unpaid stockbroker." He tipped his hand, palm up, to catch the rain. "That's why I'm out here on this lovely day. I had intended to tell him last night, but he was late getting to the boat. Then he seemed so out of sorts afterward that I didn't have the heart to tell him."

"Did he say where he had been?" Emmy asked. According to Pierce, Clark's alibi was the boat parade. No one had mentioned that he was late getting there, except for Dennis.

"No. He just asked Jay and me to cover for him. But I'm done covering things for Clark."

"Then you can tell me where you were the night of the lighting, when everyone was looking for you," Emmy said.

Fear flashed in his eyes, and Emmy was sure he was going to run, so she talked quickly. "The farther away from the crime scene you were, the more likely you are to be cleared."

He took a deep breath. "You're right. I was in Ms. Carmichael's room at the Cottage. I hacked into her computer because I wanted to find out what she knew about Clark's financial situation and my involvement in it, and Jay asked me to find out what she knew about him."

"And what did she have on Jay?" Emmy asked.

"Like I said before, it's not my place to say."

Emmy thought back to the note at the pageant. "Something to do with a woman named Candy Mason?"

"Yeah. How did you know?"

Emmy didn't want to explain the whole thing about the note and the pageant. "Lucky guess, and I'm going to make another one. Jay's charity is fraudulent."

Dennis let out a long breath, as if he'd been hoping someone would figure out Jay's secret so he didn't have to keep it to himself any longer. "Worse than that. The charity is based on a false premise, and he kept the money he brought in for his rock and roll lifestyle."

Motive.

"Was that what was written on the pages you stole from Ms. Carmichael's notebook?"

He hung his head. "Yes."

"Where are those pages now?"

He dug into his pocket and pulled out a bit of wadded up paper. "I was actually on my way to throw these into the ocean."

Emmy took the pages from him and read:

*The young guy isn't funny at all, and I know for a fact he's a complete and utter fraud. His mother isn't dying of cancer. I've known her for years. I have proof he's keeping the money for himself.*

"Candy Mason is his mom. Of course."

"Apparently she was a really terrible mother," Dennis said.

"But that's no reason to kill her off, even virtually, and then profit from other people's sympathy." Emmy was so angry with all of them she thought about calling Pierce to arrest Dennis for breaking and entering. She wasn't sure if it was worth it. Besides, if anything, it proved Dennis didn't kill Ms. Carmichael. "Is there anything else I should know about your trip to Ms. Carmichael's room?"

He looked down like he wasn't sure, then finally he said. "Something your dad told me when I ran into him just before the tree lighting has been bothering me. I didn't tell the police about it, but I think you should hear it."

Emmy's chest tightened, "What was that?"

"He told me he had the means, and if he got the chance, he would bury Penelope Carmichael for what she did."

## Chapter 34
# Spilling the Tea

"Emmy!" Ms. Lee said as soon as Emmy walked into the tea shop. "I was wondering when you would come to get the tea."

"Right, sorry, I've been busy, but I'm dying to try some of your holiday flavors."

Emmy's whole body felt cold after her discussion with Dennis. She'd hoped a cup of hot tea would warm her up.

Ms. Lee took off her apron and brought a tray with one of her little pots and two cups. "Yes, I have some wonderful winter flavors. This one is Nutcracker Sweet, you'll love it, but I actually meant the 'tea,' you know, the gossip around town."

"Right." Emmy could always count on Ms. Lee to have the inside story on whatever was happening on Sharp Island.

"This is new," Emmy said, pointing to a framed and autographed picture of Clark on the wall by the counter.

Ms. Lee set down the tray and put her hand to her heart. "The handsome British comedian. I caught him in the vendor's area just before the tree lighting and had him sign that picture for me. That accent." She smiled dreamily.

Emmy thought back to what Clark had said about being accosted by a fan that took his attention away from the vendor's booths. "You're the one. You're his alibi." Emmy said.

"Am I?" Ms. Lee seemed pleased. She poured a cup for Emmy and one for herself. Then she leaned forward. "Two murders. Do you have any leads?"

Emmy picked up the cup. The tea smelled of hazelnuts and sugared candy. It was too hot to drink, so she set it back down.

"And don't tell me you aren't getting involved. I know you too well."

Emmy sighed. She wasn't really in the mood to answer questions. "Because of the time of death, there are only a few people who could have killed Ms. Carmichael. And now one of them is dead."

Ms. Lee nodded. "Most of the town was at the boat parade. It was beautiful, by the way. I've said for years that we should have continued that tradition. I'm so glad to see so many of the old traditions come back to life."

"Thanks." Emmy blew on her cup.

"Was Santa killed after the parade? I saw him on the Christmas Town boat."

"No, that was a different Santa. Nicholas, the man who has been playing Santa, was killed just before the parade. When he came up missing, my dad took his spot."

"Yes, they are similar. I've gotten them confused a few times myself. Like yesterday, when Santa Claus was here trying to find you, I automatically assumed it was your dad."

"Nicholas was trying to find me?" Emmy asked.

"He said he had something important to tell you. I gave him directions to your apartment. Which, again, I thought was strange. That's when I realized it wasn't your dad." She shook her head. "The only thing that helped me tell them apart was the Santa suit, and Nicholas wasn't wearing his when I spoke to him."

"Did he say why he wanted to talk to me?" Emmy asked.

"No. But it seemed important. He was in a big hurry. Did he find you?"

"No."

"And now he's dead."

"Yeah." Emmy stared into her tea. Nicholas was found in the alleyway near her apartment. He must have been coming to find her. What did Nicholas want to talk to her about? Was it the same thing he had argued with her father about? Was he going to tell her that her dad had stolen the star, or something worse? Or did he just want her advice on how to win back his daughter's trust?

"What time was he here?" Emmy asked.

"About 5:45, just before I was going to close up shop to go to the boat parade."

"Pierce and I were trying to find him about that same time," Emmy said. She thought about the timeline. Nicholas had left after his break, shed the Santa suit and left it in the Christmas village. Then he came to find her. Somewhere along the way he had been murdered. Why?

"Did you hear him say anything?" Emmy asked.

"He kept muttering, 'She was already dead when I got there,' and, 'He's the only one who knows the truth.'"

"Who's the only one who knows the truth?" Emmy asked.

"I don't know. I assume that's what he wanted to talk to you about."

Emmy wished she'd met up with Nicholas before he died.

"Emmy, when was the last time you saw Clark?" Pierce asked when she answered the phone. He'd gone to the mainland to do some research on the case.

"He and the rest of the group are still at the Cliffside Inn, why?" Emmy answered.

"I need you to ask him some questions, casually and in public. Officer Peters is on patrol a couple of islands over, and I can't make it back until the next ferry. I'd like some answers as soon as possible."

"What kind of answers?" Emmy asked.

"I want to know exactly how he knew Penelope Carmichael."

Emmy was confused. "I thought he had already answered that. He said she had been stalking her for years. He actually seemed afraid of her."

"That's the vibe I got from him too, but there's been a development in the case that I think might change all of that."

"What kind of development?" Emmy asked.

"We got a hold of all of Ms. Carmichael's legal papers, including her will."

"So you found out who gets the pile of sweaters that are stored in the back of the bookshop?"

"That and a lot of money," Pierce said.

"A lot of money?" Emmy repeated. "Was the sweater business that good?"

"I'm not sure if that's where she got the money, but it turns out she had a small fortune. It sounds like she was a good businessperson and a savvy investor. She had quite a nest egg saved up."

"So who did she leave it all to?" Emmy asked.

"That's where it gets interesting. She left it all to her ex-husband, Clark Franklin."

"Ex-husband? They were married?" Emmy asked.

"I guess so. We have a marriage license and annulment proceedings from the UK to prove it. It was a long time ago. They were both very young, but he lied about it. I think that says something about his character, if not his involvement in all of this."

"I wonder if he knew she had money, or that she'd included him in her will," Emmy said.

"That's what I hope you can find out for me. Again, a casual conversation, and in public, just in case."

"I'm on it," Emmy said. "Does this mean you're looking at other suspects besides my dad?"

"I always like to keep an open mind," Pierce said, "or at least, I'm learning to."

Chapter 35
# The Ex

"You must be looking for our British friend." Anjuli wiped a pink cloth over the glass case that was filled with gingerbread, sugar cookies and a whole host of delicious treats. "I assume he'll be here soon. He's come in every morning as soon as I open since he's been on the island. He's always dressed so nicely, not like those people who come in with their pajamas on and their hair unkempt." Anjuli shook her head, and Emmy knew she was talking about Jay.

"Every day he orders a chocolate croissant to eat here and a gingerbread man to go. For a comedian, he seems very solemn. He's always polite, but also glued to his phone.

Once I walked behind him and glanced at it—I wasn't spying or anything—it looked like something financial. He was shaking his head."

"Like he didn't understand, or like he didn't like what he was seeing?" Emmy asked.

"I would say both. But maybe you should ask him about it." The bell dinged, and Clark walked in.

Emmy could tell he was both surprised and dismayed to see her. He covered it quickly with a wide smile.

"Our lovely hostess. What brings you here this early in the morning? Except for a few to-go orders, I'm used to having all of this to myself." He made a wide gesture to encompass the patisserie.

"I have a lot on my mind, I guess," Emmy said.

"Of course, how insensitive of me. Would you like to sit down and talk about what's been going on?" he gestured to the display case. "Pick out something delicious, my treat."

It was the invitation Emmy had been hoping for, and not just because she loved the pastry. She asked for a crème pat filled croissant and took a seat across from Clark.

"How are you doing, Emerson? It must be such a shock to have two additional tragic deaths in your little town. Do you have any idea what happened to Mr. Star?"

"Not yet. Pierce is looking into it. I'm just trying to do damage control."

"I can only imagine." Clark nodded his head sympathetically.

Emmy waited a few beats, trying to figure out how to ease into this conversation and steer it the way she wanted it to go. "What about you? Where are you headed after here? Do the Three Wise Guys have another gig?" She wondered if Dennis had broken the news to him about the split.

He shook his head. "Sadly, this group hasn't worked out the way I thought it would. Jay is a newcomer with a decent future, but he isn't there yet. Dennis has his moments. He does almost as good a Granny Gray as I do, but he lacks the comedic timing and the drive that's necessary in a very cutthroat business—pardon the inappropriate pun. Frankly, he's too old to start a career now. I took a chance on him. I probably shouldn't have."

Emmy saw her opening. "How old were you when you started in this business? I mean, my stepmom was a fan from back in the day, so I watched a lot of *Comedy Train*. But there was one before that, *Improvapalooza* or something like that, right?"

"Improvaganza." Clark said.

"Of course. I've only seen a few bits from that one, but it was very good."

Clark sat back with a satisfied look on his face. He obviously enjoyed talking about himself. "It was a slow, but steady climb. We didn't have things like social media in those days, so we had to do a lot more legwork. I spent a lot of time in seedy little comedy clubs. I even did a bit of street performing in London back in the day."

"That must have been pretty discouraging," Emmy said.

"Oh, it was, but I pressed forward. I loved the idea of bringing a smile to people's faces and making them laugh, so I persisted."

"And now here you are. A success story." Emmy said.

"Thank you," he gave a little bow.

"But maybe not as financially successful as you had hoped at this point."

His self-satisfied expression faded. "That's quite a personal question. You must have been talking to my loud-mouthed companions." He folded and unfolded his napkin. "The honest answer is no, I don't have the money I once had or hoped to have by this point in my career."

"Any chance there might be a windfall coming your way anytime soon?" Emmy watched his face. She wanted to see if he knew what she was getting at—if he knew about Penelope's will.

"Something from Dennis?" he laughed. "Not likely. He's at least as bad at money as he is at comedy." His eyes narrowed. "Unless you think I had something to do with the disappearance of your lovely star. I heard a rumor that it was missing and quite valuable."

Emmy stared at him for a second. "How do you know about that?"

"Rumors fly when bodies go down." It was the same thing Estelle had said. "Yes, the bling queen has been talking about it. She hinted that your dad had something to do with it. I can't speak to that. I only know I didn't have any idea it was that valuable until she mentioned it."

"No. I wasn't talking about the star. That's a whole other mess to unravel. I was talking about something else that might lead to extra money for you. Something, or someone from the past."

Clark looked at her for a long time. "What are you getting at, Ms. Fox? If you have something to say, or something to ask, ask it. I don't like all this beating around the bush."

"Okay then. Pierce found Penelope Carmichael's will. She left everything to her ex-husband. In other words, you."

"She did?" Clark looked genuinely shocked. He shook his head. "I can't imagine why she would do that."

"Maybe because she loved you, or maybe because she thought you loved her."

He waved his hand, like his marriage to Penelope was something easily dismissed. "There wasn't any love involved. She came to me after one of my shows when I was first getting started. She was on holiday in England. There was drinking, a hotel room, and an unexpected pregnancy. In those days, getting married seemed like the right thing to do, even when it wasn't. It only lasted a few months. She lost the baby. I had the marriage annulled, and we went our separate ways."

Emmy got an unpleasant taste in her mouth. She suddenly really disliked Clark. "Except obviously she didn't get over it. You lied about your relationship with her. You said she was a stalker, not someone you used and then threw away. What else are you lying about?"

Clark put his hand up. "Now hold on. It's not my fault that Penelope couldn't get over me. I never gave her any encouragement, and I was kind as long as I could be. There are just some people who get on everyone's nerves. I finally had to file a restraining order to keep her away. A restraining order she violated, by the way."

"*She* violated?" Emmy asked. "The people I talked to said you had gone to her in her booth, not the other way around. If you'd been trying to stay away from her, why were you in her booth that night? And don't tell me it was to sew up your jacket."

His mouth was set in a hard line. He wasn't nearly as good-looking when he scowled like that. "Because she had invited me, slipped me that note after the pageant. The one I showed you. I didn't want her to make a fuss about it, so I went in person to tell her I wouldn't be coming to meet with her, then or ever. She wasn't there, so I took the sweater and left."

He let out a long breath. "It wasn't the first sweater she'd made with my face on it. I wanted to laugh it off, but it was so disturbing, and besides–"

"Besides, you didn't want anyone to know she'd been your wife."

He screwed up his face as if he were smelling something foul. "Can you blame me? I mean, she was an insufferable busybody."

"An insufferable busybody who was stupid enough to fall in love with you and then stupid enough to stay in love with you."

"I can't be blamed if women find me irresistible."

Emmy bit back the reply she wanted to give him. "So she didn't tell you that you were her sole heir?"

He sat back as if he were bored with the whole affair. "No. I had no idea. What did she leave me? Her supply of knitting needles?"

"No," Emmy said. "She left you nearly three million dollars."

# Chapter 36
# Overthinking

"I know. I shouldn't have told him how much," Emmy said as she finished relating the story to Pierce. "But he was being so arrogant, so full of himself. So cruel to poor Ms. Carmichael, that I had to say something to wipe that superior look off his face."

Pierce gave her a look when she said, "poor Ms. Carmichael." She got that her sympathy for the murdered woman had increased since she found out what she had been through. And since she wasn't dealing with her constant complaining.

"How did he take it?" Pierce asked. "Do you think he had any idea that she had left that much money to him?"

"No, he seemed pretty shocked, but then again, he is an actor. He claims he was trying to save Ms. Carmichael's feelings by stopping by to tell her in person that he wouldn't be able to have a drink with her and that he never saw her, but I don't think that man has ever thought about anyone's feelings but his own."

"Do you think they talked long enough for her to let him know about the will, or to say something else that might have set him off?"

"I don't know. The more I know about everyone's connection to her, the more it feels like any of them could have done it. Dennis told me…" She hesitated. "He told me that Ms. Carmichael had threatened to expose Jay for embezzling money from his own charity."

Pierce nodded. "We've been following up on that one, too. We don't have enough proof yet to come after him, but it's coming."

"Poor Jay, and poor Ginny. The two of them have really hit it off."

"Why poor Jay if he founded a charity just to steal money from it?" Pierce asked.

"Sometimes guilt and innocence are more complicated than just the things that you do."

"Are we talking about Jay or about your dad?"

"Both. Maybe neither. I'm just saying we don't always get the full picture. People have a lot of reasons for committing a crime."

"I know that. In my line of work, we call those motives."

*Motives.*

Emmy rearranged the ornaments on the table again. In the center was the crocheted angel that represented Ms. Carmichael. Emmy moved the Santa Claus ornament, so it was in the middle too.

"Okay, connections," she said. "Ms. Carmichael was married to Clark, and she left him everything she had in her will. That gives him ample motive."

"If he knew about the money," Pierce said.

"Or if he was just fed up with her following him? But what motive would he have had to kill Nicholas?"

"Maybe Nicholas saw him kill Ms. Carmichael. You said he was the last one to go to her booth."

"She was already dead when I got there," Emmy said, remembering what Ms. Lee had told her.

"What?" Pierce asked.

"Ms. Lee told me Nicholas kept saying, 'she was already dead when I got there.' He had to mean Ms. Carmichael, right?"

Pierce nodded. "Maybe he saw whoever killed her and went to see if she was really dead."

"But why not report it?" Emmy asked.

"Because he was already violating his parole, and he didn't want to get involved with the police."

"Good point. If he saw who killed Ms. Carmichael, that would be a good motive for her killer to kill him as well. But we still don't know who that is." Emmy picked up the sequined angel. "Estelle?"

Pierce nodded. "Estelle was the first person to go to Ms. Carmichael's booth, but she was definitely alive then."

"Yeah. Everyone heard the argument about the missing box of gems. And then we found an actual diamond in a similar box. What did the jeweler say about that diamond?"

"He couldn't tell if it came from the star or not. But it could have. I doubt Estelle just had a bunch of loose diamonds lying around."

Something hit Emmy. She thought about the way Estelle was always working on the sweater with the star on it. The way she folded it up quickly when she and Pierce came into her booth. Nicholas had said it was special.

"Estelle's husband was a diamond smuggler, right? What was his business model?"

"He was bringing illegal diamonds into the country–diamonds that were mined through slave labor or other unethical processes. He smuggled those uncertifiable diamonds into the U.S., diamonds which would yield a nice black market profit."

"And how did he get them here?"

"I believe they were sewn into costumes and mixed with rhinestones and other fake jewels."

"You mean like the sweaters Estelle makes?" Emmy said.

"You think she might still be smuggling diamonds?" Pierce asked. "Investigators cleared her of any involvement in his smuggling operation."

"Maybe she wasn't involved in the business then, but maybe she learned some things along the way. I think she might be trying to smuggle diamonds out of the bazaar."

"You mean the diamonds from your family star?"

"Exactly." Emmy picked up a star ornament. "My dad picked up two stars, a real one and a fake one. He left the real one in the safe in my apartment."

"Allegedly," Pierce said.

"Allegedly," Emmy repeated. "And put the fake one in a box on the table by Ms. Carmichael's booth. Then he went back to the apartment, got his coat and got something to eat at the Big S." She moved the white-bearded nutcracker ornament that represented her dad off the table.

Pierce covered her hand. "He might still have had time to get back in time to kill Ms. Carmichael. We have three eyewitnesses who said they heard threats exchanged between them when he left the box on the table."

Emmy pulled her hand away. "My dad is a lot of things, but he's not a killer."

Pierce sighed and nodded.

"On the way to the apartment, my dad talked to Dennis, who was on his way to break into Ms. Carmichael's room. Dennis walked straight onto the stage when he came back, so he couldn't have killed her." Emmy moved the wise man ornament representing Dennis off the table.

"Landon was supposed to be guarding the star, but he was called away to fix something."

"Jay went into Ms. Carmichael's booth to look for an ugly sweater, but she wasn't there. Then Ginny asked him to come help her." Emmy moved the second wise man off the table. "That leaves Clark, Estelle, and Nicholas in the vendor's area. Clark said he was signing an autograph."

"So far we haven't been able to find the supposed crazed fan who took his attention from the vendor's area," Pierce said.

"It was Ms. Lee. She has the picture he signed hanging in her shop." She turned the tall, dark, wise man ornament around so it was facing away from the others.

"And Jay came back," Pierce pointed out.

"I'm getting to that." She picked up the Santa Claus ornament. "If Nicholas had looked into the box that held the star on Ms. Carmichael's table, he would have known immediately that it was a fake, right?"

Pierce nodded. "Right, so maybe he followed your dad to see if he had the real star. He followed him to your apartment, saw the safe, and then broke into it and stole the star when your dad went to get something to eat. Estelle said he could break into anything."

"That makes sense. But then what did he do with it?" Emmy asked.

"Assuming he was stealing it for Estelle, maybe he stashed it back in her room in the cottage. That's why he was late. He could have put it in her box of bling and then come back. That would explain how a real diamond ended up with her rhinestones."

"Right, and while he was gone, Jay came back." Emmy put the second wise man back on the table. "He said he spoke to Ms. Carmichael, but her back was to him and she wasn't acting like herself. She was quiet, and she said, 'Everything was fine.'"

"That certainly doesn't sound like the Penelope Carmichael we all knew."

"Maybe it wasn't her. Maybe she was already dead and someone was pretending to be her."

Emmy picked up the glittered angel ornament that represented Estelle. "Jay said it was a woman's voice, and at this point, all of our other suspects were somewhere else."

"Or Jay is lying, and he killed Ms. Carmichael when he came back so she wouldn't expose his fraud."

Emmy studied the ornaments again. "Nicholas was in a hurry when he came back. He saw the box on Ms. Carmichael's table and assumed it was the one with the star, the one he needed to use for the lighting. When he went to get it, he knocked over the bottle of peppermint schnapps and broke it. When he bent down to retrieve the bottle, he saw the blood and realized she was already dead."

"But by that point, everyone was at the lighting, even Estelle. Peters said she was approaching him at the far end of the square, opposite the vendor's booths, just as the lights came on."

"It also means Nicholas couldn't have seen who killed Ms. Carmichael, so he couldn't have been killed because he witnessed the murder."

She picked up the Santa ornament again. "He's the only one who knows the truth."

"Yeah, except he's dead," Pierce said.

"No, I don't mean Nicholas. It was something else he told Ms. Lee just before he died. He said, 'he was the only one who knew the truth.'"

"Who was the only one who knew the truth and about what?" Pierce asked.

"That's the problem. I don't know. I think Nicholas was on his way to tell me that before he was murdered. If we find the answer to that, we'll know who killed both of them."

"Maybe we're overthinking this," Pierce said. "If Estelle had Nicholas steal the star for her, then that would be a big motive for her to get him out of the way. And Estelle said she went back to Ms. Carmichael's booth to see if she could get her gems back. Maybe she killed her then."

"But Estelle isn't strong enough to have lifted Ms. Carmichael's body back into her chair. And she has an ironclad alibi for the night Nicholas was murdered. She had a line of people at her booth."

"Maybe she didn't do her own dirty work. She was married to organized crime for a long time. She has to have connections in that area. Maybe that's who Nicholas was talking about. I'll look into that."

"And I'll talk to her. If nothing else, I'd love to find out if my theory is correct and she stole my family's star."

"Be careful," Pierce said.

"Aren't I always?"

Pierce just shook his head.

# Chapter 37
# Canceled

"Have you seen the newspaper today?" Ramona said into the phone before Emmy got the chance to say hello.

"Newspaper?" Emmy was still groggy from her sleepless night. Today was the last day of the bazaar. She needed to figure out a way to confront Estelle as soon as possible. "Who reads the newspaper anymore?"

"I do. Every single day." Ramona said firmly. "And before you make some snide comment about my age, I'll tell you it comes straight into my inbox every morning. I enjoy getting the story without all the talking heads."

"Okay, I get it," Emmy looked at her phone. It was past eight o'clock. Where was her dad? Usually he got up and made enough racket pretending to make breakfast to wake her up so she could finish for him. "What was in the newspaper today?"

"It's about Jay, our handsome, yet arrogant, yet funny philanthropist comedian," Ramona said. "It's an expose piece about how he's been stealing from his own charity to finance his rock and roll lifestyle."

"Wow." Even though Emmy expected this was coming, it was still a shock. She got on her phone to search for the article.

"But that's not the worst part of it," Ramona continued. "His mother isn't even dead. She's living in some trailer court in Northern California. Apparently, they've been estranged for years. You'll never guess who the source was for the article."

Emmy had found the article and skimmed through it to the bottom, where the reporter thanked her source. "Penelope Carmichael?"

"Yeah. She found a way to tattle on Jay, even from the grave."

For a heartbeat, Emmy had flashbacks of another person coming back from the dead, but the reporter said that Penelope sent her the email containing her lead on the day she died.

"She carried through with her threat after all." Emmy said.

Ramona clucked her tongue. "They're falling like flies. How on earth did we manage to put together such a motley crew of thieves and liars for this bazaar?"

"I guess we should have listened to Ms. Carmichael when she said we needed a thorough vetting process," Emmy said.

"Yeah, but would that vetting process have kept her out?" Ramona asked.

Jay was standing with Ginny on the porch of the Cliffside Inn. He had his arms around her, his head on top of hers, looking out over the water.

He stepped back when he saw Emmy. His hand slid down and reached for Ginny's. They both looked miserable.

"Hey," Emmy said. They stood at the railing and watched the waves lap lazily against the rocks below for a few moments.

"The water is so smooth right now, especially for this time of year. It's hard to think about all that's going on below the surface." Jay said.

"There usually is," Emmy replied.

He sighed. "I guess you saw the article. Did you come to ask for your money back from our performances?"

"Emmy wouldn't do that." Ginny's eyes snapped a warning, just in case that's what Emmy was there for.

"No. I just wanted to see how you were doing." It wasn't entirely true, but Ginny looked so protective of Jay that Emmy didn't want her to think she'd come to interrogate him, even if that was true.

"Probably doesn't matter. You can get in the long line of people who want a refund. Our little group is breaking up anyway, and I don't think there will be a reunion tour. Clark isn't talking to Dennis."

"Why aren't they speaking?" Emmy asked.

"When I say 'not talking,' I don't mean he isn't communicating with him; more like the volume he uses in conversation is too high to consider it talking–shouting, bellowing, screaming would be more appropriate terms."

"He's right," Ginny said. "I could hear them outside the inn when I dropped Jay off last night."

"Poor Dennis. The way Clark treats him reminds me of the way my mom used to go after my dad. She ruled him—all of us, really. She was a tyrant." Jay looked at Ginny and she squeezed his hand.

It appeared Ginny and Jay had gotten close quickly. Emmy couldn't help but worry that Jay might be scamming her friend too. Maybe some interrogation was in order. "Your mom? You gave me and the rest of the world the impression that you were very close. You said she inspired you to live your dreams."

He turned to look at her, his eyes sad. "The woman I talk about in my videos is not my actual mother. Her name is Gloria Handelburg. She was the single woman who lived down the street from me. She never had kids of her own, so she basically raised me while my actual parents were fighting or otherwise MIA. I had no idea the 'Comedy for a Cure' thing would go that big. If I had, I might have been more honest in the beginning."

Emmy looked at him skeptically. "That sounds like the perfect additional sob story to get more sympathy for your cause. And by cause I mean you."

"That's not fair," Ginny broke in. "You don't know what his mom did to him. He's told me things…" She shook her head.

Ginny was in deep, and that worried Emmy. Jay was probably still lying. This was a weird shift in their relationship. Ginny had always been the one protecting her.

"Maybe you should have been honest about it from the beginning," Emmy said.

Jay avoided her eyes. "Ironically, I did it to save my real mom's feelings."

"By replacing her?"

"No, by not telling the world our family was a disaster. Somehow, it felt nicer to make up a story about the woman I considered my mom than to tell the world what a terrible person my real mom is."

They all remained silent for a few minutes. Jay's phone pinged. He looked down, and his face twisted. "More hate posts."

"I told you to stop looking at those," Ginny advised.

"It doesn't matter." He shoved the phone back into his pocket. "I'm already on a fast track to being canceled, thanks to that busybody Ms. Carmichael. I don't care so much about what happens to me. Maybe I actually deserve it, but the charity was doing well. Even though she's gone, I felt like I was finally getting to repay Gloria for everything she did for me. I was finally making something of myself and doing some good."

"By pocketing the money from the charity?" Emmy said.

"He wasn't pocketing it," Ginny said. "He was investing it."

"Investing it?" Emmy felt like she'd heard this one before. "Let me guess, with Dennis?"

Jay looked down at his feet. "Yeah. I got sucked into Dennis' investment advice. He said he could give me a great return on the charity's money. I knew it was a dumb thing to do, but he was very convincing, and Clark trusted him, so I bought into it."

"You can just get the money back then, right?" Ginny said. "At least what's left. Then you can get on your social media platforms and explain what happened and then give what's left to the American Cancer Society or something."

"I can't do that. All the money is gone. Turns out Dennis isn't quite the investor he once was, or maybe he never was. He screwed both Clark and me out of a bundle of cash, but he keeps saying it's our fault because we aren't patient enough and that it will come back eventually. I'm not any kind of financial genius, but I get that a hundred percent return on a negative balance is still less than zero."

The phone in his pocket dinged a couple more times. "I knew it was going to come out eventually, but I hoped by the time it did, I would have done enough paying comedy gigs to cover the debt."

"I'm sorry," Emmy said, because there wasn't anything else to say.

"It's okay. If it hadn't been for that Carmichael woman, neither Clark nor I would ever have known that anything was wrong."

"Ms. Carmichael clued you in that Dennis was losing your money?" Emmy asked.

"Not me, Clark. She sent him a note after the pageant. It turns out she's a bigger snoop than anyone knew. She somehow got into Clark's financial records and figured out that all of his money had gone into the deep dark hole where Dennis had thrown it."

"Maybe that's why she left all of her money to him," Emmy said, mostly to herself.

"Wait, she left her money to him?" Jay looked shocked. "But he hated her."

"It couldn't have been much, right?" Ginny asked.

Emmy had made that mistake once already, so she just said, "I just know he's named as her sole heir." She thought for a minute. "Did you see the letter she sent Clark?"

"No, he just told me about it. We confronted Dennis together. That's when he told us we needed to be more patient. He said he was working on a deal that would get us at least a fifty percent return on our investment. We just needed to wait a little longer."

"What happened then?" Emmy asked.

"We let it go. Clark said that Penelope Carmichael had probably exaggerated how bad the financial situation was. We gave Dennis another chance. It wasn't until I got the threat from her at the pageant that I took a good, hard look at what was going on."

Emmy looked at him skeptically. "And you asked Dennis to go check it out by breaking into Ms. Carmichael's room?"

"What? No, I never asked Dennis to break into anyone's room. Is that what he told you?"

"Yeah."

"Well, I didn't. Dennis only does favors like that for one person: Clark. He thinks Clark walks on water, even with the way he treats him."

"Did you know what else Dennis saw on Ms. Carmichael's computer?" Ginny looked from Jay to Emmy. "Maybe he saw the will, and knew that Clark was going to inherit the money. Maybe he was hoping to get his hands on that money too."

Jay shook his head. "He didn't mention it. I'm guessing it was a surprise for everyone."

Emmy wasn't sure that was true. "Yeah, I guess so. So what now? It sounds like you're guilty of defrauding all the people who invested in your charity."

Jay flinched. "Yeah, that's why all of this is so hard. I thought I was doing the right thing, trusting Dennis and trying to increase the money that was going to the charity. Turns out I was committing a crime. And now Ms. Carmichael's email and that article has gone viral, my career is over and I'll probably be going to jail too. The only way to save myself is if I get enough money to pay back what I took from my own charity fund. But there's not much of a chance of that, unless…"

"Unless what?" Emmy asked.

He looked at Ginny. "Unless I find a rich wife. That might be the only thing that could save me."

Ginny rolled her eyes. "Don't look at me. Emmy's the one who owns a private island."

"Well, how about it?" Jay asked.

Emmy laughed uncomfortably. "I'm not as rich as you think I am."

He shrugged. "It was worth a shot. I've been told I'm irresistible."

"Trust me. You are," Ginny leaned into his shoulder.

He stepped back. "You need to stay away from me, Gin. I've basically screwed up my whole life." The miserable look on both their faces made Emmy pity him even more. "When do you think your boyfriend is coming to arrest me?"

"Can't you do something to help him?" Ginny looked at Emmy with pleading eyes. "There's got to be something off about Dennis' investments. Could you have your dad look into it?"

"My dad?" Emmy asked, shocked.

"Yeah. He's kind of an expert on the whole shady investments thing. He'd probably recognize it if Dennis was doing something illegal, and if he was, maybe it would get Jay off the hook," Ginny said.

Something like hope lit up Jay's expression. "Do you think you could ask him?"

"I'll try," Emmy said, but wasn't sure if one con man could ferret out another.

## Chapter 38
# On the Dot

"Y ou have some crazy stuff going on that island of yours. What's the body count up to now?" Avery Covert, Seattle Time reporter, asked over one of Anjuli's eclairs. Avery had written the article outing Jay's charity. She had also written a favorable article about Sharp Island's disastrous fall festival that had saved Sharp Island's reputation.

Emmy had gambled on the idea that she could get the reporter to give her more details about what Penelope had told her about Jay. To sweeten the deal, Emmy had made a side visit to the patisserie on her way to the newspaper office in Seattle to pick up some pastries. The reporter had mentioned that the eclairs were her favorite.

"These are to die for," Avery said after taking a long bite. "And on your island, that might actually be true."

Emmy hoped Officer Peter's comment about Sharp Island being known for murder wasn't coming true. She sighed. "When did you get Ms. Carmichael's email about Jay?"

Avery wiped Bavarian cream from her fingers onto her napkin and consulted her notes. "The email came on Wednesday."

"Why didn't you publish it right away?" Emmy asked.

"This may or may not surprise you, but we've received a lot of emails like that from Ms. Carmichael. I needed to do some research to make sure her claims were accurate."

Emmy thought for a minute. "What time on Wednesday did the email get there?"

Avery pulled out her phone. "Sixish on Saturday evening."

"Six in the evening, exactly?" Emmy repeated.

She looked at her notes again. "Actually, 6:45."

"Really?"

"Is that significant?" Avery leaned forward, eager for the scoop.

"It might be," Emmy said thoughtfully.

"Okay, if it is, and if you figure this out, promise me you'll let me interview you about solving yet another island mystery."

Emmy sighed. "I guess I owe you for all the good publicity we had after our disaster of a fall festival. But I don't want to keep another Sharp Island murder in the spotlight."

"Leave the spin to me. I love your little island. I can make it work."

"I'll think about it," Emmy said. But what she was really thinking about was how Ms. Carmichael couldn't have sent the email blasting Jay at 6:45. She was likely dead by then.

Someone else had to have sent it.

As soon as she got home from meeting with the reporter, Emmy went looking for her dad. Jay had sent her the files with the financial information he'd gotten from Dennis. He hoped that her dad could look at them and figure out if Dennis had done something illegal.

The apartment was quiet. There was no food cooking, or attempting to be cooked. There was no coffee, or even a teakettle on the stove. Her dad's snores weren't rattling the walls of the guest bedroom. She suddenly realized it had been a long time since she'd seen him.

"Dad?" Emmy said. She checked the guest room. The room was empty and the bed was made. "Daddy?" she called again.

Then she saw the note on the nightstand.

*Emmy,*

*I've made a lot of mistakes, but this isn't one of them. I didn't take the star, but I can't live with myself if you think I did. I'm going to find out what happened to it and clear my name. I think I have an idea of who it is. You aren't the only sleuth in this family. I'm going to figure this thing out and bring your diamonds back to you. I know how important it is to you. Don't worry about me. □*

*Love, Dad*

"He's taking this into his own hands and trying to catch a thief who is most likely also a two-time murderer? What is he thinking?" Emmy said after she showed the note to Pierce. She'd found him working on the case in the little police station.

Pierce tried to suppress a laugh by making it seem like a cough.

"What? This is serious. My dad doesn't know what he's doing. He could get hurt. He needs to leave this to the professionals; he can't just–"

She stopped. Pierce was still snickering. "What is so funny?"

"You." He laughed again. "How many times have I told you to stay away from my investigations because you might get hurt? Now someone else is doing it to you and you don't see the irony? Maybe it runs in the family."

Emmy made a face at him. He was probably right, but she was too scared and annoyed by what her dad was doing to admit that. "But he's also a convicted felon. If he does something stupid, his parole could be revoked, and he'll be back in prison."

"And if he does nothing, the evidence suggests he's a diamond thief, and the same thing might happen."

"But it's my star. I told him I don't want to press charges…" She shook her head. "I'm just worried about him, okay? I just wish I knew where he was."

Pierce moved to the computer on his desk. "That one I can help you with. He still has his ankle bracelet, right? I can track it."

Emmy's eyes shone. "Really?" Then her heart sank. "Unless he takes it off."

"Then he would be in violation of his parole, and there's not much I can do for him." Pierce said seriously. He saw the look in her eyes and kissed her on the forehead. "We'll find him, talk some sense into him, and if you don't want me to file a report about the missing star or your missing father, no one needs to know about any of this."

"Because you think he did it. You think he took the star and lied about it," Emmy said.

"I didn't say that." Pierce went back to his computer. He checked a couple of files and then waited. Emmy leaned close to the screen, but she couldn't tell what Pierce was doing.

"That's interesting," he said suddenly.

"What?" Emmy asked. Pierce tapped on the screen, and the map became bigger. Emmy looked at the dot in surprise. "Why would he go there?"□

# Chapter 39
# Enola

The last time Emmy had stood outside the building that once housed the Hartman, Fox, and Rogers investment firm had been just before her high school graduation. She had gone to meet her father for dinner. They were going out to celebrate her acceptance into the way too expensive university of her choice.

They'd gone to the nicest restaurant in town. Her graduation present was a diamond necklace. He told her how proud he was of her and not to worry about the expensive tuition, and that she had plenty of time to choose a major. He said he'd take care of everything. He always had.

The lower half of the building had been converted into a high-end department store. There were still professional offices for lease upstairs, where her dad's office had been. Emmy paused in front of the building, remembering how many times her dad had brought her there. She remembered sitting at his big desk. When she was a little girl, the receptionist always had candy for her. Once she had even brought Emmy a hot chocolate when she brought in her dad's morning coffee.

The receptionist she remembered hadn't been there the last time Emmy had gone to his office. She had been a thin woman with a pointed nose, thick glasses, and shoulder-length brown hair. As she thought back, she realized that Penelope Carmichael had been sitting at the desk in the front of the building.

She had no way of knowing that the woman at the desk was already planning to bring her dad down. Neither of them had any idea that Emmy would one day be trying to find Penelope Carmichael's killer.

"Any idea why he would have come here?" Pierce asked.

"Nostalgia? This was where his office was," Emmy said.

"The signal definitely shows his ankle bracelet is here. Do you think he's hiding out in his old office?"

"Maybe. It's worth a look." But Emmy knew it couldn't be that simple.

Pierce made a couple of phone calls, and soon the building manager met them at the back of the department store.

"I can get a warrant if you'd like, but it would be easier if you just let us go inside," Pierce said.

"No need." The man inserted the key into an elevator at the back of the department store.

The department store had taken over the lobby where the receptionist's desk had sat and where the big conference room was, but the elevator was familiar to Emmy.

"Do you remember which office was his?" Pierce asked as they reached

"Of course," Emmy said. "The corner office on the fourth floor. He had a great view of the city."

"Even better," the building manager said. "Most of the offices that are that high up are vacant. The economy isn't what it was when this building was built."

Emmy led them down her own memory lane—the burgundy carpet, the dark wainscoting, the big door at the end of the hall.

Pierce consulted the app that tracked her father's ankle bracelet. "It looks like he's in here."

The manager reached to unlock the door, but it swung open before he turned the key. Emmy walked inside, feeling nostalgic, even though nothing was the same. There was still a desk in the vacant office, but it wasn't the desk that her dad had used. There was also a big table, a small couch, and a couple of empty file cabinets. Her dad's ankle bracelet sat on top of the empty desk. Next to it was an old coffee cup with the name 'Enola' printed on it

.

Emmy leaned close to the coffee cup. It was from "Bayview Brewers." It was the high-end coffee shop where her dad's secretary had always gotten his coffee. Emmy had gone there with him a few times.

Pierce picked up the coffee cup gingerly. "He wants you to meet him at this coffee-house, alone."

"Right," Emmy said. "Not very subtle."

"Did he come all the way here to give you that message? It seems like there would have been an easier way to do it. Maybe even one that didn't violate his parole."

"My dad likes to make a show, to do things big and complicated."

"Are you going to go?" Pierce asked.

Emmy hesitated for a long moment. "I don't think I can answer that without incriminating myself."

Pierce looked resigned, but he nodded. "Right." He swept the coffee cup and the ankle bracelet into an evidence bag. "I'll take these down to the station here. Do you think you can make it back to Sharp Island, *Enola*?"

"Yeah. No problem."

"From what I hear, Bayside Brewers isn't as nice as it may have been eight years ago. If you decide to grab a cup of coffee, be careful."

After Pierce left, Emmy looked around the room. She wanted to meet with her dad, but she wasn't quite ready to go yet. She had a feeling there was something more that he wanted her to find here. It was so strange to be back in his office. Here her dad had been king or this office. She felt it every time she visited him here. Despite that, he'd let her climb under his big desk, even when he had clients in his office. She remembered drawing pictures in the thick carpet with a coffee stirrer.

*"It's our secret, okay?"*

Something pricked her memory. There was something under his desk. Something she'd found when she was drawing under his desk. Something he told her to keep secret.

Emmy squeezed underneath the desk, feeling her way along the carpet underneath, but it wasn't there. Maybe they had redone the carpet, just in the same color.

She stayed on her hands and knees, looking around.

"Is everything okay?" The building manager appeared at the door.

Emmy stood up, embarrassed. She was about to give up and leave, but then she realized the desk in the room was in a different place than her dad's desk had been when she was a little girl.

"Fine, but can I have another minute?"

"Of course." The man nodded and pulled the door shut behind him.

She got back down on the floor and found the spot where his desk had been. She ran her fingers over the carpet until she felt the edge of the cut carpet piece and pulled it up. Underneath, there was a loose board. She pulled it up and found a locked safe. Emmy looked at the dial for a few seconds, then put in the numbers that represented her mom's birthday. The safe opened.

Inside was a file. Emmy pulled it out and read through it, her eyes getting wide.

## Chapter 40

# Homeless for the Holidays

"Y ou said you found Penelope's financial records on her laptop. How closely did you look at them?" Emmy's dad asked as she settled into the now run-down little coffee shop a few blocks from his old office.

He looked every bit like the "unhoused" person Anjuli had mistaken him for when he first came to the island. This time, Emmy knew it was on purpose. He'd been in hiding from her, from the police, maybe even from a killer.

"Not very close. Just enough to see that her sweater business had been very lucrative."

"Maybe a little too lucrative?" Her dad said. "Did it ever occur to you to ask how a former temp receptionist and part-time sweater vendor had that much money to leave to the ex-husband who'd spurned her?"

"No, it all looked legitimate to me. The figures added up." Emmy held her breath, waiting for him to tell her it was because she wasn't good with math, or that she was so easily distracted that she didn't see the issue. That somehow she had missed something important.

Instead, he said, "I don't blame you. I'm guessing that neither Pierce nor any of the financial professionals they hired to look into where the money came from saw it either. Believe it or not, a craft fair is a decent place to launder money—a lot of cash transactions and not too many receipts. She was very good at covering her tracks. If I didn't know her exact tricks, I might have missed them, too."

"And you know her tricks because she learned them from you," Emmy said.

He hung his head. "So you understood the files I left for you?"

Emmy nodded.

He took a deep breath. "On the record, Penelope Carmichael was a temp receptionist at the firm I worked at. She saw something fishy was going on and reported it to the police. In reality, she knew something fishy was going on because she was right in the middle of it. She helped me cover up the embezzlement for a cut of the profits. When she realized the whole deal was about to go sour, she turned me in. No one knew she was up to her eyebrows in the scheme herself."

"If she was that deep into it and if you had all of those records showing how far her involvement went, why didn't you bring them out at the trial?"

He nodded. "I guess you could call it 'honor among thieves.' I didn't know she was the whistleblower until I was already in prison. Those files were as incriminating to her as they were to me, and the police hadn't found them. I wasn't about to tell them where they were. That's why she was so afraid of me when she first saw me. She was sure I would be out for revenge. Honestly, I was pretty mad about the whole thing. More mad that she'd gotten away with it while my life was ruined, but I had no intention of ratting her out. I wasn't a snitch like she was."

"Why didn't you tell me all of this after she was murdered?" Emmy asked.

"Same reason as before. Having files that showed the extent of that woman's betrayal only made me look more guilty—of murder this time."

"But what does all of this have to do with her murder, or Nicholas's murder?" Emmy asked. "Who wanted them both dead?"

"I was actually hoping you could help me figure it out. It wasn't until yesterday that I thought about the files I had left hidden in my old office. They seemed important, and I knew I needed to see if they were still there. The rest is up to you."

"I need to think about this. I need..." Emmy scanned the restaurant, but there wasn't much on the table: one salt shaker and a few loose napkins. "I need the ornaments from Pierce's tree."

"What?" her dad said. He was looking at her as if she'd lost her mind.

"I mean, I need some kind of visual representation of all the suspects so I can think this through."

They both looked around for a minute. Finally, her dad said. "Got it!" He picked up the grungy backpack and pulled out a tin box of Christmas cookies. "How about these?"

"Where did that come from?" Emmy asked.

"I got a quick gig playing Santa at a church Christmas party last night. I didn't get paid, but it came with a place out of the rain, a free dinner, and a bunch of leftover cookies."

Emmy suddenly felt terrible. Her dad wasn't in disguise. He'd actually been living on the streets, trying to figure out who stole the star to clear his name.

Emmy arranged the cookies on the table. She put an ugly sweater cookie in the middle and then added a Santa. Around them she added an angel with sugar sprinkles for Estelle, a piece of shortbread for Dennis, a scone for Clark, and a snowman for Jay.

"Where's the cookie for me?" her dad asked.

"Did you kill anyone?" Emmy said.

"No."

"Then I don't need one for you."

She stared at the cookies. "We know how they are all connected, but what we don't know is why Ms. Carmichael, or Nicholas for that matter, had to die."

"They all had motives," her dad pointed out.

"Motives to kill Ms. Carmichael, but not Nicholas."

"If he was in on the theft of the star and Estelle thought he might rat her out or run off with half the jewels, that would be a reason to kill him," her dad said.

"That's what we thought originally, but Estelle couldn't have killed Nicholas. She was at her booth with a long line of people from the time Nicholas ended his shift, right until the lighted ship parade, and the way he was killed..."

"He would have bled out pretty quickly," her dad said. "Maybe she hired a hit man?"

"I thought about that. But it was a pretty risky way to do a hit. Why would a professional hit man choose a knitting needle? Not the most effective weapon. It was up close and very personal. She had to have been killed by someone who knew her and had a grudge against her."

"You're really good at this." Her dad smiled at her with something that looked like pride. "I never imagined you had the kind of skills it would take to solve a crime."

"Thanks." Emmy glowed in his praise, but his mention of skills made her remember what Jay had asked her to do. "If I sent you some files, could you see if you can find any discrepancies? Jay thinks Dennis has been cheating him."

"Of course." Her dad seemed pleased that she'd asked him.

Emmy got on her phone and shared the files.

"I'll take a look at them while you hunt down a killer," her dad said.

"Thanks." Emmy stared at the cookies, thinking she was missing something. She picked up a star cookie from the plate and put it on the table in front of them. "What if the two crimes weren't related?"

"The two murders?" Her dad asked. He was already looking at the file she'd sent.

"No, the theft of the star and the two murders." She pushed the star to the edge of the table.

"We're pretty sure the star going missing was a collaboration between Estelle and Nicholas, right?" Her dad said. "They're the only ones who make sense."

"But they don't make sense for either of the murders. Nicholas was at the booth after Penelope was already dead. Estelle has an alibi."

"Okay," her dad moved the cookie representing Estelle out of the circle. "Who does that leave?"

"Our three wise-guys," Emmy said. "All three had a motive to kill Ms. Carmichael, but I don't see where any of them had a motive to kill Nicholas." She sat staring at the Santa Claus cookie for a long time. "Unless…"

But her dad wasn't paying attention to her. He was focused on a tall, broad-shouldered woman walking into the coffee shop. It was his parole officer.

He ducked down in the booth and leaned closer to Emmy. "You didn't tell Pierce where you were meeting me, did you?"

Emmy ducked down too and whispered. "I didn't have to tell him. Your hint wasn't that subtle. But he said he'd give us time to talk. Maybe she just came by here."

"I don't believe in coincidences that are that big," her dad said.

Emmy didn't either, but she also didn't believe Pierce had been the one to tell the parole officer where her dad was. "It might just be better to turn yourself in," she said.

He reached across the table and squeezed her hand. "Not when there's a killer on the loose. I can't protect you if I'm in jail." He pulled a red coat and a Santa hat from his bag. Emmy didn't know where the costume had come from, but she guessed he'd stolen it from the church where he had played Santa, if that part was even true.

"Dad, I don't need your protection, I need–"□

He pulled the red cap down over his eyes. "I'll contact you as soon as I can."

He ho, ho, hoed his way out of the coffee shop. The parole officer barely looked up as he walked by. Coincidence or not, she didn't seem to recognize her dad in the Santa outfit. As he stepped out of the door, something worked its way into Emmy's mind.

What if Nicholas wasn't the murderer's intended target?

Emmy opened her phone and went to YouTube. She scrolled past the "Comedy for a Cure," videos she'd been watching earlier and pulled up another sketch where Clark was dressed as Granny Gray. She played the video and listened.

It tickled something in her memory. Jay had said Ms. Carmichael talked to him after he'd come back for the sweater. But Ms. Carmichael was already dead.

Then who was talking to Jay? She'd thought it was Estelle, the only other woman left in the vendor's area. But what if it wasn't?

What if it was someone who only sounded like a woman?

Emmy realized it could have only been one person. One person who had an interest in killing Penelope, because she had told him about the will.

What if the killer hadn't meant to kill Nicholas at all? What if that murder was a case of mistaken identity?

## Chapter 41
# Message from the Grave

T he ferry ride back to town was long and excruciating. Emmy wished she hadn't lost track of her dad. She hoped he was hiding somewhere safe, on the mainland and far away from the person who had killed the wrong man.

Her phone buzzed just as she got off the ferry. She looked down, hoping it was a text from her dad. Instead, it was a message from Avery Covert, the Seattle Times reporter. The message read:

*It came from her cell phone.*

Emmy stared at the message for a minute. She didn't know what the message meant, but she didn't have time to try to decipher it right now. Pierce was standing at the ferry dock, waiting for her.

"I was starting to get worried." Pierce wrapped her in his arms as soon as she got off the ferry back at Sharp Island. "Did you figure out what part your dad played in all of this?"

"I'm not sure," Emmy said. "I need to ask you a legal question."

"If your dad violated his parole, there isn't much I can do," Pierce answered.

"It's not that. What would happen to the inheritance if someone made a lot of money illegally and then left that money to someone in their will?"

"The person inheriting the money would have to forfeit the inheritance. Why?"

"That's what I thought. I need to find my dad," Emmy was cursing herself for letting him leave the coffee shop. "I think he's in danger."

"Why would he be in danger?"

"Because I don't think Nicholas was the person who was supposed to die the other night. I think it was my dad."

"Why would someone want to kill your dad?" Pierce asked.

"He's the only one who knows Penelope Carmichael made her fortune not by knitting and selling sweaters, but by embezzling money. He said she was just as deep into what was going on with his company as he was, but she became a whistleblower and never got caught. She sat on the money for years, maybe even made some legitimate investments, but the fact is, most her money was made by doing something illegal."

Pierce nodded. "Which means the money Clark stands to inherit would be forfeited."

"And maybe he doesn't want to risk losing all that money. That would give him a motive to kill Ms. Carmichael and a motive to kill my dad, only he got it wrong and killed Nicholas instead. That's why I couldn't figure out who had a motive for killing Nicholas."

"Any idea where Clark is now?" Pierce asked. "Has he left the island?"

"They were all supposed to be leaving on the next ferry. I don't know where my dad is. We need to find him before Clark does."

Pierce pursed his lips. "You're not going after a killer, again."

"Don't worry about that." Emmy had done enough confronting killers on her own. "I'm going back to my apartment. If my dad comes back to the island, hopefully he'll go there."

"Okay, but stay put. I'll let you know when I find Clark."

"Dennis?" Emmy stepped back, surprised. The comedian was standing in the alleyway between her apartment and the square, talking on the phone.

"It's in the bag," he said into the phone before hanging up.

"What are you doing here?" She asked.

He slipped the phone into his jacket pocket. "The usual. Looking for a quiet place to have a phone conversation."

"You always seem so busy."

'Yeah," he laughed nervously. "Comedy never sleeps."

"But most of what you are doing isn't for the sake of comedy; it's for the sake of one comedian, Clark. Jay tells me he has you at his beck and call. That you're so sure he's going to be the one to kick-start your career that you'll do anything he asks. How far are you going to let him push you?"

The look of fear on Dennis' face grew. But he shoved his hands in his pockets and tried to appear casual. "I don't know what you're talking about."

"What did you find on Penelope's computer that you didn't tell me about? Her will maybe? Did you tell Clark what you found?"

Dennis let out an exhausted sigh. "I didn't have to tell him about the will. He'd already talked to Penelope about it. They got together after the pageant. She told him I was cheating him, only I wasn't. I'm just not a very good investor."

Emmy considered that. Dennis could be just as bad at investing as he was at comedy, or he could have been playing dumb to cover his tracks. "And she told him about Jay and his charity scandal."□

"Yeah."

"She sent Jay a note too, something about a person who wasn't what they seemed. I guess she meant Jay. Did you ever tell Jay you knew he was lying about the charity?"

"Why would I do that?" Dennis asked.

Something stirred in Emmy's mind. Something she couldn't quite pinpoint. Something important.

"You ran across the email she'd intended to send to the papers. You told Jay you'd deleted it, but you're actually the one who sent it. Why?"

Dennis shook his head. "Petty jealousy? Jay is half my age and already more famous than I probably ever will be. He's barely worked a day in his life. He deserved to go down. People who lie and cheat their way to the top deserve to be punished."

His face had changed. He was no longer afraid and unsure. He had a look as if he were confident in his own virtue. It was a look she remembered seeing on Ms. Carmichael's face.

"What did Clark know about the will?"

"She told him she had money to spare, and that she wanted him to stop playing games. She said she would take care of him for the rest of his life, that she'd already provided for him if anything should happen to her. She asked him to marry her. She even bought herself a diamond."

"The one we found on the floor of her booth?"

"I don't know anything about that. I just know he had no intention of marrying her. He wanted the money, needed the money for the lifestyle he thought he deserved, but that lifestyle didn't include her."

"So he killed her."

Dennis didn't answer. "He's the logical suspect, isn't he?"

*The message was sent from her cell phone.*

It suddenly clicked what Avery had meant by that text. Emmy had asked her if she could find out where the email describing Jay's charity fraud had been sent from. "Her cell phone," was the answer.

Based on the timeline it had been sent right after she died. That's why Emmy had assumed Dennis had sent it after he hacked into Ms. Carmichael's laptop. And she was right. Dennis had just admitted that he had sent the email to the newspaper.

*From her phone.*

The phone that was found in Ms. Carmichael's booth after she died.

## Chapter 42
# The Wise Ones

Emmy stared at Dennis. He didn't know that by admitting he'd sent that email to the newspaper, he was also admitting to murdering Penelope Carmichael.

"Emmy, what a lovely surprise," Clark said as he joined them in the alleyway. Pierce must not have caught up with him yet.

"I thought you'd be gone by now," Emmy said.

"No. I wanted one more look at this beautiful island. Do you know if any of the property here is for sale? It would make a lovely out of the way place to spend my vacations."

"Thanks to Ms. Carmichael's generosity," Dennis grumbled.

"Yes, thanks to her."

"Do you have any idea why she left you all her money?" Emmy asked.

"I think any of us would be hard-pressed to figure out what Penelope Carmichael was thinking. But as I said before. People seem to find me irresistible," Clark said.

"I'm not sure why," Emmy answered. She was aware that at one point she had felt that way herself.

Clark grimaced. "Ouch. I'm not sure I deserve that."

"I'm pretty sure you do." Emmy said. "You weren't very nice to Ms. Carmichael, even if she found you irresistible. But I guess it doesn't matter. She left you a fortune, so she must have seen something in you that was redeemable. Did you ever find out how she made all of that money?"

He stopped walking and turned. "Selling her creations and wise investing is what I gathered. Penelope was always a practical little lamb. Not that it matters now."

"But it would matter if the way she made her money was less than legal," Emmy said.

For a second, fear crossed his face. "Penelope? Something illegal? The woman was justice herself, raining fire and brimstone down on anyone who stepped out of line."

"You'd think so. But money can corrupt even the most self-righteous person. His fists were clenching and unclenching as Clark spoke. She couldn't tell if the two of them were working together, if Clark had talked Dennis into killing Penelope, or if Dennis had his own reasons for murdering her.□□

Dennis continued, his face getting red. "If she thought what she was doing was right, if she had a greater cause in mind, like winning you back, maybe she might have fudged a little in her bookkeeping."

"Fudging the books was what Mr. Fox did, not Penelope," Clark said. "Speaking of your father, have you seen him lately? I have some unfinished business with him." His voice was still polite as ever, but there was a deadly calm behind it.

Emmy caught the look in Clark's eye. It was a dark, angry look she hadn't seen from him before. "No. I think he's still off island."

"That's too bad. I wonder what might bring him back in a hurry and what he'd be willing to trade for a lifetime of silence," Clark said.

Dennis stepped forward and grabbed Emmy around the waist. Before she could move or scream, he pressed something cold against her throat.

"Another knitting needle?" Clark looked disgusted. "I told you to bring a weapon."

Dennis' face darkened again. "So far they've proved pretty effective. They keep people from making any noise after they get stabbed."

Clark shook his head. "I'm counting on Ms. Fox to stay speechless without that crafty instrument being thrust through her pretty little throat."

Emmy swallowed, her throat constricting against the sharp point pressed into it. "Where do you think you can take me? My dad is somewhere in Seattle. Pierce is already looking for you. You can't just kill me, then you lose any kind of leverage you need to keep my dad quiet."

Clark smiled. "You are very smart, Ms. Fox. All of those things are true, except for one. Your dad is on the island. He came on the same ferry you did." Emmy's blood ran cold because she knew he was telling the truth. "He was fairly prompt once I explained the consequences for his daughter if he didn't come."

Dennis pushed her toward the bookshop while Clark kept talking. "I think it speaks to his character that he came so quickly. The Wayne Fox Penelope wrote to me about all those years ago was selfish, ruthless, and untrusting, but here I find a loving father who would do anything to protect his daughter."

"Why does it matter so much to you?" Emmy asked. "My dad said that Penelope was very good at covering her tracks. The missing chunk of money could still be attributed to my dad. It's his word against the financial portfolio of a dead woman, and he's a convicted felon, so who is going to listen to him?"

"You make a lot of good points, Emerson, and I could almost agree with you, except Penelope mentioned that your father kept a careful record of all his transactions, legal and otherwise. That record is somewhere, and I need to know it's destroyed before I leave this island."

Dennis dragged her to the door of the bookshop. It had been long-since closed, and the doors locked. "Unlock the door, Emmy. We don't want to keep your dad waiting."

Emmy fumbled for the keys in her pocket, trying to stall, wondering where Pierce was now. She might be able to get away from Dennis. He seemed pretty weak. Clark appeared stronger, even though he was much older. But if she escaped, what would happen to her dad?

Wayne Fox sat in the large chair next to the fireplace in the bookshop. It struck Emmy that it was the same chair her Uncle Edward had sat in the night she first met him, the chair he'd been lying underneath after he was murdered. The lights were off, but someone had built a roaring fire. On the table in front of her dad was the file Emmy had read from the safe in his office.

He rose as soon as they walked in. "Let my daughter go. I have all the files you want. All hard copy. I didn't dare leave anything on the computer."

"Very nice," Clark said.

Dennis pushed Emmy forward, the knitting needle still digging into her throat.

"Throw them in the fire, all of them," Clark said.

Emmy's dad stood and threw the documents into the fire. His face glowed red as the flames grew and consumed the pages. "There," he said. "Now let Emmy go."

'It's good," Clark nodded, smiling. "But not good enough. I can't exactly just let you walk out of the bookshop, can I? Not with everything you know."

Emmy met her dad's eyes. They were wide with fear. Not fear for himself, she realized, but fear for her. She tried to signal to him to stay calm. It was two against two, and Dennis wasn't much of a match. Really, what kind of weapon was a knitting needle, anyway?

She flipped around and grabbed for it, but as she tried to disarm him, Dennis reached into his coat and pulled out a gun. She stumbled back as he held it out in front of her. "Go, stand by your dad."

"You can't just kill us here," Emmy pointed out as she moved next to the chair where her dad was sitting. "Pierce will figure it out."

Clark laughed. From under the table he produced a familiar box. It was the box that Penelope had made to put the star in.

"What your boyfriend will see is that you solved another crime. You figured out that your dad was the one who had stolen the diamonds from your priceless family heirloom. To cover his tracks, he killed both Penelope and Nicholas—the two witnesses to the theft. When you confronted him, he accidentally shot you. When he saw what he had done, his grief was so intense that he shot himself. Another Sharp Family tragedy, right here in the same bookshop where your uncle died."

Dennis pressed the gun into Emmy's father's hand and held it there. He raised the gun to point at Emmy.

"Don't do this, Dennis," Emmy said. "You quit your job to live your dream. This will never get you there. Clark will never help you. He's only interested in you for what he can get from you. He laughs at you behind your back. He told me you have no talent, no future, that you're too old."

Dennis glanced from Emmy to Clark. His insecurity showed through his grimace of determination. Beads of sweat that had little to do with the fire in the fireplace behind him rolled down the sides of his face.

"Why are you listening to her?" Clark demanded.

"Do you think I have talent?" Dennis asked.

"Of course you have talent. Once these two are out of the way, you and I will be the funniest guys around. We'll have plenty of money to spend and fame to go with the fortune. You just have to hold it together."

Dennis' hand holding the gun shook.

"Hold steady," Clark said. "We have three million dollars on the line, plus whatever this thing is worth." He lifted the lid of the box.

Inside was a bare, silver star-shaped frame.

## Chapter 43
# Gone to Plan

"The diamonds are gone?" Clark looked at the empty box, dumbfounded. "How could you have let it out of your site long enough for someone to strip it of everything that's valuable?"

Dennis looked at the box, obviously just as shocked as Clark that the star-shaped frame was bare.

"You're such a moron. I don't know why I ever invited you to be part of this? Nothing has gone to plan since I included you. You've lost the star, you chose the most asinine way to dispose of Penelope, and then you killed the wrong Santa Claus."

Dennis turned the gun on Clark. "Actually. Everything has gone to plan." The shake in his voice and in his hand was gone. He gestured with the gun. Go to the corner, Clark."

"What are you doing, Dennis?" Clark looked offended.

"It's like you said, *you* can't just walk out of here. You murdered two people. You're the one with the motive. You're the one who stands to lose three million dollars. I'm just the village idiot."

Clark looked at him, shocked. "But, Dennis."

"I'm afraid you're not as irresistible as you think you are," Dennis said. "But you will make a decent scapegoat."

Clark joined Emmy and her dad in the corner of the room. "We can share the money." Clark's voice sounded small and pitiful.

Dennis smiled. "Too late for that, my friend. Ms. Carmichael wasn't good at keeping her passwords secure." He turned to Emmy and her dad. "Like a lot of people I know. Once I got into her laptop, it was a simple matter to break into the accounts where she had so carefully laundered her money. Even easier to set up a transfer to my untraceable account. See, I did learn something from when I worked under you, Wayne. I was always a little miffed that you and Penelope didn't let me in on your game from the beginning. I could have been a rich man at a very young age. I could have made enough to live my dream of being a comedian. Instead, I lost my job. I had to work and struggle until I nearly killed myself."

He turned to Clark. "And you, Clark, you never respected my comedy. You only wanted me for my money. Funny how the funny business works. After your untimely death amidst a quadruple murder scandal and the humiliating downfall of Jay Gold. I will be the reigning king of comedy."

Emmy and her dad exchanged a look. Dennis was delusional. How was Clark's death going to make him into a famous comedian?

"That's not how fame works," Clark appeared incensed. "You have to work your way to the top. You have to actually be funny."

"I guess I'll just have to settle for being rich." He turned the gun on Clark.

"Duck!" Emmy yelled, lunging for Dennis. She took him out at the knees. The gun fired, hitting the wall behind Clark as he went down. The gun clattered to the floor. Dennis ran to the door.

Emmy's dad knelt down beside her. "Why would you do that? That was incredibly stupid." He took a breath and then wrapped his arms around her. "Are you okay?"

"Yeah," Emmy got to her feet. "Is Clark?—"

Clark moaned in response.

"He's fine," Emmy's dad picked up the gun.

Emmy stood. "I'm going after Dennis. You keep Clark covered."

"We should both go after him," her dad said. "Clark is not going anywhere soon."

"No, I've got it. I'm about half his age, and he's not armed anymore. Not even with a knitting needle."

## Chapter 44
# Chaos and Camels

E mmy took off at a sprint in the direction Dennis had gone. As she ran she fumbled for her phone, trying to call Pierce.

She lost track of Dennis as he ducked into the square. The animals from the petting zoo were just being loaded into a trailer to head back on the ferry. He rushed between the three reindeer, knocking the lead rope off two of them. They bolted into the woods. The third reared up and broke free. The sheep were being herded into the back of a truck. Dennis scattered them as he ran. They swarmed in all different directions.

"Emmy!" Pierce's voice carried through the phone. She'd finally connected with him. "What is going on?"

"I'm... chasing... Dennis... through the square..." Emmy struggled to find Dennis and struggled for breath. For a man who looked so out of shape, Dennis was fast.

"Dennis?" Pierce asked. "I thought that Clark–"

"Long story... Just get down here."

"What is that noise?" Pierce said.

"Chaos..." Emmy panted. "The animals...they're loose."

The square had suddenly become filled with animals: a neighing donkey, reindeer with their harness bells jingling. A stray dog nipping at the heels of the swarming sheep, and in the midst of it the camel sat, still saddled, watching the whole thing with half-closed eyes, chewing as if it didn't care what was going on.

She made eye contact with a confused Kirsten, who a few minutes before had been casually chatting with the owner of the animals. "Help!" Emmy said.

It took just a second for Kirsten to regain her composure, then she yelled, "Help!" too.

Landon came from the back of Santa's workshop. Ginny and Jay came out of the tea shop. Brighton and Stan came from the Pirate's Cove, Ramona came from the patisserie, and Madelyn stepped out of her tech shop.

"We need to round up the animals, and we need to find Dennis!" Emmy yelled. Just as she said it, she spotted him. He had mounted the camel. For a moment, it stayed seated, chewing unconcerned. Something flashed in the sunlight. Its eyes opened wide and jumped to its feet. Dennis clung to the saddle and kicked the poor beast.

Pierce arrived, and they stood next to each other, dumbfounded, as Dennis maneuvered the camel through the throngs of people and animals and then headed off into the woods.

"I had no idea Balthazar could move like that," the animal trainer said. "A knitting needle? Who'd have guessed?"

"Where does he think he's going?" Pierce asked. "What part of 'this is an island' does he not get?"

"I don't think he knows where he's going, either." Emmy said. Then she started laughing. The image of Dennis, clinging to the camel's back, making his escape, "He looks like some half-crazed, not very wise man."

Pierce looked at her as if she were losing it, and maybe she was. "I'll go get my patrol car."

"I'm coming too," Emmy said.

Together they left the chaos of the town square behind, got into Pierce's car, and pursued the camel and its crazed rider down the road.

"I'm a little fuzzy on my camel-chase etiquette," Pierce said. "Lights and sirens or running silent?"

"I'm going to go with running silent. That poor beast has to be so spooked at this point that it doesn't know which way is up," Emmy said.

"Good point," Pierce said. "You want to fill me in on the events that led up to us chasing a wannabe comedian riding a camel through the woods?"

"Well, for starters, I know my dad is innocent, at least of the murders and stealing the star, and I know who killed Penelope and Nicholas."

"Time to hoof it, pun intended." Pierce said as the camel took a well-worn horse trail into the woods that his patrol car couldn't follow. He parked the car, and they both got out to continue the chase on foot. "Based on current events, I'm guessing our camel jockey is also the murderer?"

"Good guess," Emmy said. Pierce caught her hand as she slipped on the muddy path.

"And the diamond thief?" Pierce asked.

"That's where things get a bit more complicated," Emmy said.

"More complicated than this?" Pierce asked as they got closer to the cliffs at the top of the island.

"Yes, and no," Emmy said. "It's not 'chase a camel into the woods' complicated, but it's which thief or thieves are we talking about?"

"Can't wait to hear all about it, after we take care of this one," Pierce said as they got to the top of the ridge and found the camel, once again sitting like on the ground like it had nothing better to do. "What do you think happened to…"

"Don't come any closer," Dennis was standing at the edge of the cliff. "I didn't want it to end this way, but I'll jump if you keep pushing me."

He looked over the edge, and Emmy could almost hear him contemplating the headlines now. *Rising Comedy Star Pushed to the Edge in the Quest for Fame and Fortune.*

She and Pierce looked at each other and stepped back. Dennis stayed at the edge of the cliff.

"You don't want to do this," Emmy yelled to him.

He humphed. "Of course I don't want to do this. I want to be rich and famous. I want to go to big parties and be surrounded by adoring fans. I want to be remembered as something other than a washed up semi-talented investment banker. But you've left me no other choice."

"No. You've left yourself with no other choice." Dennis turned just in time to be wrapped up by Emmy's dad. "You were mine the minute you threatened my daughter." Both men went down. They struggled for a few minutes before Emmy's dad ended up sitting on a subdued Dennis.

Pierce stepped forward and put the handcuffs on Dennis.

Emmy helped her father to his feet. "How did you get here so fast?"

"Shortcut, up the steep part on the other side," her dad wheezed. "Remember, I used to do a lot of hiking around here. Many, many years ago."

She wrapped him in her arms. "My Daddy. My hero."

Chapter 45

# All That Glitters Isn't Bling

"It looks right, if a little bare," Emmy looked at the silver frame of the star sadly. The diamonds were all gone.

"I guess they figured that the star itself would be too easy to trace. The diamonds themselves were never graded or inscribed, so they would be easy to pawn."

"We can try it," Madelyn said. "If it fits, we'll know that's what happened."

"I guess so."

Emmy went up the lift for the second time. She was too despondent this time to even care about the height. They'd figured out who had killed Penelope Carmichael and Nicholas Star. Dennis would probably spend the rest of his life in jail. Clark too. Hopefully, Jay would be acquitted. Despite everything their Christmas celebration had been a chaotic success. That should have made her happy, but the only thing she could think of was how she had lost all the diamonds in The Sharp Family Star.

Madelyn disabled the alarm and took the fake star down. Emmy put the frame into the clips. The tree and the square lit up in the early-darkening evening. There was a lot less fanfare and joy than there had been the first time the square had been lit.

"What do want to do now?" Madelyn asked.

"Put the fake star up for the rest of the season. It's not the real thing, but it's pretty. Most people won't even know the difference."

Emmy looked out over the island as the lift lowered. Sharp Island really was a beautiful place to live. The town glowed from Christmas lights on every building. More lights shone from ships in the harbor, and the town square still looked like a Christmas wonderland.

"There are more important things than bling," she said out loud as the lift reached the ground. But that thought gave her an idea of where she might find the rest of the diamonds.

"Emmy, so good to see you," Estelle said, but her eyes told Emmy she was the last person the bling lady wanted to see.

"I'm so glad I caught up with you," Emmy replied.

It was two days before Christmas. Emmy had tracked Estelle down to another bazaar in a small town just across the border in Canada. The bazaar had closed and most of the booths had been packed up. Emmy hoped she wasn't too late.

"I'm glad you finally caught up with *them*," Estelle said. "It's scary to think we were all working that closely with a couple of murderers. And what about the diamonds? Do you think they'll ever be recovered?"

"We're still working on that," Emmy said.

Estelle folded the last of her bedazzled apparel into the box. It was the sweater she'd been working on in her booth the last time Emmy had seen her, a beautiful white cashmere with a glittering silver star in the center.

"Did you finish it?" Emmy said.

Estelle shut the box. "It's mostly done."

"Can I see?" Emmy lifted the lid. She examined the sweater. "No glue gun here. Penelope was obviously wrong about your craftsmanship. How do you get the gems to stay on? This isn't the technique you taught in the class."

"It's a very complicated process. It involves setting the gems in a metal clip that I then hand-sew onto the garment–piece by piece." Estelle reached to shut the box.

Emmy put her hand in the way so Estelle couldn't get the box closed. She ran her hand down the front of the sweater, fingering the dazzling bits that covered it. "The gems on this one are a much higher quality than you usually use, aren't they?"

"Yes, yes," Estelle glanced around.

"This sweater is beautiful. Would you consider selling it to me now?"

"Oh no," Estelle's laugh was high-pitched and strained. "I made it as a gift for a friend." She turned. "But I have one that's similar if you're interested." She opened another box and started digging through it. "It's not as elaborate, but the gems I used for this one are exquisite and the fabric is so soft. Come closer and I can show you. I believe the red is more your color, anyway."

Estelle's hand shot out, the sharpened knitting needle aimed toward Emmy's throat. She caught Estelle's hand before she made contact. The two struggled for control of the needle. Estelle was stronger than Emmy had imagined. As she fought off the needle, Emmy looked around for something to help her.

A glint of silver in the top corner of the booth caught her eye. She kept one hand on Estelle's arm to keep the needle away from her; with the other she reached for whatever it was. Her fingers tightened around a heavy object.

She turned and brought it down hard on Estelle's head. She dropped the knitting needle, turned and staggered before she crashed to the ground, dragging a box with her and burying herself in an avalanche of bedazzled sweaters, hats and scarves.

Pierce stood over Emmy, shaking his head. "You were supposed to wait for me to contact the Canadian authorities."

"Sorry, I didn't want her to get away." Emmy held up the sweater. "The diamonds all seem to be here."

"What did you hit her with?" Pierce asked as Estelle moaned.

"This." Emmy pointed to a heavy silver stapler on the floor of the booth. On the back, printed in neat block letters, it said:

**PENELOPE CARMICHAEL**

## Chapter 46
# The Real Thing

"You never told me how she ended up with the star," Kirsten said. "Especially since Dennis had the frame."

Emmy added another of her mother's ornaments to her first Christmas tree in her apartment. It had taken until Christmas Eve to put it up. "He was the one who stole it originally. He followed my dad back to my apartment, and got lucky because the code for my door was my mom's birthday. It was a combination my dad had used when he worked with Dennis."

Pierce was shaking his head.

"Don't worry. I changed the code on my door," Emmy said.

"But how did Estelle end up with it?" Ramona added a hot pink camel ornament to the tree. She'd picked it up at the bazaar as a present for Emmy.

"He had it with him when he came back to murder Ms. Carmichael. He was on too tight a timeline to have hidden it before that. He must have stashed it somewhere in the booth. Estelle saw him. She went to find Officer Peters after Dennis went on stage. She was dazzled by the star at the tree lighting and didn't have time to say anything. Then the body was discovered, and she decided to keep her mouth shut. Maybe so she could go back and get the star."

"When we didn't find the star, she insisted on taking Penelope's premium booth so she could get to it and slowly remove all the diamonds."

"We completely emptied that booth. Where could Dennis have hidden it so that we wouldn't find it?" Pierce asked.

"Probably in the compartment under the booth," Landon said, popping a piece of popcorn into his mouth from the bowl Kirsten was trying to string.

Everyone turned to look at him. For a second, no one said anything.

"There was a compartment under the booth?" Pierce finally said.

"Just in that one. I built it so that it looked like part of the floor. Unless you knew it was there, you couldn't see it. Extra storage space was one reason it was a premium booth," Landon replied.

Why didn't you tell anyone?" Emmy asked.

Landon shrugged and ate another piece of popcorn. "No one asked, and no one told me the star had been stolen."

Kirsten sighed and moved the bowl out of his reach. "We need to work on your communication skills."

Jay and Ginny laughed from the corner of the room. They were snuggled on the couch, replaying Jay's last viral video. It was the video he took when all the animals had scattered and Dennis had jumped on the unsuspecting camel.

"At least Dennis had the chance to go viral before he went to jail," Ginny said.

"I told you. Chaos is pure comedic gold," Jay said and then kissed her.

Emmy's dad set out a tray of fresh sugar cookies from Anjuli's. "Are we ready for the big lighting?" He asked, gesturing to Emmy's little tree.

"Almost. I need to make sure it's all connected." Pierce slid under the tree and reached for the cord.

Emmy stepped back, admiring how beautiful her tree looked adorned with her mother's favorite ornaments. She looked around her. It felt good to have all the people who were important to her in the same room, celebrating Christmas Eve together. For the first time in a long time, that included her dad.

Pierce crawled out from under the tree. Still on his knees, he looked up at the top with Emmy. "It seems like it's missing something."

"I know," Emmy said. The top was bare. "Nothing will compare to the big star. I get that; I just feel like it still needs to be something unique and beautiful. There wasn't a tree-topper in my mom's ornaments, so I decided I needed a new tradition, something all my own, only I couldn't find anything that quite fit."

"Maybe you just haven't looked hard enough." Pierce said. From inside the thick branches at the bottom of the tree, he pulled out a white box with a silver bow. Still on one knee he turned to her.

Emmy's breath caught in her throat.

Pierce stood and opened the box. Inside was a replica of the Sharp family Christmas star. "I had this made when I thought the other one was gone for good."

Emmy pulled the star from the tissue paper. "It's beautiful, perfect. Everything I didn't know I was looking for."

Pierce put his arms around her waist and looked deep into her eyes. "That's exactly how I feel."

Emmy's dad looked between them at the star. "Is this the real thing?" He asked.

Emmy leaned in to kiss Pierce. "Absolutely."

**The End**

# Chapter 47
# Revenge at the Retreat: The Proposal

R ain poured outside the picture window at the front of Pierce's apartment. Emmy leaned against him, their legs propped up on his dark leather ottoman, a toasty fire crackling in the hearth. They were both reading the same true-crime book. It had become their favorite Sunday evening routine through the rainy winter months. Emmy's best friend, Ginny, had accused them of being boring, but after all that had happened on Sharp Island, Emmy felt like they'd earned some time to be boring.

"Did you get to the part where–"

"Shh," Pierce put his finger on Emmy's lips to stop her from talking. You read faster than I do, remember? You promised no spoilers."

"But the ex-wife's new boyfriend was–"

He leaned over and kissed her. This method was more effective in keeping her quiet. His lips moved across hers for a minute before he pulled away to just a few inches from her lips. "I said, no spoilers."

"Keep interrupting me that way and I'll forget everything I just read," Emmy replied.

He leaned in again. "Deal."

Her phone rang from somewhere in the depths of the couch.

Emmy sat up fast, banging her lip against Pierce's teeth. "Ouch!"

Pierce traced his finger over her bottom lip. "Sorry."

"Have you seen my phone?"

Pierce put his hand over hers. "Don't–"

"I have to get it, you know that." Emmy dug through the couch, trying to track the impatient buzz of her cell phone.

"Right," Pierce sighed and pushed back the ottoman to help her look.

They were used to being interrupted. They both had jobs that required them to be available to answer the phone at any time or place. He was a police detective; she was the controlling owner of Sharp Island, a small island in the San Juan Islands of Washington State.

Things had been quiet for both of them—maybe too quiet. As Emmy continued her search, she imaged what kind of catastrophe waited on the other end—a problem with the sewage system, or maybe a call to settle a dispute between shopkeepers. Worse, it could be a call to settle an argument between Ramona, her dead uncle's ex-wife and Madelyn, her cousin's widow.

"Got it," she said, as she caught the phone between her fingers and extracted it from the depths of Pierce's couch. It stopped ringing as she tried to answer. She read the caller ID. "Unknown number."

"Probably a spam call." Pierce surveyed the disaster left in the wake of her search. Couch cushions, two paperbacks, and an upended bowl of popcorn covered his usually spotless living room floor.

"Sorry," Emmy said, I'll get the vaccu–"

"Later," Pierce pulled Emmy toward the cushionless frame. "Where were we?"

"In the middle of a murder," Emmy teased.

"That's not how I remember it." He pressed her down on the couch and moved his face toward hers.

"What happened to the ambitious detective who was all about advancing his career and solving murders?"

"He found something more important to focus on," Pierce said as he moved in for the disrupted kiss.

Emmy's phone rang again. She put it to her ear as Pierce moved from her lips to her neck. She tried not to sound breathless as she answered, "Emerson Fox speaking."

"Emerson Fox." The woman's tone made Emmy slide away from Pierce and sit up straight.

"Yes."

"The famous heiress and amateur detective from Sharp Island?" The voice purred.

"Yes. I mean, I'm Emerson. What can I do for–"

"Oh, my dear. It's what I can do for you. This is Dr. Melinda Showell." The woman stopped as if her name should dispel any questions Emmy might have.

Emmy didn't recognize the name. "Melinda Showell? I'm sorry, I don't–"

Pierce caught her attention. "Melinda Showell?" he mouthed, his eyes wide.

"Yes," the woman continued as if she hadn't heard the question in Emmy's voice. "I know it must be a shock to hear from me directly. Normally, I wouldn't be calling in person. I have any number of assistants I could have..."

Emmy covered the receiver with her hand. "Who is Melinda Showell?" she whispered to Pierce.

He gestured to the TV, but Emmy still didn't understand. He grabbed the remote and scanned through the listings.

"You see," Dr. Showell continued, "this project is very close to my heart, and I wanted to make sure you understood that from the outset. I didn't choose your quaint little island for my couple's retreat at random."

Pierce stopped on a preview image of a tall, slender, sixty-something woman in a blue pantsuit standing on a stage. There was a couple on the couch behind her. She was holding a microphone and addressing a large audience. The caption read, "Love, Life, and Learning–taking your relationship to the next level with Dr. Melinda Showell, couple's therapist."

"Right, of course, Dr. Showell." Emmy worked to keep her voice steady. She had never seen the TV show or heard of Dr. Showell until that moment. She couldn't imagine what this woman wanted to do on Sharp Island. "Wait, did you say 'couple's retreat'?"

"With my new book coming out, I've decided the best way to spread my influence and still maintain my very personal touch would be through an intimate couple's retreat." She paused as if she expected Emmy to fill the void with applause. "I've chosen Sharp Island to host the retreat and the accompanying reality television show."

"Reality...TV...show?" Emmy conjured up scenes from the reality TV shows she had binged with her roommates in college, all sex and scandal and bare skin. Emmy and the Founder's Council had been working to improve Sharp Island's image, to sell it as an idyllic family vacation destination, instead of a place only known for murder. "I don't think–"

"No need to think, Emerson dear. We'll do all the thinking for you. My retreat will be just what your little island needs to warm things up for the summer tourist season.

And you're invited to participate, of course. Any relationship, even one with a handsome police detective, could use a little therapy."

It unnerved Emmy that a famous relationship guru and a complete stranger would know anything about her relationship with Pierce. It struck her that this was all a scam. "I don't know who you really are, but I–"

"None of us really know who we are, do we? We all wear different faces–public and private, and often the face we show the world isn't our true identity. That was something I explored in depth in one of my earlier works, *The Masks We Wear.*"

"I didn't...I don't–"

"Oh, I don't expect you to have heard of that one. I published it well before I became the famous relationship expert I am today. I believe it's out of print, but if you're concerned about an identity crisis, I would definitely..."

"It is her," Pierce hissed. "She sounds just like she does on her podcast."

Emmy stared at him. She didn't know whether she should be more shocked that someone famous had sought out Sharp Island for a reality TV show, or that Pierce had listened to a relationship podcast enough times to recognize the host's voice.

"...But I'm wandering off-topic. We don't have time to go into depth about how you identify yourself and those around you. My agent has already sent the paperwork to Kirsten, your island event planner. I just wanted to reach out to you in person. As I said, this project is very important to me. Even though I could have held my retreat at any location, your little island is the one I have chosen."

"I would need to–"

"No need to thank me now," Dr. Showell said. "There will be plenty of time for that later. As they say, 'my people will talk to your people.' We'll see you in April."

"April isn't exactly..." But the line had gone dead.

"Did I hear that right? A couple's retreat and a reality TV show?" Pierce asked.

Emmy clung to the phone, stunned. "Yeah. Here. On Sharp Island."

"What possible reason would someone like Dr. Showell have to hold a retreat here? I mean, Sharp Island is great but–"

"I don't know." Emmy perched on the edge of the bare couch, her thoughts tangling like a line from the fishing charters Brighton Redding had added to his fleet. Turning down this opportunity would be crazy—Sharp Island's economy ran on tourist dollars, and a reality show would put them on the map in ways the Founder's Council had barely dreamed about.

But she suspected there was more to the offer than Dr. Showell was letting on. She talked in circles, always assuming, never asking or explaining why she wanted to use Sharp Island for the show. Emmy wasn't sure what Dr. Showell's motives were and *motive* was a word Emmy had explored in depth through three murder investigations. People didn't choose places like Sharp Island by accident. They chose them because they were small. Isolated. Easy to control.

She sat back, wondering if Pierce's faraway look meant he was thinking the same thing. Emmy was sure Dr. Showell had an agenda. She could only guess what disaster awaited the island when Dr. Showell's retreat became a reality.

Keep reading now!

# Also by Jennifer Shaw Wolf

Revenge at the Retreat

Emerson Fox knows better than to trust reality TV. When an ambitious producer pitches Sharp Island as the perfect backdrop for his couples' retreat show, Emmy hesitates-events on the island have a nasty habit of ending in murder.☐

But the publicity will definitely boost the upcoming summer tourist season, and the producer promises everything will be fun, therapeutic, and squeaky clean, but he's hired renowned relationship guru Dr. Melinda Showell—whose brutal 'therapy' sessions are about to make everyone on the island wish they'd stayed single.☐

Then the contestants arrive—including Emmy's jilted ex-fiancé and a powder keg of exes with unfinished business. Dr. Showell's "counseling sessions" drag painful secrets into the open-including what Emmy's boyfriend, Detective Pierce Hamilton, has been hiding from her. When the therapist pronounces their relationship dead on arrival, Emmy's humiliated. When Dr. Showell turns up actually dead, Emmy's investigating.☐

With an island full of couples nursing grudges and keeping secrets, the suspect list is as tangled as the relationships themselves. Now Emmy must solve a murder, save the show, and figure out if her romance with Pierce can survive-all while dodging the man she left at the altar. But the killer is watching, and Emmy's getting close to a past that was meant to stay buried.□

Can she unravel the truth hidden in Dr. Showell's unorthodox therapy sessions before she becomes the next victim?

The Body in the Bookshop

Inheriting a bookshop and the island that comes with it could be the solution to all of Emmy's problems, or it could be the last thing she ever does.

Emerson Fox's ADHD has left her with a do-nothing degree, a jilted ex-fiancé, mounds of student debt, and a knack for forgetting important things while focusing on obscure details. When a disastrous blind date leaves her stranded in a quaint bookshop on a tiny island in Washington's Puget Sound, the last thing she expects is to find the bookshop's owner has been murdered. Even more shocking, he's left a will that names her as his long-lost niece and sole heir to his bookshop and the entire island. Emmy can't claim her inheritance until she unearths a long-buried family secret, convinces the only police officer in town (and the other half of her disastrous date) that she's innocent, and finds the focus she needs to solve her uncle's murder.

The Haunting in the Hall

Since inheriting Sharp Island, Emerson Fox has everything under control, except that the island's water system is failing, the only one who knows how to fix it was recently found floating in the water tank, and the ghost who historically foretells doom showed up at her first Town Hall Meeting--just before she was almost killed by a falling chandelier.

To solve the mystery and save the island Emmy must team up with an old enemy turned event planner, an over-the-top ghost hunting podcaster, and convince her ultra-logical detective boyfriend to follow the trail of a ghost. The second book in the Emerson Fox series pits our intrepid heroine against the Sharp Island Phantom, a fall festival of epic proportions, and of course, murder.

Seeing may not be believing in this twisted mystery full of ghostly sightings, deep dark secrets, and a masquerade ball to bring down the house (or maybe the Town Hall).

### The Second Kiss

Jess never told anyone about her first kiss, her crush on the too-old-for-her boy next door, or what his departing gift meant to her.□

Jacob has been gone for six years, and a lot has changed. The shy, awkward little girl he left behind has grown up. Jess is a high school senior with plans, popularity, and a football star boyfriend. Just as everything she's worked for falls apart, Jacob is back—assigned to the Army base near her home. Is this her second chance at love, or will Jacob only see the little girl he left behind?

Kiss Me Goodbye

Long-distance love is hard enough. Long-distance love during wartime feels impossible. Jacob is in Iraq. Jess is at college, trying to build a new life. Between grainy video calls and messages that never quite capture what they need to say, their newly rekindled relationship feels like it's held together by hope and heartbreak. And then there's someone else—someone who isn't half a world away.

When tragedy shatters everything, guilt, blame, and an unfathomable loss threaten to destroy what they've built. In the wreckage, Jacob and Jess face an impossible choice: Can their love survive what war has taken? Or is letting go the only way to save each other?

A stunning sequel to *The Second Kiss*, this is a story about love, loss, and discovering what's worth fighting for.

### The Extra

Desperate for cash, a starving student takes a job as an extra on a B-list horror movie and finds herself in a fight for survival.□

To get your free copy of "The Extra," subscribe to my mailing list, and get access to free content visit my website at:

jennifershawwolf.com

### Dead Girls Don't Lie

Jaycee and Rachel were best friends. But that was before. . . before that terrible night at the old house. Before Rachel shut Jaycee out. Before Jaycee chose Skyler over Rachel. Then Rachel is found dead. The police blame a growing gang problem in their small town, but Jaycee is sure it has to do with that night at the old house. Rachel's text is the first clue-starting Jaycee on a search that leads to a shocking secret. Rachel's death was no random crime, and Jaycee must figure out who to trust before she can expose the truth.

### Breaking Beautiful

Allie lost everything the night her boyfriend, Trip, died in a horrible car accident - including her memory of the event. As their small town mourns his death, Allie is afraid to remember because doing so means delving into what she's kept hidden for so long: the horrible reality of their abusive relationship.

When the police reopen the investigation, it casts suspicion on Allie and her best friend, Blake, especially as their budding romance raises eyebrows around town. Allie knows she must tell the truth. Can she reach deep enough to remember that night so she can finally break free?

### Meant to Die

Ever since her twin sister died at birth, Miranda has walked with the dead. But what she knows about death has kept her from living life. Then she meets Remy, a little girl with a different view of life and death. Remy sees people on the brink of a violent end, people who were never meant to die. When Remy shares her visions with her, Miranda has to decide whether to team up with this fearless girl and a restless spirit to solve a string of decades-old murders. But can someone who's spent her life in fear find the courage to catch a killer, even if it means she might be the next to die?

To my family, for putting up with so many chaotic Christmases.

www.ingramcontent.com/pod-product-compliance
Lightning Source LLC
Chambersburg PA
CBHW022042240626

47154CB00007B/2529